DARK HARVEST

WARHAMMER™
HORROR

WARHAMMER™
HORROR

DARK
HARVEST

JOSH REYNOLDS

WARHAMMER HORROR
A BLACK LIBRARY IMPRINT

First published in Great Britain in 2019 by
Black Library,
Games Workshop Ltd.,
Willow Road,
Nottingham, NG7 2WS, UK.

10 9 8 7 6 5 4 3 2 1

Produced by Games Workshop in Nottingham.
Cover illustration by Maxim Kostin.

See Warhammer Horror on the internet at

blacklibrary.com

Find out more about Games Workshop
and the worlds of Warhammer at

games-workshop.com

Printed and bound by CPI Group (UK) Ltd, Croydon, CR0 4YY

WARHAMMER™
HORROR

A dark bell tolls in the abyss.

It echoes across cold and unforgiving worlds, mourning
the fate of humanity. Terror has been unleashed, and
every foul creature of the night haunts the shadows.
There is naught but evil here. Alien monstrosities drift
in tomblike vessels. Watching. Waiting. Ravenous.
Baleful magicks whisper in gloom-shrouded forests,
spectres scuttle across disquiet minds. From the depths
of the void to the blood-soaked earth, diabolic horrors
stalk the endless night to feast upon unworthy souls.

Abandon hope. Do not trust to faith. Sacrifices burn
on pyres of madness, rotting corpses stir in unquiet
graves. Daemonic abominations leer with rictus
grins and stare into the eyes of the accursed. And the
Ruinous Gods, with indifference, look on.

This is a time of reckoning, where every mortal soul
is at the mercy of the things that lurk in the dark.
This is the night eternal, the province of monsters
and daemons. This is Warhammer Horror. None shall
escape damnation.

And so, the bell tolls on.

CHAPTER ONE

BLACKWOOD

When I awoke, the rain was pattering against the canvas overhead. The wagon smelled of ghyroch and gunpowder. My back ached, and my head was ringing like a duardin smithy. I could taste last night's mistakes in the back of my mouth, and my skin had that greasy, gritty feeling that comes from too many baths in water barrels.

For a moment I looked around, wondering what had woken me. Then I realised that the wagon wasn't moving. I cleared my throat and called out, 'Have we stopped?'

No one answered me. Then, 'Blackwood? That you?'

'It's me, Lucio,' I said.

The drover leaned through the front flap and gave me a tepid smile. 'I thought you'd sleep right through it.'

'Right through what?'

'Come up and see.'

I sat up and winced. Everything hurt, the way it always did when I slept rough, which was altogether too often for my liking, these days. Sometimes it felt as if I'd spent half my life sleeping in the backs of supply wagons or in tents. At other times, I realised that was a charitable estimate. I tried not to think about it too much.

I squinted against the gloom. There was no lantern, and for good reason. The wagon was packed to the canvas with crates and barrels full of guns and gunpowder, the primary exports of Greywater Fastness. If it belched fire or spat lead, it came from the foundries of the Fastness. Business was good, especially these days. The dead rested uneasily in their graves, and shot was more effective than prayers.

I wasn't the only one sleeping in the back with the merchandise, though I was the only one awake. When they were off-duty, the drovers were allowed to rest in the wagons, if there was room. I made my way to the front as carefully and as quickly as I could, trying not to disturb anyone. I had enough problems as it was. The last thing I needed was an angry mule-skinner trying to knife me.

I didn't like leaving the city. Especially to go into the wilderness. I'd had enough of that to last me a lifetime. But sometimes you have to do things you don't like. Life is like that. And then you die.

The buckboards were wet when I hauled myself out onto the front of the wagon. So was Lucio. He wore an oilskin cape and broad-brimmed hat, but neither had done him much good. He didn't seem to mind. He offered me an apple. 'We got us a right fine quagmire here.' I didn't bother to ask where 'here' was. I'd realised where we were as soon as I saw the gun-towers – Mere Keep. The edge of civilisation, as far as many inhabitants of Greywater Fastness were concerned; where Sigmar's light faded, and the dark of Ghyran began.

The immense gatehouse-keep straddled the only road out of the city, its foundations set deep in the muddy ground the way only duardin stonemasons could manage. Built of heavy, black stone, dredged from the marshes centuries ago by labour gangs, it held a dozen wide portcullises within its sturdy frame. Each of these gates was closed at the moment, causing much consternation among the waiting travellers.

Above the portcullises, a long, reinforced parapet supported a battery of cannons and their crews. Greycaps, armed with hand-guns and fire-casters, patrolled the palisade walls and gun-towers that stretched out to either side of the gatehouse and folded back along the road leading to the city like the walls of an immense corridor.

Once, the road had been bigger and there had been others. Now there was only one thin snake of raised stone and packed earth, squeezed between two expanses of blasted heath and mire. One way in, one way out. Even that had cost a generation of blood and fire to keep, and annual sacrifices to maintain.

I rubbed the apple on my sleeve, trying to find an unbruised spot to bite. 'So what's going on? Why aren't the gates open?'

Lucio shrugged. 'Don't ask me. I just drive the wagons. Scribe made a mistake somewhere, probably. Chantey is fit to be tied.'

'I bet.' Chantey was the master of the caravan I was hitching a ride with. He was unhappy at the best of times. Most caravan-masters were. It wasn't the sort of job that attracted those of cheerful disposition. 'Where is he?'

'He and some of the other masters went looking for somebody in charge.' Lucio leaned over the side of the buckboard and spat. 'Good luck to them, I say.'

'You get paid either way, right?' I said, and he laughed. I bit into the apple and watched as Greycaps and scribes threaded their way among the line of covered wagons that waited to depart through one or another of the portcullises. The apple had a bitter taste, like much of the fruit grown in the city's allotments. Something was wrong with the soil, but everyone pretended not to notice. Or maybe we'd all just grown used to it, like the rain.

I risked an upward glance. The sky was the colour of slate. Grey on grey. Some said the weather was proof that Sigmar had abandoned us, that he was angry with us for our crimes. Though just what those crimes were, no one really knew. Others insisted it was punishment from the Everqueen, or even Elder Bones. All I knew for sure was that I couldn't remember the last time I'd seen the sun, or felt anything other than damp.

'Is it true you used to be a priest?' Lucio asked me.

I laughed. 'Who told you I was a priest?'

'Just something I heard.'

'Gossip is a sin,' I said.

It was his turn to laugh. 'I just thought it was funny is all.'

'Why?'

'On account of you breaking legs for Caspar Guno.'

I took a bite of my apple. 'You shouldn't say such things. You never know who might be listening.'

He had the good sense to look afraid. The truth was, I didn't break many legs, if I could help it. A man who can't walk can't work. Arms were my speciality. And occasionally necks. But only rarely. Most people were only too happy to pay tithe to Caspar Guno. Those that weren't… well. Guno employed men like me for a reason. In my learned opinion, working for him wasn't much different to serving Sigmar.

Atop the palisade, Ironweld cannons began to boom. Lucio started in his seat, and the ghyroch pulling our wagon began to low. The great bull-like beast was covered in shaggy, moss-like hair and had a rack of branch-like horns that rose higher than the top of the wagon. Massive, stony hooves splashed mud everywhere as it stamped in growing agitation.

It wasn't the only one doing so. Animals up and down the

line of wagons began to bellow, squawk and whinny. I saw two Chamonian axe-beaks claw at the mud with their talons, their metallic feathers shimmering in the rain, and a half-grown demidroth drool acidic spittle and lash its scaly tail as its duardin rider tried to calm it.

Lucio extended his goad and scratched the ghyroch between its shoulders, soothing it. 'There's something on the wind,' he said, softly. As if afraid someone might hear him.

'Besides gunpowder?' I said, as the stink of the volley washed back over us. Living in the Fastness, you got used to the smell quick, or your sinuses burned out. It was everywhere in the city, in every stone. It wafted across the Ghoul Mere in black banks of powder-fog, staining the trees and turning the rain to acid. Was it any wonder the sylvaneth hated us?

'They say the treekin are on the march.'

'Who says, Lucio?'

'Greycaps,' Lucio said.

'How drunk were they?'

'Less than me.' He looked around. 'Listen to that.'

I didn't ask what he meant. I could hear it well enough – had been hearing it since I'd woken up. I'd thought it was just the rain at first, but it was the sound of trees. Of branches swaying in the rain and wind. Only there was no wind. The sound beat against the air with a constant pressure beneath the more bellicose thunder of the guns.

Maybe Lucio's Greycaps were right. I wondered if I ought to cut my losses and go back to the city. But that wasn't an option.

'It's nothing,' I said. 'Just a lot of noise.'

'Doesn't sound like nothing. I haven't seen them this agitated since...' He trailed off. I knew what he'd been about to say. Since the last time the treekin had decided to tear the Fastness down, stone by stone. They'd failed then, as they always failed. But we lost ground nonetheless. We always lost ground.

'Guess I picked a bad time to leave the city.'

'You after somebody?'

'Why would you say that?'

'Only reason I can think of that a man like you goes anywhere is if you're after someone – or they're after you.' Lucio looked at me. 'So which is it?'

'Bit of both,' I said, after a moment.

It had started with the coin. A message from a dead man. Or someone as good as.

When it found me, I considered ignoring it. I'd broken almost every oath I'd taken when I'd abandoned the azure, after all. What was one more? I wasn't a priest any more, and the promises I'd made while I was one were just ashes as far as I was concerned.

But here I was, on a southbound wagon. I took the coin out of my pocket. It was Aqshian, a kind minted in some backwater city of the Great Parch. Not even real gold. It was stamped with the face of some petty king who'd probably long since been forgotten. Only, the face had been scratched out. That was how I knew what it meant.

I flipped it across my knuckles, trying to distract myself. Ten years on, I was fairly good at it. You can ignore almost anything, if you convince yourself there's no point in seeing it.

I knew who the coin was from, even if I didn't know who'd sent it, or how they'd found me. I'd spent a decade making myself hard to find and thought I'd done a good job of it. I'd even changed my name. 'Blackwood'.

The coin said otherwise.

I didn't like that, people knowing where I was. Who I was, or who I had been, for that matter. The coin was from someone who should've known better. I intended to tell them so. That was part of the reason I was going to Wald. Or so I told myself.

The truth is… the past, like the dead, doesn't always rest

easy. There's always someone looking to dig up what's better left buried.

I tossed my finished apple to the ghyroch. 'I'm going to go find Chantey. See what the hold-up is.'

'He's in a foul mood,' Lucio warned.

'So am I.'

As I climbed down, I looked back, past the wagons and inner defences, towards the distant forge-glow of the city. Greywater Fastness crouched at the end of the fortified road like a tiger herded into a cage.

I made my way around the wagon, sinking into the mud with every step. I pulled my coat tight about me, grateful for the heavy magmadroth leather. It was tough enough to turn aside most blades smaller than a sword, and kept out all but the worst of the weather.

I looked around. The gatehouse was a fortress in and of itself. Stables and animal pens occupied the north, while a forge anchored the south. Even with the rain, it was busy. Hammers rang as horses were shod. Block-and-tackle frames lowered goods to waiting wagons, as scribes hurriedly weighed cargoes and noted the results in logbooks.

It had to be self-sufficient. Every year, a little more of the mere vanished. Every year, the trees pressed closer to the road, further isolating the city from the rest of the realm. Every year, the Greycaps demanded more funds for guns and towers and walls to defend what was left. And every year, the Council of the Forge and the Grand Conclave gave it to them.

Given that they'd started out as a regiment of backwater hand-gunners it was almost impressive. The Greycaps had gone from a shifty crew of garrison soldiers to overseeing the defences of a city of several million.

The forecourt was crowded – drovers and sellswords diced or argued; food-sellers circulated, offering steaming bowls of broth for cut-rate prices; pilgrims gathered against the walls and sang hymns, rang bells or simply read loudly from the Canticles of Thunder. A steady tide of humanity, filling an ever-shrinking space – a microcosm of the realms themselves.

Despite the crowd, I spotted Chantey easily enough. He was right in the middle of all of it, as usual, along with a few other caravan-masters. They surrounded a put-upon Greycap in a vaguely threatening manner, and took turns yelling at the stubbornly unresponsive soldier. Several of them were waving scrip papers or badges of licence, as if it would do any good. If the Greycaps wanted the gates closed, they were staying closed.

Chantey turned as I drew near. He stepped away from the others, a sour expression on his hatchet face.

'Blackwood.' He said my name as if it were something unpleasant. I didn't hold it against him. Fallen priests aren't exactly high on anyone's list of desired companions. And I'd fallen harder than most.

'What's going on?'

'Something has the Greycaps riled up.' Chantey ducked his head and water spilled off the broad brim of his hat. 'Troggoths again, maybe. Or a mere-gargant…'

'Or Pale Oak,' one of the other caravan-masters said. Everyone fell silent at the treelord's name. If the sylvaneth were on the warpath again, there wasn't much chance of anyone going anywhere except back to the city.

'Whatever it is, it's something that ought not to be so close to the road, this time of day,' Chantey said firmly. 'They'll see it off, never fear.'

'Are they still going to let us through?' I asked.

'Eventually. Might be a few hours.' Chantey was from somewhere else, and his accent was a medley of all the places he'd ever lived. He fished a filigreed pocket watch from his coat and popped it open. The hands of the watch were stylised lightning bolts, and the runes were Azyrite. The Fastness was on celestial time, like all of Sigmar's cities. 'It's going to play merry hell with my schedule.'

Chantey led convoys south to Headwater Breach and back twice a month. That was the direction I needed to go, so I'd wrangled a berth aboard one of his wagons.

I flicked rain from my eyes. 'We'll make it in time, though?'

He looked at me. 'I said we would.'

'You also said there'd be no delays once we got past the New Fen Gate.'

'You can walk, if you like.' He snapped his pocket watch shut and put it away.

'If I thought it'd get me to Wald faster, I might.'

Chantey grunted. 'Don't see why you'd want to go there, of all places, anyway.' He looked at me speculatively. 'There's nothing in Wald except eels and moss.'

'My business, isn't it?'

He grunted again, but didn't press the issue. Chantey had once had a profitable side-business delivering the bodies of vagrants to the ash-grounds for cremation. I had helped him out a few times, enough to earn me some goodwill, along with a ride.

Up on the palisades, Greycaps were ringing bells and shouting. Handguns popped and cracked, splitting the curtain of rain. I heard a sound like trees bending in a great wind. I knew that sound. We all did, everyone who made Greywater Fastness their home.

The caravan-masters shared nervous looks. Even Chantey had lost the usual pugnacious gleam in his eyes.

'They're not attacking,' said the Greycap, the one Chantey and the others had been berating. His voice was soft, as if he weren't speaking to anyone in particular. 'They never do. We have a truce.'

And then he laughed. A sort of high-pitched, raggedy sound. He looked worn out and worn down. Unshaven, his uniform threadbare and stiff with stains. His hands were shaking and his eyes moved quickly, as if searching for something.

All of the soldiers looked the same. They were men riding the broken edge. They'd been out here too long, enduring the wild hours with no relief. I'd felt that way myself, often enough. There was only so long you could bear it. Every man had his breaking point. I knew that better than most.

Something slammed against the eastern wall. And then to the west. An echoing boom that made the wooden walls bow and flex alarmingly. Greycaps scrambled back from the ramparts as cannon crews redoubled their efforts.

'If they're not attacking, they're doing a pretty good job of making it look like they are,' Chantey spat.

'They can't attack,' the Greycap said dully, as if it were a mantra. 'We have a truce.'

I heard something like the skitter of leaves over lead roof tiles and felt a chill race through me. I knew that sound. The treekin were laughing.

'Maybe somebody needs to remind them,' I said, as my hand fell to my knife. It was the only weapon I carried these days. It was a good knife, but it was still just a knife. I had never been any good with a sword, and I wasn't about to pick up a hammer again. I couldn't afford a pistol and wouldn't have known how to use it, even if I'd had the comets to spare.

Chantey had his own blade half-drawn when the gun-towers on the palisade walls started up. The ghyrochs lowed in plaintive agitation. Everyone was nervous, even the beasts. Whatever it was was moving past the gatehouse, along the western walls. Greycaps scrambled to keep pace, and I could hear the order to fire being given.

'They're not attacking,' the Greycap said again, his voice high and thin. 'Not really. They're just… just playing, you see. Trying to draw us out. It's harmless. Harmless.'

'Doesn't sound harmless,' Chantey growled.

The volleyguns in the gun-towers spat rhythmic hails of lead into the rain. I heard the sound of trees in the wind again – a vast sighing that seemed to grow deeper and louder with every passing moment. It echoed through my bones and I felt it, down deep inside me. Like the memory of a song once heard and never forgotten.

The sylvaneth were singing. Somewhere out in the rain, out among the trees, they were singing. I wasn't the only one who heard it. I thought the Greycap was weeping, but it was hard to tell in the rain. Chantey pulled off his hat and closed his eyes. The guns stuttered to silence, as the song danced across the ramparts.

I'd heard that melody before, once and in another realm. But it had the same anger, the same sadness I'd heard back then. They hated us so much that it hurt them to feel it. Like a wound that never healed. The song – the attack – was a way for them to remind us of how much they despised us. How little we mattered.

The song reverberated through me, louder and louder, until I thought my head would burst from the pressure. And then, suddenly, it was done. As quickly as a man might snap his fingers, the song ended. The bells on the walls fell silent and the only sound was the rain and the lowing of ghyrochs.

The Greycap wiped his eyes, and made the sign of the hammer. Chantey put his hat back on, and I realised he'd been praying. I released a breath I hadn't recalled taking.

Chantey was the first to speak. He looked at me. 'Still want to go, then?'

I didn't trust myself to reply, so I just nodded.

Behind us, the portcullises began to open. The swamp road was clear.

CHAPTER TWO

THE COIN

I couldn't sleep.

It wasn't just the dreams, though those were bad enough. I felt every jolt and bump as the wheels passed through muddy potholes. This far out from the city, the road was in bad condition. Rain pelted against the canvas roof. Distant thunder rumbled, like the warning growl of some great beast. I was getting used to it. The wagon didn't leak as much as where I normally resided, and it didn't smell of bird droppings and foundry smoke.

I leaned back and peered through the wooden slats of the wagon. The rain made it hard to see much past the closest trees. In the occasional flash of lightning, I spied the broken remnants of statues, overgrown with clinging brambles and moss. They marked the places where the road had once diverged, or so I'd heard. Those paths were lost now, swallowed up by the swamp as it grew and spread, urged on by the rains.

The first settlers to Greywater Reach had drained the meres and harvested the trees and burned away everything else to build their city. But somehow it had all come creeping back over the decades, slowly but surely strangling the Fastness off from the rest of the realm. We deserved it. Whatever anyone says, we deserved it. Not just because of the devastation we left in our wake, but because we couldn't stop. Can't stop.

Sigmar won't let us.

I tossed the coin up and caught it as I watched a group of drovers and sellswords play cards by the light of a moss lantern. I flipped it over and over, but it always landed on the scarred side. I wondered if that was an omen.

I should have ignored it. Tossed it in a canal or given it to a beggar. Instead, I'd found the first wagon going south and begged a berth. Some things you just can't let go.

We'd worked out the signal together, all of us. Me and Murn, Osmal and Feyros, Glaspell and Arda. I remembered that night, just south of Broker's Bay. One of the last good nights, before it all went wrong.

The coin hadn't come into my hands alone. It had accompanied a letter, written in a regimental cipher. A request for reinforcements, written by a dead man and sent from a place I'd never heard of.

Wald. Even the name sounded strange.

It was one of the swamp-cantons – those isolated fiefdoms that littered the marshes of the Greywater Reach. There were maybe a hundred of them, some no larger than a town. Others consisted of several small villages, banded together under the leadership of a feudal lord, or a lone fortress.

They were left to their own devices by the Grand Conclave, mostly because no one remembered that they existed save around tithing season. Even then, it was a dedicated tithe-collector who braved the swamps to collect whatever pittance was to be had from those particular backwaters. If the swamp didn't get them, the inhabitants would.

I'd never travelled the swamps, even at my most desperate, though I'd heard there was work aplenty for sellswords. Their lords were a famously fractious lot. A man could make a good living travelling from canton to canton, changing masters with the seasons.

Evrek Murn wasn't that sort of man, though.

He and I hadn't parted on good terms. Maybe our relationship had cooled even before everything went wrong. The last time I'd seen him, he'd tried to kill me, and I hadn't been drunk enough to let him. A day later, or earlier, and things might have been different.

I didn't blame him, not really. I hadn't just ruined my life. I'd ruined his as well. Him and the others. Osmal, Feyros and all the rest. They'd made their choice, but I was the one who had given it to them in the first place.

But just because I understood didn't mean I was going to put my neck on the block. Especially now. Ten years was a long time to become comfortable with guilt. I'd made my peace with what had happened, insofar as I could.

I'd been wrong and the bastards I'd killed that night had been right. I was going to pay a heavy toll for what I'd done, whether tomorrow, or another ten years from now. But until then, I'd do everything in my power to keep the wolves of Azyr from my door. Even if that meant killing one of the few people remaining who might still be a friend because he knew where I was. Knew who I was.

But even having made that decision, I couldn't help but wonder why Murn had done it. What had possessed him to take such a risk – and why me, of all of us?

I'd briefly considered the possibility that it was a trap. Murn could hold a grudge, no doubt about that. But it had been a long time. I hadn't even realised he was in Ghyran, much less alive. It made me curious about the others and how they'd fared since we'd parted ways. I tried not to think about it. If they were smart, they'd done the same thing I had and gone into hiding. If they hadn't, then they were likely dead. Or worse.

If it was a trap, I was ready. It would make things easier if it was and I almost hoped Murn was planning something. I tapped the pommel of my knife as I considered the coin. 'A standard in every city, a comet in every purse,' I recited softly.

I closed the coin in my fist as one of the drovers flung down his cards and stood, grabbing a nearby crate to keep from falling over.

'That's it. I'm out a day's pay thanks to you and these damn cards, Gint.'

'So come back tomorrow,' Gint said, eliciting laughter from the group. He was a lanky sort, dressed in clothes that hadn't seen much wear. I knew his type. Wherever men worked, there was always a Gint. Always good for a laugh or a game, always there when it came time to be paid, but curiously absent whenever the duty roster was being drawn up.

The loser made an obscene gesture and lurched awkwardly to the front of the wagon. The game continued. New bets were laid down and money changed hands with increasing frequency. One by one, the players left as they ran out of money, or went back on duty. Eventually, only Gint and one other remained.

I wanted to go back to sleep, but knew it would be useless. Instead, I watched the remaining two drovers play cards through half-closed eyes. Constellations was a game of infinite regional and cultural permutations, few of which I'd ever understood. Osmal had tried to teach me once, but I'd never acquired the knack for it.

One of the drovers laid down a spread of cards. 'Hanged Man,' he said. 'Read 'em and wail, Gint.'

Gint flashed yellow teeth in a smile and said, 'I see your Hanged Man, and match with a Lion of Azyr. Beat that, Melf.' He set his cards down, and spread them with a quick flourish.

Melf stared at the cards and frowned. 'What...?' he began.

I saw his hand inch towards the skinning knife on his belt. Gint reached for the pile of motes between them, apparently heedless of the other drover's growing anger. As he moved, something slipped from his frayed sleeve and fluttered onto the pile. I groaned inwardly. Gint froze, his smile slipping.

Melf caught his wrist. 'Cheat,' the drover growled.

'Not in Hammerhal,' Gint said quickly.

'We're not in Hammerhal.' Melf jerked his knife from its sheath and slammed Gint against the side of the wagon, scattering coins and cards. Gint yelped.

'Kill him quietly, or not at all,' I said, without moving. 'I'm trying to sleep.'

Melf turned, eyes narrowed. 'Stay out of this, sellsword.'

'Or what?' I sat up. Melf raised his knife. I drew mine. 'I have a knife too. And I'm not a sellsword. Just a traveller, trying to get a bit of shut-eye. Now put that toy of yours down, before I turn it sideways and shove it up your arse.'

Melf hesitated. Despite his size, he wasn't a warrior. He released Gint and reached for the coins. 'Leave them,' I said softly. Melf froze. 'Consider it a stupidity tax. Now go find another wagon.'

Melf paused, as if weighing the odds. Then, with a snarl, he stumped to the back of the wagon and dropped to the ground. I watched him go. I was glad I hadn't had to kill him. Chantey wouldn't have been pleased.

'You saved me,' Gint said. He made to gather up the coins, but I stopped him. I gestured with my knife, and Gint scrambled back, eyes bulging.

'No,' I said. I picked up the coins. Gint visibly swallowed his protest.

'Stupidity tax?' he said.

'Everyone pays it, one time or another. You shouldn't have cheated.'

'I wasn't cheating. I was playing by a different set of rules.'

I laughed. I'd heard that one before. 'Is that what you call it?' I sat back and counted the motes. A tidy sum. Enough to buy a bottle of something nice, at least. And maybe a meal to go with it. I tossed a few coins to Gint. The drover scooped them up and made them vanish.

He settled down and shuffled his cards idly. 'Gint,' he said.

'What?'

'My name. Pallas Gint.'

'Harran,' I said, after a moment. 'Harran Blackwood.'

'Pleased to meet you, Harran. Care to give me a chance to win some of that money back?' Gint continued to shuffle the deck with one hand. I was impressed with his dexterity, if nothing else.

'No.'

'Ah well. Can't blame a fellow for trying, eh?' Gint peered at me, all smiles. I didn't trust a man who smiled that much, or that easily. 'You're not one of Chantey's regular sellswords. I've taken money off all of them.'

'Are you a drover or a gambler?'

'Both. Herding ghyrochs and bramblehorns is as much a gamble as a game of constellations.' Gint continued to shuffle his cards. 'Where are you heading?'

'Who says I'm heading anywhere?'

Gint snorted. 'You don't have the look of a man going nowhere.' He leaned back. 'Like I said, I know sellswords. Mostly, they look bored. They're marking the days. A lot like drovers, in that regard. One day is the same as the next, unless your luck turns.'

'My luck turned a long time ago.'

Gint smiled. 'But you're still in one piece. Sigmar protects, eh?'

'Not that I've noticed.' I almost laughed. Faith is a joke. The gods are hungry millstones, grinding up the faithful. We're currency, a way of keeping score. That's all. I know, because I saw it first-hand. I meddled in the affairs of heaven, and I paid the price.

I'm still paying it.

But I didn't say any of that.

Gint shifted uncomfortably. 'Not a Sigmarite, then? No matter. I'm not much of one for faith, myself. Rather trust my own two hands, you might say.' He shuffled the cards. He paused. 'Not a Nagashite, are you?'

I did laugh at that. 'No.'

'Good. Not that I have anything against Elder Bones and his lot, you understand,' Gint said quickly. 'Death is just a part of life, if you catch my meaning.' He made the sign of the hammer, if badly. 'Gods, eh? Not for men to understand. Keep your eyes on the horse in front of you, that's what my father says.'

'A wise man.'

Gint snorted. 'Not especially. But sometimes he has good advice.' He paused. 'Going to Headwater Breach, then?'

'No.'

'One of the other cantons?'

'Not really your business, is it?'

'Depends on how you look at it, friend. We're sharing a wagon. It behoves us to get to know one another.'

I snorted. 'Did your father tell you that as well?'

Gint laughed. 'No. I came up with that one on my own.' He paused again. 'What's in Wald, then?'

I looked at him. 'Who said I'm going to Wald?' It wasn't a secret. Chantey knew where I was going, so likely the whole caravan did, by now. Drovers gossiped like fishwives. But why had he pretended not to know, only a few moments ago?

'Are you?'

I leaned back. 'What of it?'

Gint shrugged. 'Not a nice sort of place, way I hear it.'

'And what do you hear?'

He shuffled his cards. 'There's a new lord there.' He selected a hand, frowned and reshuffled the deck. 'That always means trouble.'

'Not always.'

'Always,' Gint said firmly. 'People go missing in Wald.'

'People go missing in the swamp all the time.'

'True.' He selected a new hand, laying the cards out one at a time. 'But a lot of those people were around Wald when it happened. Funny that.' He looked up at me. 'Someone you know go missing?'

'You ask a lot of questions.'

'You're the one who didn't want to play cards.'

'I still don't. What else do you know about Wald?'

Gint frowned. 'Some of the other drovers could probably tell you more.'

'Maybe. I'm asking you.'

Gint sighed and began to shuffle his cards again. 'Used to be a proper town. Started as a logging camp, I think. Then the waters rose and it turned into what it is.'

'Which is?'

'Like I said... an unpleasant place.' He grimaced and cut his deck. 'All of them are, really. No one lives out in the swamp-cantons unless they have to.' He began laying out the cards again. 'The sylvaneth only abide by the truce if you're on the road. Everyone else is free game. Never understood why anyone would risk that.'

'Maybe they know something we don't.'

The wagon creaked to a halt. Cowbells clattered as horsemen rode up and down the line of wagons, calling out the time. The caravan was stopping for the night. Gint put his cards away and rose.

'Finally. I was getting tired of all that jostling.'

'Could be worse,' I said, hauling myself to my feet. 'You could be walking.'

Gint shuddered. 'Sigmar forfend.'

I heard a bleating scream from outside the wagon and peered out the back, Gint at my elbow. 'Bramblehorn,' he muttered. 'Stinking beasts.'

Bramblehorns were akin to sheep, though their thick, shaggy, coarse wool was the colour of moss, and their curling horns were barbed and deadly looking. The animals were hardy and capable of surviving even the most adverse conditions. They also didn't like being herded.

Shepherds rode among the flock, keeping them to the road and safe among the wagons. I winced as a big ram bleated fiercely and charged a shepherd's horse. The horse reared, pawing the air, and the rider cursed. A blunt spear thudded down, catching the ram in the flank. The animal spun and launched itself at the second shepherd, bleating loudly. The shepherds urged their horses towards the troublemaker. It took a deluge of blows to calm the animal and drive it back in amongst its flock.

'Chantey brought a hundred head,' Gint said. 'If we make it to Headwater Breach with sixty, it'll be a miracle. They say you get used to the smell. And the dung patches wagons nicely. Keeps them watertight.'

As we watched, a ewe was separated from the flock, and its hooves tied. The wailing beast was hauled onto a brawny drover's shoulders and had its throat cut. Its blood filled a line of plain wooden bowls.

'Looks like they're already filling the gheist-bowls,' Gint murmured. 'Bit early. It's not even dark yet.'

'Better safe than sorry,' I said, as I climbed down out of the wagon. The gheist-bowls were an old tradition – Shyishan, maybe. How it had come to Ghyran, I couldn't say. But it had become a custom of late, in these days when the dead were more prone to rise. Only sensible, really, given the state of things. It might even work, though I suspected that only lesser gheists would be appeased by such meagre fare.

I didn't like gheists. They didn't like me much, either. I wondered if it had something to do with me having been a priest. Maybe I was just unlucky. Whatever the reason, I could see them, and they could see me. Even the weak ones – the little threadbare nothings that haunt every roadside grave and forgotten place.

I hated them more than the others, if you can credit it. The nasty ones, the ones that anyone can see, they're simple things. All hate and spite; two things I know intimately. But the others, the little ones, they just… watch. Sometimes they try to speak, which is worse. Most people can't see the little ones. Or maybe they can, and pretend not to.

That's what I do. But sometimes I can't help but look.

It was still raining, causing the branches of nearby trees to twitch and dance in ways I didn't like. Farther back, where the light of the lanterns didn't reach, I caught a glimpse of a soft radiance.

'You see it too?' Gint asked. 'Think someone's out there?'

'Don't look at it,' I said. 'It's hag-light.' Some people called it ghoul-shine. Whatever name you used, it was death to follow it. It would draw a traveller into quickmud or cause them to become hopelessly lost, if they weren't careful.

'I've never seen it before,' Gint murmured. 'The way it bobs along, just out of the corner of your eye. Like it's trying to get your attention…'

'It is. It's trying to lure you off the road.'

Gint looked at me. 'You sound like you know an awful lot about it.'

'And you don't. You sure you've been out here before?' I asked. I wasn't suspicious of him, not exactly. But something about him was making me nervous, and I didn't like it.

Gint laughed and slapped me on the back. 'Maybe I'm just lucky.'

He ambled off. I watched him go.

Out in the swamp, the hag-light bounced and bobbled, and I could feel something watching me. Something – someone – was out there. Just at the edge of the light. I peered closer and saw duardin faces glaring back at me from within hoods of greenery.

Lonely plinths and posterns rose among the trees, and all of them had faces. The duardin were obsessed with faces, with giving eyes and mouths to everything they built. But they were being worn away by the swamp. Every sign that someone had once sought to tame this place was being strangled or submerged. I could feel the malice in the trees.

The swamp hated us. It hated the roads and all who travelled on them. It hated and watched and waited. As it was watching us now, watching us creep through its fiefdom, like furtive invaders. Like a cat, watching a mouse.

I heard a sound, like the babble of distant voices. A hasty susurrus, rising like a wind, full of pain and confusion. I heard the splash of unseen feet, and saw what might have been handprints forming on the sides of a nearby wagon.

The gheist-bowls began to twitch and slop, as if something were drinking greedily from them. As the blood vanished, the drinkers faded into view. Pale and fat, like grubs. Bloated, in the way of dead things too long in the water.

I wondered how many people had been drawn into the deep places by the hag-light. How many of them had drowned?

One of them turned to look at me. Its eyes were empty, red holes. Raw wounds in the white dough of its face. Its mouth moved.

For a moment, I fancied it was trying to say my name.

Suddenly cold, I turned away.

CHAPTER THREE

GHEIST-STORIES

It didn't take long for the caravan to make camp.

The half a dozen wagons were pulled up into a square formation, with only the lead wagon outside the block – almost
like a gatehouse. Campfires were dug in the hard turf of the
road, between each wagon, to be filled in at first light. The fires
were as much for light as they were for cooking and warmth.
The swamps were a bad place to be caught in the dark.

The animals were walked down the slope and into the soggy
grass to feed. The ghyrochs grumbled and shoved aside crooked
branches in their eagerness for mouthfuls of leaves. The bramblehorns milled beneath the trees, tearing up hunks of grass.

Drovers sat atop their horses, crossbows and spears at the
ready, just in case something decided to make a meal of one
of the beasts. Sellswords stood sentry between the wagons,
watching the encroaching dark for any sign of trouble. Bells

had been hung from every wagon, in reach should anyone see anything.

'Shouldn't you be doing something?' I said to Gint. He shrugged and leaned against the back of the wagon.

'They look like they've got it handled.'

'You're a lazy bastard, aren't you?'

'I prefer to think of it as conserving energy,' Gint said. 'Besides, I'm being paid to drive a wagon, not set up camp.'

'You've been playing cards since we left Greywater Fastness.'

Gint grinned. 'Relief driver. I'm not on duty until we start heading back.'

Gint was the sort who had an answer for everything. He was getting on my nerves.

'I'm hungry.' I pushed away from the wagon and left him there.

The rain had slackened to a phantom drizzle, and was barely noticeable. Scrap wood, gathered from the edges of the road, served as fuel for the campfires. No one thought to take wood from the trees. Not these days. That lesson had been learned early and well, and every caravan-master enforced it, if he had any wit at all.

As I neared one of the fires, Lucio and another drover made room for me with terse nods. The campfire was crowded. A dozen men, at least, a few duardin and even an aelf or two. With the work seen to, the drovers relaxed, drinking and singing incomprehensible songs for the dubious enjoyment of their fellows.

A chicken was turning slowly over the fire. Drovers sliced off portions with their skinning knives. A bow-legged shepherd with gold teeth and bad breath fed bits of gizzard to a whining knot of dogs. A sharp-featured swordswoman, clad in tatterdemalion finery beneath a battered scale mail shirt the colour of a cat's eye, strummed a lute with more enthusiasm than skill.

'Play us that Greenglades ditty, Taelya,' Gint said, as he sat down beside me. The sellsword laughed and plucked a mocking note.

'Only if you sing it, Gint.'

'I thought we were trying to avoid troggoths, not attract them,' one of the other drovers said, prompting a round of laughter. Gint made an obscene gesture, but was smiling. The woman with the lute – Taelya – began to play a merry tune. One of the mercenaries, a Calderan clad in flowing silks of red and yellow, attempted to dance to the off-kilter music, eliciting hoots of laughter from the others.

There was an easy companionability to it all that I realised a part of me still missed. Once, I'd huddled around similar fires, with similar men and women, listening to Osmal boast about his prowess in bed, or to Feyros elaborating on some obscure philosophical point. Murn had often sung for us. He'd had a pleasing voice. Able to sing the stars down from the skies, as Feyros had put it.

I shook the feeling off. The past was dust. I distracted myself with food and drink. I used my knife to saw off a slice of chicken, and watched the lutenist play. She caught me watching her and smiled invitingly.

I turned away. Out of the corner of my eye, I saw her shrug and go back to playing.

'Not interested?' a deep voice growled.

I turned. 'Not at the moment.'

The duardin was big, even seated. Compacted slabs of muscle, flattened and stretched, until only the vaguest resemblance to the human form was there. His beard spilled across his barrel chest, and the golden clasps that decorated it winked red in the firelight. His crest was almost as tall as I was standing, the dark hair held at attention by the sides of his golden helm, wrought in the shape of a rearing serpent. A fyreslayer, one of several Chantey had hired to act as guards.

'Besides,' I added. 'Not much privacy.'

'Never known that to stop your kind,' the duardin said. He

bared big, flat teeth in a wide smile. It was meant in a friendly way, but was still intimidating. 'Drink, manling?' the fyreslayer continued, proffering the wineskin he held. 'Aqshian piss-water, but at least it's bitter.'

I took the wineskin and nodded my thanks.

The first swig nearly made me choke. The second went down smoother, but not by much. It tasted of embers. Blinking back tears, I handed it off.

'Cindermilk?' I asked.

Gint took a pull and coughed. 'Chantey has a supplier in Hammerhal. He sells it in the markets up north. Stuff doesn't curdle for ages.' He sucked in a breath and passed it on. 'I like it a bit sour, myself.'

Taelya was playing softly now – a mournful sort of tune. I took another pull of the cindermilk when it came around, enjoying the warm flush that filled me now that I was expecting it. Two sellswords began to play some Ghurdish variation on constellations. Gint watched them avidly, and I wondered whether he was planning to deal himself in.

I handed the wineskin back to the duardin.

'Soldier, were you?' he said.

'No.'

'But you've seen battle.'

I nodded. 'Too much of it.'

The duardin shook his head. 'No such thing. A good fight is like good meat, good drink, but for the spirit. It keeps the soul aflame.' He reached into the fire and snatched up an ember. He bit into it, chewing with apparent relish. 'Orm,' he said, spitting sparks.

'Harran.'

Orm took a deep pull on the wineskin and passed it to a drover. 'You're no sellsword, then. No drover. Not a shepherd, either. You don't smell bad enough.'

My reply was drowned out by a shrill bellow, echoing from the darkness beyond the fire's light. It reminded me of a stag's cry, only fiercer and more savage. No one moved. 'Troggoth,' Gint said, flipping over the top card of his deck. He didn't sound certain, but no one disagreed. 'Something's got it riled up.'

'It sounds close,' I said. My grip tightened convulsively on the hilt of my knife. I'd fought troggoths before. I wasn't in a hurry to repeat the experience.

'It won't come any closer,' Orm said. He sounded more certain than Gint, but not by much. 'They rarely do. Most of the ones on this route know better. It's just letting us know that we're in its territory.'

'Sounds strange,' Lucio said. 'Not like any troggoth I've ever heard.'

Gint shrugged. 'Might be sick.' He shuffled his deck of cards, his movements nervous. 'Never known troggoths to get sick, though.'

'Saw one with the Rot, once,' a sellsword named Akkas muttered. He was a stocky man, barrel-chested and bandy-legged. He wore armour made from ghyroch hide and a steel-pot helmet that covered most of his head. The shield propped up beside him was circular and battered, and the sword he carried was little more than a cleaver. 'It died,' he added.

'Most things with the Rot do,' I said. The Rot wasn't natural, like many of the plagues that still haunted the byways of the realm. It was a dark gift, bestowed upon the mortal races by a mad god. It ate away at flesh and muscle, until only maggot-riddled bone remained. Worse than moss-leprosy, for at least with the moss you felt no pain. The Rot wasn't so considerate.

'It's the ones that don't die you have to watch out for,' Orm growled.

'It's been a long time since we've seen any of their sort,' Lucio said. He looked around nervously, as if seeking Rotbringers in every shadow. He wasn't the only one.

'But their memory lingers like a stink,' Gint said.

I'd fought Rotbringers before. I remembered the way it had felt, as my hammer pulped purpling flesh and maggot-riddled bone. It wasn't like fighting men. The Rot had come with them, decades ago, and had lingered long after the last of them had perished. Sometimes it flared up again, in out-of-the-way places.

I'd seen the aftermath of that as well, more than once. I'd heard the screams, as the afflicted were locked in their own homes, and the torches were lit. I'd watched the smoke from the pyres rise, and smelled the stink of burning meat. A worse smell, somehow, than any stink I'd encountered on the battle-field. And made all the more awful by the fact that the screams had continued long after they should have stopped.

I watched the motes of ash rising up as the campfire crackled and snapped, devouring the scrap wood that was used to feed it. It reminded me of the chapel, of the smell of smoke in my nose, and the sound of weapons. The sound of death.

The sound of the storm.

I remembered the ugly amethyst light of Feyros' magicks, as he spat obscenities and spells in the same breath. Osmal's scream, as a knife dug for his vitals. Murn, yelling out Sigmar's name as he fought. I remembered doing the same.

I remembered climbing the steps of that crumbled dais, and Cassian waiting for me there, his golden mask – Sigmar's mask, the face of the God-King – in his hand. The look in his eyes as I swung my hammer towards his head. Not wrathful or fearful. Sad. As if he understood the enormity of my error.

As if he forgave me.

Thunder boomed, off in the distance. I jumped.

'Harran?'

I blinked.

Gint held up a card. 'Care for a game?'

Orm snorted. 'You call that a game?' He laughed. The sound

was like rocks crunching together. 'That's nothing but bluffing for coin. A real game requires skill.'

Gint seemed unperturbed. 'You're only saying that because I beat you last time.'

Orm flushed. His eyes glinted with danger. 'You cheated.'

'And you *got* cheated,' Gint said blithely. He shuffled the deck. 'Not my fault you couldn't catch me.'

'I want my gold back, Gint.'

'Then play me again.' He smiled. 'No cheating this time, I promise.'

'Your promises aren't worth the air you wasted speaking them.'

Gint laughed and looked at me. 'How about you? Let me win some of that money back, eh?' He flicked a card into a nearby bucket. He repeated the gesture twice more. He was skilled, when it came to cards.

'No.'

Gint made as if to protest, but Orm beat him to it. 'Going to Headwater Breach, then?' he asked, looking at me.

'Way I hear it, he's going to Wald,' Akkas said. 'Though Sigmar alone knows why.' He burped, and used a knife to pick at something in his teeth.

'Bad place, that,' a drover said. He was a heavyset man, grizzled and weather-beaten. He stank of bramblehorn, and had a thick beard, plaited in Lyrian fashion, bound in clasps of iron.

'Oh?' I asked. 'And what do you know about it?'

'Yeah, Gunter. What do you know about it?' Gint said.

'I been riding herd on this route since you were squalling for your mother's milk,' Gunter said. He thrust his knife into the remains of the chicken carcass dangling from the spit, and prised loose a chunk of meat. 'Been to Wald a time or two.' He chewed thoughtfully. 'Not a good place.'

I glanced at Gint. 'So I'm told. What makes it not good?'

The drover sucked grease from his fingers. 'None of the cantons

are, really. Can't be. Got to be hard to live out here, in *her* lands.'
Silence fell for a moment. Men glanced instinctively at the trees.

We all knew who the drover meant. She had many names – the
Everqueen, the Lady of Leaves, the Singer Beneath the Boughs –
but whatever one called her, she was no friend to men. Especially
those from Greywater Fastness. This land, this *realm*, was hers,
whatever the church said, and her children prowled the wilderness.

Several of the drovers murmured prayers, and one of the sellswords – a Verdian – pulled a charred piece of wood from the
edge of the fire and knocked on it. Orm made a curious gesture
and spat between his spread fingers.

'Don't say her name, whatever you do. Not out here.' The
duardin stirred the fire fiercely, casting up a swathe of sparks.

'I didn't say her name,' Gunter protested. 'I know better. How
long have I been doing this?' He cut off another slice of chicken.

'Since I was squalling for my mother's milk, apparently,' Gint
said.

'Quiet,' I said. I looked at Gunter. 'What do you know about
Wald?'

'Nasty place,' the drover said.

'Besides that.'

'Used to be bigger. Logging camps. Farms. Then, the waters
rose and swallowed most of it. All that was left was what was on
high ground. Everything else was drowned.' The drover cleaned
his knife on his trousers and sheathed it. 'Place has been sliding
into the mud ever since. Waters rise and fall here like ocean tides.
Some days, the swamp retreats, and some days it advances.' He
looked at me. 'They don't like strangers, there.'

I smiled. 'Do they anywhere?'

Gunter shook his head. 'I've heard stories. About folk going
to Wald and never leaving. About a pedlar found strung up and
hanging from a tree, his body all cut to ribbons like he fell in a
thorn bush. Or the tithe-man who went missing.'

'Tithe-men always go missing,' a sellsword said, from across the fire. 'Usually with a saddlebag full of comets.' This witticism was met with laughter.

Gunter shook his head. 'You mark me – Wald doesn't belong to us. There is them that say you can see lights dancing on the waters, and hear the eels singing when the water's low. But when it's high, things come walking up out of the deep places. Hungry things.' He pushed himself to his feet. 'I only hope we're past the place by then.' He sloped off without a parting word, leaving the rest of us to get on with our evening.

No one was much in the mood to talk after that. Even Taelya's playing died away to a few notes, plucked half-heartedly. Eventually, she got up and left. The other sellswords followed suit, one by one. Gint joined them, murmuring something about sleep.

I stayed where I was, watching the fire. I think, eventually, I slept.

Or at least it felt like sleep. My limbs were like lead, and my thoughts circled one another slowly. But my eyes weren't closed, and even as the fire burned to a red murmur, I saw something unfold from the edges of the swamp.

At first, I took it to be a stag. Perhaps drawn by the light, the smell of food or the other animals. But it moved wrong, and was far too massive. I'd only ever seen beasts that big in Ghur. And the way it appeared... absent one moment, there the next.

It stepped over and past the unheeding sentries, silent and towering, blotting out the clouds and the stars beyond. Its antlers stretched up and out, spreading as if to fill the sky. With it came the sound of splashing and an eerie trilling. As if something in the waters celebrated its coming. A smell like wet bark and blood rolled over me.

The animals stirred, lowing and bleating, huddling together as the towering shape stepped over them soundlessly. Restive horses pawed the mud, whinnying as their riders murmured calming

words. They could not see what the animals saw. What I saw.
Could not see the antlers scraping the sky, or hear the sound of
creaking boughs.

I felt the spongy ground shift beneath me as it drew close.
I tried to make myself as small as possible. I closed my eyes,
hoping it would go past, whatever it was. I felt the ground trem-
ble, and knew it was close. Knew, without looking, that it was
leaning over the wagon, leaning close, thrusting something that
might have been a face down towards me. I heard a rustling,
soughing sound.

Wake up.

I bolted upright, heart thudding. Bleary-eyed, I took in the
camp. The fires were burning low, and most were still asleep.
I looked around, but saw no great shape, smelled no musk of
wet bark or blood.

Just a dream, then. And not as bad as some. I ran my hands
through my hair, and made to lie back down when I saw Gint
pad past. He was moving quietly, his gaze fixed on something –
or someone. Curious, I rose and followed as quietly as I could.

If Gint was up to something, I wanted to know what.

CHAPTER FOUR

HAG-LIGHT

Gint slipped past the sentries easily. They weren't watching for anyone sneaking out of camp – only a lunatic would do that out here. Leaving the road was tantamount to suicide. But Gint seemed determined. When I spotted the hag-lights, I realised why.

They danced across the surface of the water or along the branches of the trees. He splashed after them as they retreated. He said something but I couldn't make it out.

I'd told him not to look, the fool. Obviously he hadn't listened. Gint was nothing to me. But I followed nonetheless. I couldn't tell you why. Maybe it was because I'd got used to following my instincts in such matters. Working for a man like Caspar Guno had taught me that much. The moment you ignore your instincts is the moment you end up face down in a canal, your throat open ear-to-ear. Then again, if I hadn't followed my instincts, I wouldn't have had to work for Caspar Guno in the first place.

The swamp swallowed us up with barely a whisper. From within the shroud of trees, it seemed endless, stretching in all directions as far as the eye could see. A chill mist rose from the waters, clinging to the bases and branches of the trees and the tottering piles of semi-collapsed stone. The shadows seemed to be waiting for the sun to slip, and then they spilled out from beneath the trees at every opportunity.

Gint vanished. I had him in my sights one moment, and the next – gone. I struggled over to where he had been, blundering through bulrushes and past mouldy stone markers. I could hear the bending and snapping of branches all around me, as if something heavy were moving very swiftly. I drew my knife, knowing it would do no good, but glad to have it regardless.

'Gint,' I shouted. 'Where are you?'

...where are you...

...where are you...

It wasn't my voice I heard echoing back at me. To my left, something laughed. It was the laugh of a child, but sinister. Stripped of innocence and joy. A malign sound. The suddenness of it, incongruous in my surroundings, stopped me dead. I listened, detecting only the soft sounds of the swamp. The hum of insects, and the rustle of vermin. The murmur of wind through the highest branches. A twig snapped behind me.

I turned, looking back the way I'd come. I could just make out the glow of the campfires. It seemed farther away than it ought to be. To my right, there was a hint of movement, as if someone – *something* – had ducked out of sight, just as I turned. Another laugh, softer than the wind.

'Come out,' I said, even though I knew – *hoped* – they wouldn't. 'You want me, come and get me.'

Bravado had carried me through unpleasant circumstances more than once. A bellyful of spite can keep a man on his feet even when he ought to be dead. Showing you were harder and meaner than anyone else kept you alive on the streets of the Fastness.

My words were swallowed by the trees. No reply came. Part of me was glad. I knew what this was. They were trying to distract me. To keep me from reaching Gint. They'd chosen him as their prey, not me. Another reason I should go while I could. But I didn't.

'Gint,' I called out. 'Damn it – *Gint!*'

Gint... int... int...

More laughter, eerie and sibilant.

Look... You can see him...

I didn't. I saw only the vague hint of a man, moving rapidly away through the water and shadow. I could hear him though, splashing.

Look... There he is...

A tree rose up in my path, its bark shaggy with moss. It stank of standing water, and seemed to totter on broken roots. Gheists clung to it, watching me with empty holes for eyes. They tried to speak, but no sound came out. Which was just as well. I wasn't in the mood to listen anyway.

Look... Over there... there... there...

I turned. Insects swarmed me in a humming cloud. I swiped at them, trying to clear the air. I was in the dark now, the light of the camp blotted out, and voices all around me. Branches tugged at my hood and coat. I chopped at them with my knife, to no avail.

Go back... Stop... Go back...

I pressed on. Brambles tore at my legs and hands. The hag-lights clumped thick and radiant to either side of me. I could hear the sylvaneth murmuring all about me. Laughing at me. Of course they thought it was funny.

Only death awaits you-ou-ou-ou...

I could see them now – thin shapes, moving from tree to tree, illuminated by the dancing hag-lights. I pushed through the reeds and hanging branches, trying to follow them, but they darted away before I got too close. I found myself staring at the camp. They'd led me in a circle, without me noticing.

Go back... Go back...

I heard a cry and turned. 'Gint?' I asked, more softly than I intended. There was a snort and a stamp, as of a great hoof. Things that might have been antlers set the branches to rattling. I remembered my dream, and wanted to run.

The thing turned and bolted, crashing through the brush. Without knowing why, I followed. Maybe it wanted me to. Maybe I just wanted to prove I wasn't afraid. Regardless, it led me away from the light, away from the camp, deeper into the dark.

Voices – sounds – spun around me in a dismal cacophony. Were the sylvaneth following me, or were they trying to get out of the way of whatever I was pursuing? I didn't have long to think about it. The beast – the stag? – leapt over a fallen tree and galloped through a cloud of hag-lights, scattering them to reveal my quarry.

Gint hadn't got as far as I'd feared. They'd been waiting on him, or maybe just for anyone foolish enough to leave the safety of the camp. The sylvaneth surrounded him. I couldn't tell how many. Things of mist and bark, circling, jeering, clutching. They had faces like demented infants and screaming women. Their curved claws pulled him back and forth, as if he were a toy they were fighting over. His arms and face bled from dozens of small cuts already – soon, they'd butcher him. Once they'd finished arguing over the privilege.

He was dazed and crying out with every slash and poke. He was trying to say something, to talk to them maybe. Gint was the type to think he could talk his way out of anything. Not this time. They knocked him to his knees. I knew then that they'd decided to end the game. They froze as my guide galloped past, sending waves of water up and scattering the hag-lights. It gave a shrill cry as it vanished into the trees.

Old instincts are hard to ignore. While they were distracted, I charged one of the sylvaneth, and knocked it sprawling into the water. The rest turned on me, hissing and shrieking. I slashed out with my knife, driving them back as I made my way to Gint's side. They swiped at me, but none came close, as if uncertain. It wouldn't last.

'Gint, wake up,' I snarled, grabbing his arm. 'Get up, fool!'

He looked at me in a daze. 'What... Harran?'

The sylvaneth snarled and wailed, circling us. I could see more of them, creeping about through the trees, cutting off all routes of escape. 'Get up, damn you,' I said, trying to get him on his feet. 'Get up or I'm leaving you here.'

As I spoke, a sylvaneth sprang towards us. I lunged, catching it in mid-leap. The knife jolted in my hands, and I twisted it, piercing bark and releasing a spurt of sap. The sylvaneth screamed and jerked away from me, staggering back.

'The meat bites,' it shrilled, in a voice like rushes rustling in the wind. 'It bites with iron!'

'Tear it with bark and stone,' another screeched. 'Pulp it and grind it. Break its bones and make it dance.' The others hissed in similar fashion. But none seemed willing to make the first move. It was as if something held them back.

I've never been one to look a gift horse in the mouth. 'Come on,' I said. I caught hold of Gint and hauled him stumbling after me. I could make out the ruddy glow of the campfires reflected on the water. We hadn't gone as far as I'd thought.

'Where are we going?' he gasped. Behind us, I heard screeches and the snap of limbs as the sylvaneth gave chase. I didn't look back, though Gint did. From his curses, I could tell it wasn't a pleasant sight. 'They're right behind us,' he said.

'Head to the light,' I said. 'Don't stop, whatever you do.'

I should have known better. Such words were tantamount to a challenge. Gint stumbled and fell, spluttering. I heard a rushing sound, like water surging over its banks. As I hauled him roughly to his feet, something tore at the edges of my coat.

A shrill caterwaul of scraping branches and popping roots filled my ears. The cacophony threatened to deafen me. Water surged up, and other things besides – reaching, grasping, *coiling* things. I heard Gint scream. Brambles erupted from the black water and lashed about me as I turned, knife in hand. They bit into my flesh, and tore my clothes. I strained against them, gripping a nearby root, desperate not to be dragged under those waters. I knew that if I went, I wouldn't surface again.

I felt my fingernails lift and tear, as splinters slid beneath them. The brambles tightened about me, biting into my legs and stomach. 'Harran...!' Gint began, grabbing for me. I shoved him back with my free hand.

'Go, you idiot,' I shouted. 'Keep moving.' Then I lost my grip and was dragged, thrashing, towards the dark beneath the trees. I twisted, stabbing at the woody vines that held me. My knife was sharp, and I was desperate. Serum spurted, and the vines contracted, as if in pain. I stabbed again and again, bracing myself against the trees. Water rushed up and swirled about me, cold and clutching. There were bones in it, brown from their time in the mire. I was shouting now, old snatches of half-remembered prayers and catechisms. Just words – a mindless, animal bellow of protest.

I glimpsed shapes that hunched and skulked. Ghostly faces that were not faces, not really, leered in and jagged splinter-teeth champed in excitement – or maybe frustration. I slashed frantically, fiercely at the brambles. They released me, gouging me bloody as they pulled loose and slithered back into the water. I was bleeding from dozens of small wounds, and my hands were raw and red.

I struggled hurriedly to my feet and staggered after Gint. He was already halfway to the light when I caught up to him. Both of us were bloody and flagging, but stopping now meant a nasty death, or something worse.

As I ran, I shouted, 'Ware the camp! Ware!' Gint joined his voice to mine as we burst from the treeline, staggering through knee-deep waters towards the glow of welcoming light. I have never been so glad to see any place as I was that camp, in that moment.

At first, I feared no one had heard us. Then an alarm bell began to ring. I saw torches spring to life as men and women poured out from between the wagons. I heard voices shout in fear and shock as we stumbled into the light.

However, the sylvaneth were nothing if not persistent. They came in a rush, hot on our heels. Gint was knocked sprawling and I nearly lost my head. I lashed out with my knife, hacking at whatever came in reach. I recognised the one I had wounded before, even as it bore me backwards, against the embankment. I stabbed it again and again as it tried to throttle me. Sap spattered my clothes and hands as its splintery fangs snapped at my face.

Crossbow bolts punched into it, knocking it back. It staggered and screamed.

'Fire, you idiots,' Chantey bellowed. 'Fire and axes.'

'I've got plenty of both,' Orm roared as he splashed down towards the sylvaneth, axe slashing out in a wide arc to drive the treekin back. Behind him came Taelya, Akkas and several other sellswords. All bore torches in their hands, and the sylvaneth retreated. But they didn't go far, merely to the edge of the light. They prowled there, hissing and creaking like trees caught in a windstorm.

'Everyone get out of here,' Orm shouted. 'Back onto the road, all of you.' He paced at the edge of the light, axe at the ready. 'They won't follow us onto the road.'

'How do you know?' I demanded, as I shoved Gint up the embankment.

'Trust me, manling,' Orm growled. He swung his axe at a sylvaneth who got too close. The treekin retreated, snarling. 'I've done this before. All of you – fall back'

The sellswords didn't need to be told twice. Akkas and Orm fell back more slowly, never taking their eyes off the sylvaneth. A dozen treekin pursued them, without haste. I could hear more of them, moving in the dark. From above came Chantey's voice, calling for more light, and the squealing of frightened animals.

Then from out of the swamp came a shrill bellow, like the cry of a stag. For a moment, everything stopped. The sylvaneth seemed to turn as one, heads cocked. 'The Old Stag,' one of the creatures chittered. 'He calls!'

...the Old Stag...

...the Old Stag...

'No,' another hissed – the one I'd hurt. 'This is our meat. Our prey.' The sylvaneth lunged forward, quicker than thought, and knocked both Akkas and Orm sprawling. Akkas' sword spun from his grip. It raised both fists over the stunned mercenary.

'Akkas,' Taelya called out. I snatched up Akkas' fallen sword just as the sylvaneth slammed both fists down on his shield. The metal buckled, and I heard the mercenary's arm shatter. Akkas fell back into the water, cursing. I took two, swift steps towards him. The sylvaneth reared back, as if startled, leaving itself open. I struck.

The sword was not well-made. It was not a kingly blade, or even a soldier's weapon. It was a tool. Nothing more. But it did the job.

The sylvaneth's head rolled free of its neck, and fell into the water with a deep splash. The body followed, a moment later. Both vanished beneath the water.

Silence fell. The treekin stared at me, and I felt something take root in my soul. A niggling fear that I'd crossed some line I hadn't noticed before. Then, one by one, they slipped back into the trees and were gone, as if they had never been.

Panting slightly, I turned to check on Akkas. 'Took its head off with one blow,' he said, as if not believing his own eyes.

'Seemed the thing to do,' I said. 'Are you...?'

'Still alive,' the Ghurdish sellsword said, in a voice tight with pain. Taelya helped him to solid ground, Orm following them.

'Thanks to you,' Taelya added.

I shook my head. 'Orm would have done it, if I hadn't.'

'But he didn't,' Akkas said.

Orm shrugged. 'Not being paid to keep you alive, am I?'

'I'm not sure why I'm paying any of you,' Chantey spat. He was waiting for us at the top, a torch in his hand. He glared at me. 'What were you playing at, Blackwood? Even a fool like you should know better than to leave the road, especially at night!'

'It was my fault,' Gint said, before I could reply. 'I thought...' He trailed off. Chantey stared at him as if he'd sprouted a second head.

'You thought what? Maybe they'd want a game? Maybe you wanted to break the truce and get us all killed, eh?'

'We weren't the first to break it. Look at these tracks,' Orm said. He crouched near one of the wagons. 'Something was wandering out here.' He traced a deep print, cut into the muddy ground. 'Like a stag's hoof, only too large. And... wrong, somehow.' He gestured with his axe. 'And there, on the wagons... See those marks?'

There were scrapes on the wood, as if something sharp had been rubbed against the side of the wagon. The marks were almost a pattern, if you squinted. As if whatever it was had marked the wagon. I glanced back at the swamp, but there was nothing there save darkness.

'I want the guard doubled for the rest of the night,' Chantey said. 'And someone set Akkas' bloody arm.' He looked at me. 'That goes for you too, Blackwood. You're on watch.'

'I doubt I could sleep anyway,' I said.

Chantey nodded. He paused. 'You should have left him.'

'I thought about it.'

He snorted. 'Should have thought harder. Sometimes, there's a toll that needs paying, like it or not.' He clapped a hand on my shoulder. 'I think you know that better than most.'

I nodded, and looked around. Gint had vanished. He hadn't even thanked me. Not that I'd expected it. I realised I was still holding Akkas' sword. I looked down at it, at the sap staining it like blood. I made a half-hearted attempt to clean it, but it was impossible.

'You'll need to hold it in the fire,' Orm said. 'Have to bake it off.'

'Akkas can do it himself then.' I planted the sword in the ground before me. 'Thank you,' I said, after a moment.

Orm grunted. 'I'm paid to defend the caravan, manling. That includes you.' He peered at me. He indicated the marked wagon. 'That was the wagon you rode on, wasn't it?'

'What of it?'

Orm shrugged. 'Perhaps nothing. But none of the other wagons were marked in such a fashion. Scratches, mud, but nothing like that.' He looked away. 'The spirits in this place are young, by the reckoning of this realm. Like children, they're spiteful – but not wise. Cruel, but lacking in cunning.'

'You sound like you've had first-hand experience.'

Orm chuckled, but there was no mirth in it. 'We of the Baeldrag have long had dealings with them.'

'Friendly dealings?'

'No. They have no friends, those folk. Like the forest, they are hard and wild. Treacherous, and as changeable as the seasons. Just like their queen.' Orm looked around. 'But best, perhaps, to keep such thoughts to ourselves. They hold grudges as well as any of my kin.'

He looked at me knowingly.

'Something, perhaps, to keep in mind.'

CHAPTER FIVE

WATER-ROAD

We reached the canton of Wald a few days later.

I'd spent my time wisely. Every drover and sellsword in the caravan had stories, and I'd gathered them the way Gint gathered coins. Most of them were the same refrain, over and over again – *Wald was sour, Wald wasn't for strangers* – but here and there were other stories. Bits and pieces of tales told by pedlars and realmwalkers... stories of laughter in the night, and creaking shapes lolloping along isolated tracks. Of strange processionals through the swamps, and rough voices raised in song.

Nothing that made me want to stay any longer than I had to or gave me any insight into why Murn was here, and why he'd risked so much to contact me. I wondered if he knew what calling on me meant – whether he suspected I'd come to shut him up, if for no other reason. Maybe he was counting on it. That would have been like him. Murn had always been one for risks, especially in the right cause.

When I wasn't cadging stories, I dozed. It was hard to sleep at night, with the silent trees looking on. The animals agreed, and I shared their unease, even if no one else did. And when I dozed, I dreamed strange, green dreams. Not my usual dreams of fire and the stink of incense, but dreams of wet shadows, and soft, green, pulsing things.

I didn't like it.

Something was waiting for me in Wald. I could feel it, like a beast circling just beyond the fire. Waiting for me to let my guard down. I was determined to make sure that it would be sorely disappointed.

Outside the wagon, a bramblehorn groaned in protest as a drover swatted it back onto the path. The swamp edged closer to the road, and the horsemen were careful to keep the bramble-horns from straying. There was precious little safe ground away from the road out here, and nowhere close to hand to forage.

I heard Gint laugh, and looked over at the card players. As usual, Gint was winning. I didn't know whether or not he was cheating this time, but it wouldn't have surprised me. It never stopped the other drovers and the sellswords from trying to take his money regardless. Akkas and Taelya were among them. The Ghurdish warrior had his arm in a sling and was awkwardly try-ing to sharpen his blade one-handed. I'd dulled it when I'd taken the sylvaneth's head off. Taelya was playing cards, and losing badly by the looks of it.

'That's it, Taelya,' Gint said, throwing down his hand. 'A full bastion. Beat that.'

Taelya threw down her cards in disgust. The sellsword had her lute strapped to her back, and as she reached for it, she said, 'Just for that, I'm going to write a song about you, Gint. And not a flattering one.'

'Given how you play, that's not much of a threat,' Gint chortled. The sellsword rose to her feet, looking as if she might just brain him instead. But she turned away and plucked sourly at the strings of the lute. She kicked my outstretched feet aside.

'What did I do?' I asked, looking up.

'Nothing,' she said, and strummed the lute. 'More's the pity.' She sat down beside me and let her legs dangle off the back of the wagon. 'Still planning to leave us at the next stop?'

'Yes.'

She nodded. 'Be better if you didn't. You're good with a sword. Chantey would hire you, if you'd ask him to.'

'I have something I have to do.'

She indicated my knife. 'That sort of something?'

I looked away. 'Does it matter?'

'Not to me.' She strummed her lute for a moment. 'You saved Akkas, so I owe you.'

'You two close, then?'

'Close enough.' She plucked a sour chord. 'Care for a bit of advice?'

'If it's free.'

'I did some work up around the barony of Mossreach a few years back...'

I indicated her sword. 'That sort of work?'

She grinned. 'The only kind that pays. Anyway, the old baron hosts a feast every winter solstice. Lord Wald was among the guests. Right bastard. Arrogant.'

'So, like nobles everywhere?'

'He's different. Most of the petty lordlings in these parts like to claim they've got Azyrite ancestry. Like to pretend they're descended from Sigmar himself, rather than just jumped-up backwater aristocracy. But the Walds claim a different sort of lineage.' She leaned over and spat. 'Jade-bloods. All Ghyranites. Not from Verdia or Lyria, though. Somewhere farther south.'

That was unusual. Most of the cantons around Greywater Reach were ruled by star-bloods – descendants of the first Azyrite colonists to arrive in Ghyran. 'They've been here a while, then,' I said.

Taelya nodded. 'You might say that.' She scratched her chin. 'They've been here since there was a here, the way it was told to me. Their roots go deep.'

'I'm not planning to get in their way, if that's what you're worried about.'

'You might not have a choice.'

'Oh?'

'You're looking for someone, aren't you?'

I paused. 'Maybe. Why?'

'People go missing in Wald.'

'So I hear.'

She looked at me. 'A while back, I heard from some acquaintances of mine and Akkas'... the Lord Wald was looking for sellswords. Needed guards, or so they said.'

'That's not unusual. The swamps are dangerous, even at the best of times.'

'They didn't need them for defence.' She plucked at her lute. 'They needed them for transport duty...'

That caught my attention. Enforced transport was a common sentence for criminal behaviour in Greywater Fastness. You got stuffed onto a prison barge with every other lowlife and debtor that the Greycaps had caught that day, and sent somewhere downriver. Generally, a term of forced labour was what awaited you at the end of your involuntary pilgrimage. Occasionally it would mean service in one of the penal regiments, or being press-ganged onto a ship heading for Thyria. Sometimes, it just meant a stint of hard labour.

'I didn't realise the swamp-cantons transported their criminals.'

'They don't,' she said, playing softly. 'The transports were coming to Wald.'

'Why?'

She shrugged. 'I didn't ask, and they didn't say.'

I sat back. 'Well, it's none of my business either, is it? Thank you, though.'

'For what?'

'The warning.'

She nodded. 'What you did for Akkas – I owed you.' She strummed her lute. 'And Gint is a fool, but you did right by him.'

A bell began to ring, somewhere further up the line.

'Looks like we've arrived,' Taelya said. She slid from her perch and landed lightly on the ground. 'Watch yourself, Blackwood,' she said, as she strode off. 'Keep that knife of yours close.'

I leaned out of the back of the wagon, ignoring the rain that plastered my hair to my scalp. I watched the wagons behind us sway to a halt along the muddy stretch of road. As always, the ghyrochs protested loudly, their heavy hooves sinking deep into the marshy ground as they lumbered to a stop. Clouds of insects rose about the straining animals and spread out in shimmering waves as the wagons rocked on their axles.

The trees were thicker here, rising from the water in clumps. They reminded me of watchtowers, overseeing the approach to a castle. Rushes blanketed the shallows, and the grass on the causeway was akin to an animal's pelt. Everything was green and damp, and reeked of the swamp. It reminded me of my dreams.

For a brief moment, I considered doing as Taelya had suggested. A man like me could make his fortune in Headwater Breach. Caspar Guno wasn't the only usurer in the Jade Kingdoms, and men like that always needed someone like me.

Maybe afterwards, when I'd done what I'd come out here to do. Maybe then I'd go somewhere else. Somewhere smaller than the city. Quieter. I took the coin out of my pocket and turned it between my fingers.

If Murn was really alive – if he'd really sent the coin – there was only one way this could end. I'd put too much effort into hiding myself to let him ruin it now.

What would it be like, to kill someone I'd thought of as a friend? Would it be hard? Or worse – easy? I wondered if Murn had asked himself the same thing the last time we'd met. Regardless, I wasn't going to make the same mistake he had. If Evrek Murn was still alive, he wasn't going to be for much longer.

'So, we're here then?' Gint said, from behind me. I snapped my fist shut about the coin and shoved it back into my pocket.

'Looks like.'

He sat down beside me. 'I never said thank you, did I?'

'No.'

He nodded. 'I'll get around to it.' He peered at me. 'Some luck, you finding me as quickly as you did. I thought they were going to kill me.'

'They were,' I said. I didn't see any reason to mention the stag, or the fact I'd almost abandoned him. 'Why did you go out there?'

Gint frowned and waved an insect out of his face. 'I saw something.'

'What?'

'I don't know. Maybe it wasn't anything at all. Or maybe it was just a trick.' He laughed. 'No sense worrying about it now. Looks like that old Zirc fortune teller was wrong.'

'Was she?'

'Said I'd die in the swamp. And yet here I am.'

'Plenty of time yet.' I climbed down out of the wagon. 'I'd advise you to stay close to the fire from now on, Gint. At least until you reach Headwater Breach.'

He called out after me, but I ignored him. I went and found Chantey overseeing the unloading of several crates of powder and shot. 'This is the place,' I said.

He didn't look at me. 'It is.'

'You said you'd show me the way to Wald from here.'

'I did.'

'Well?' I looked around impatiently. All I saw was trees and water.

'There it is,' Chantey said. He gestured, but I didn't see anything.

'There what is?'

'The staithe there. See it? Just under those trees.'

I squinted, trying to see through the rain. 'I see some stones.'

'That's it.' Chantey sounded pleased with himself. Like he'd pulled a fast one on me. 'The only road to Wald is through the swamp. Wagons can't get there, not without getting bogged down. A horse could do it, maybe. But the locals use skiffs.'

'Wonderful.' I looked at him. 'They'll send a boat?'

'A skiff. Yes, eventually. We pile the merchandise, they come and collect it. Payment is left in the trees.' He knocked on the nearest one, and something clattered. I looked up and saw an oilskin bag dangling from a branch.

'Efficient. And neither of you has ever cheated the other?'

Chantey looked offended. 'All a man has is his reputation.'

'And I know yours.'

Chantey grimaced and turned away. 'Not wise, cheating your customers. Especially Lord Wald.' He sounded nervous as the name passed his lips.

'No, I suppose not.' I adjusted my bedroll. Everything I needed, other than my knife, fitted into a woollen blanket, folded over and slung across my chest, Freeguild-fashion. Another trick learned in the regiment. A change of socks, a few slim books, some trail-jerky and what little coin I had to hand. 'I wish I could say it's been pleasant.'

Chantey snorted. 'Better than some trips.' He paused. 'I won't say no, if you change your mind. You're good with a sword, and I need the extra hands...'

'I have business in Wald,' I said, as I studied the trees.

They were too close together for my liking. The branches

rustled in the rain, and it sounded like laughter. Chantey seemed to hear it as well, and he swallowed nervously.

'Do as you will, Blackwood. We'll be coming back this way in a week If you're still alive...'

I nodded. 'I might need a ride.'

Chantey nodded and clapped me on the shoulder. 'Sigmar keep you, Blackwood.'

'Why would he start now?' I murmured, as the caravan-master turned away. I watched them unload casks of black powder, and crates of crossbow bolts. I thought about what Taelya had said and wondered what Lord Wald needed so much ammunition for. It was dangerous out here, true enough, but from what I could see, it was enough to outfit an army.

'Lot of casks. I wonder who they're planning to shoot, eh?'

I turned to see Gint striding towards me, a pack slung across one shoulder. 'What do you think you're doing?'

'I'm going with you,' he said, cheerfully.

'No, you're not.'

'Looks like I am.' He sat down on his pack, and started shuffling his cards. 'I was getting tired of pretending I knew what droving was anyway. Besides, I'm thinking of settling down. Maybe get married.'

'To anyone in particular, or just whoever?'

'Oh, you know these Verdian backwaters – plenty of women, not enough men to go around.' He paused. 'Or is that the Thyrian ones?' He shrugged. 'Either way, bound to be more interesting than riding in the back of that wagon, taking money off shepherds.'

I stared at him. Then I sighed and turned away. 'Fine.'

'No argument?'

'Would it do any good?'

'Not a bit.'

'Then why would I waste my breath?'

Gint laughed. We watched the drovers finish unloading the cargo. Ten cases of bolts, ten casks of powder. Chantey only retrieved the money when they'd finished. It took the caravan some time to get moving again, but when it did, I felt a sense of unease. As the clattering of wheels and the bellowing of the ghy-rochs faded, silence rushed to fill in the void. The mist rose up strong and quick with it, choking us off from sight of the road.

Gint whistled nervously – a habit of his I could see I was going to dislike immensely. For a time, there was no noise save the slap of water against stone and the fading clatter of the wagons. The creak of branches. The soft, steady fall of rain across the water and trees.

It was almost peaceful. That was probably why I didn't trust it. I'd learned the hard way that peace was an illusion. A veil, drawn over something ugly and savage. Life, by its very nature, could not be peaceful. Nothing existed save that it consumed something else. In my experience, nowhere was that more apparent than Ghyran.

'How long do you think we should wait?' Gint asked.

'Until the boat arrives,' I said. I sat down on a sunken stump and watched the water swirl about the stones. There'd been a proper dock here, once, I thought. But the swamp had taken it, like it took everything. The consumed, and the consumer.

'Want to play a hand or two, while we wait?'

'No.' The gheists were back. They watched from the water, bobbing white faces just beneath the surface. I closed my eyes, and they were gone when I opened them.

Gint sighed. 'I'm already regretting this.'

'You could still catch up with the caravan, if that's the case.' I didn't look at him. 'I doubt there's anything waiting for you in Wald.'

'Well, we won't know that until we get there, will we?'

'No, I suppose not.'

'So, what do you do for a living?' Gint asked. 'You never said.'

'No. I didn't.'

Gint nodded, as if I'd said something pithy. 'Lucio says you break legs.'

'Lucio talks too much.'

Gint laughed. 'That he does. He also says you used to be a war-priest. One of Sigmar's own battle-hounds.' He paused. 'I didn't think that was the sort of career one could give up.'

'It was a calling, not a career.' I gave him a look. 'It's also none of your business.'

Gint nodded again. 'True, but seeing as we're friends now, I thought I should show some interest.'

I laughed. 'How did you come to that conclusion?'

'You saved my life. In Darezi culture, that means you're responsible for me.'

'I'm not Darezi. Neither are you.'

Gint smiled. 'Good tradition, though.' He looked out over the water. 'Lucio says you work for Caspar Guno. That's a long fall from serving Sigmar. If you don't mind me saying so.'

'I do.'

He raised his hands, as if afraid I was going to hit him. 'No offence meant. It's just... Guno's a thief. A killer. Worse, he employs thieves and killers.'

'How is that any worse than the gods?'

Gint stared at me. After a moment, he said, 'I'm starting to see why you're not a priest any more.'

I turned away. 'You don't know anything, Gint. So be quiet. You want to come with me? Fine. I won't argue. But do us both a favour and keep your too-clever mouth shut.'

Gint snorted, but thankfully didn't say anything else. After a few moments, however, he said, 'Just one hand of cards. For fun, not money – I swear.'

I didn't bother to reply. I was too busy listening to something.

Barely there at first, like the sound of a distant wind. But getting louder, until it became a soft rush of voices. Many voices, all whispering at once.

The sound dripped down, like honey sliding down a stick. Soft but close. Gint's eyes widened, as he caught sight of something above my head. 'Harran,' he whispered.

Almost against my will, I looked up. Above me, in a knot in the trunk of the tree, something pale nestled. At first, I thought it was a bird, or maybe a clump of leaves, but then it unfurled and looked down at me with eyes like two holes and a smile made of splinters. Gint yelped and stepped back, nearly sinking into the mire, as the sylvaneth extruded itself from the knothole with boneless, crinkling ease.

It observed us with black, empty eyes – as if we were some strange, new species it had discovered. 'What do you want?' I said, fighting to keep my tone even. The sylvaneth weren't human, though some among them resembled us superficially. But they could be talked to. Bargained with. Humans had done it before.

It spoke, and its voice was like the scratch of a branch across a shutter. More insistent now than before, but I couldn't understand anything it said, unlike the ones we'd encountered earlier.

I tried again. 'I don't understand. What do you want?'

Instead of answering, it fell to the ground in a lump. Gint pushed away from it as it unspooled, rising up and up, that pale face bobbing on top of a body that was nothing more than a tangle of brambles and sticks.

Something like a hand stretched towards me, almost gently. I swept my knife out, parting the fibrous fingers from the limb. It screeched and I turned.

'Run.'

CHAPTER SIX

EEL-SOAK

We ran in the only direction available to us – into the water.

Behind us, the thing screeched and exploded in pursuit. I heard branches crack and leaves whip about in a frenzy. The trees seemed to shudder about us as we splashed through the deepening waters. It was not just one voice now, but many, all screaming in almost infantile frustration. I realised Orm was right. They held a grudge.

They were all around us, pale faces squirming with rage and eagerness as they glared out from between trunks or from within the canopy overhead. The bottom stirred beneath us, heaving and clutching at our legs. The bark of the trees seemed to bite my palms as I grabbed hold of branches for support. Vines caught at my throat and hair, and I heard Gint cursing and floundering to my left, though the thickening mist made it hard to see.

If they'd truly wanted us, they could have had us. This was

just a game, despite their seeming fury. They were playing with us. Showing us their power. But why? Spite? Revenge? Maybe there was no answer. Maybe it was simply because they could.

Gint yelped and fell against a sunken log. I splashed to his side and dragged him up. Silence descended. Gint looked around, eyes wild. 'What are they waiting for?'

'I don't know. Be quiet.'

'But–'

'I said be quiet!'

He fell silent. From overhead came the soft crack-crack-crack of rain striking leaves. The sky opened up, and the drizzle became a downpour. I wiped water from my face. Behind me, something trilled. The sound sent a tremor through me.

'What was that?' Gint whispered.

'Not a sylvaneth,' I said. 'At least not any I've ever heard.' Rain slid down the back of my neck and beneath my clothes. Another trill, closer this time. Something splashed. I turned, and saw a flash of spotted flesh, slipping beneath the water. A chill ran through me. 'Damn it.'

'What? What?' Gint asked.

'Leopard eels.'

A trill sounded somewhere to my left, and I heard the splash of rudimentary paws hauling a heavy body through the reeds. Beneath the water, a great weight brushed against my leg, and I was nearly thrown from my feet.

Gint cried out. 'Something went by me!'

'We need to get to higher ground,' I said. I saw a fin split the surface of the water and slide towards us. And then another, and another. I spotted a thick, arthritic-looking tree, its branches hanging low over the misty surface of the water. 'Come on!'

I caught hold of Gint and dragged him towards it, not daring to look back as the hunting trills of the eels grew louder and louder. When we reached the tree, I shoved him forward.

'Up – *climb*!'

'What about you?'

'I'll be right behind you – go!'

I turned as the first of them burst into the open. It was a lean thing, lethal and ugly. Longer than a man was tall, it was a twisting, murderous abomination, with wide, heavy jaws set into a protruding snout. A stiff, serrated dorsal fin ran the creature's spotted length, and a dozen tiny, vestigial, grasping paws dotted its flanks.

It arrowed towards me, surging up and out of the water in a single, convulsive motion. There was no time to follow Gint. I managed to interpose my knife as its slimy, spotted length coiled about me. I slashed out, and there was a keening sound. The coils tightened spasmodically, nearly crushing the breath from my lungs.

The eel snapped at me as I hacked and stabbed at it. Spots crowded at the edge of my vision as it squeezed. Warmth gushed over my hand, and the eel's length whipped away from me.

It let out a piercing shriek as it thrashed through the reeds. Tiny paws clawed uselessly at the air. More spotted shapes shot towards it, and the shrill cries ratcheted up to agonising volume as the eels devoured their wounded fellow alive. I forced myself to my feet and splashed towards the tree, hoping to get above the chaos.

Just as I was about to reach it, an eel slammed into me, knocking me back down into the water. I surfaced, gasping, and slashed at it, driving it back. Out of the corner of my eye, I saw that the other eels were finishing off the injured one. It wouldn't be long before they started on me again. I could hear Gint shouting from the tree above, but I had no breath to answer him. I rolled over as the eel that had knocked me down reared up, readying itself to strike. Sacs of translucent flesh bulged beneath its gills, and I had just enough time to throw up a hand. Venom hissed as it spattered my forearm. Screaming in pain, I lunged, driving my knife into the eel's skull. It fell back, carrying me with it.

I tore my weapon loose as the others turned towards me, jaws wide. Before they could strike, however, something hissed through the air, parting the membranous fin on one creature's back. The eel whipsawed in apparent surprise, and dived into the water. I saw a crossbow bolt sticking out of a nearby tree, and turned as someone whistled. A low-hulled skiff nosed through the mist. A woman, grey-haired and clad in a ragged shawl, stood at the prow, a crossbow in her hands. She whistled again and gestured.

'Over here, lad, unless you fancy getting eaten.'

I sheathed my knife and splashed towards our rescuer. Gint was already in the boat, of course. 'Leopard eels,' the old woman said, as she helped me clamber into the skiff. 'They come up when the waters drop, to hunt. Nasty buggers.' She set aside the crossbow and picked up a wooden pole.

'So I see,' I said. I looked at Gint. 'Are you in one piece?'

He nodded. 'Thanks to you. That's twice now you've saved my life.'

'I wasn't keeping track,' I lied. My hand burned from the eel's venom, and I hissed in pain as I flexed it. The old woman clucked her tongue as she thrust her pole into the water.

'Lucky it only hit your hand. If it had got you in the face, you'd be blind. Or dead.'

'Still hurts.' As the skiff scraped through the reeds, the air shook with the hunting trills of the eels. They'd scattered at the newcomer's arrival, but hadn't gone far. 'They're not giving up,' I said.

'They never do.' The old woman gestured. 'See that satchel? Get me one of those bottles out, if you're of a mind.'

I looked at Gint and he rolled awkwardly towards a battered satchel. After a moment's rummage, he extracted a clay bottle, stoppered with cloth. 'What is it?'

'Eel-soak. There's a flint and tinder in there as well.'

The hunting trills were getting closer. I saw long, lean shapes slithering through the nearby water. Gint found the flint and tinder and handed it to our rescuer.

'Hold the bottle,' the old woman said. She struck a spark, but the cloth in the bottle refused to catch. 'Damp,' she grunted, trying again.

'Hurry,' I said. The trills were loud now, piercing. The skiff rocked as something passed beneath it. I spotted serpentine shapes twisting just below the surface of the swamp. There seemed to be dozens of them, and more gathering every moment. I reached for my knife. I didn't fancy my chances against so many.

'They smell your blood. Drives them crazy.' Her voice was mild, as if this were something she dealt with every day. 'Might also be the bait I tossed out, before I noticed you there in the water.'

'They're getting closer,' I said. Every trill caused my injured hand to ache. Yellow, bulbous eyes glared at us from beneath the skin of the water.

'Patience,' the old woman said. She struck flint to tinder and a spark caught at last. 'Ah. There we go.' The bottle began to smoke, and I gagged. The smell was reminiscent of rotten eggs. She hefted it. 'And here you go, you spotted bastards.'

She grabbed up one of her reed baskets and set the bottle inside. Then she dropped it over the side. Smoke was frothing from the top of the bottle now, and spreading low over the water. The leopard eels retreated from it, trills changing tenor, becoming raucous shrieks.

The old woman laughed. 'Smells this bad to us, I can only imagine how it smells to them. Drives them away, though. Sends them diving deep.'

'What is it?' I coughed, dragging myself up into a sitting position. Gint moved to help me, and I waved him away.

The old woman looked down at me. 'Told you – eel-soak. Made from charcoal and eel bile. Let it soak overnight, until it hardens. Crush it up, and set it alight. Can rub it on your clothes, as well. Keeps them from scenting you, sometimes.' She picked up her pole again, and got the skiff moving. As she did, her sleeve fell back, revealing a tattoo marked on her forearm – a chain, looped about a cannon. 'Doesn't last long, though. Rain will clear it in a little while, but we'll be safe by the time they come back, never fear.'

'My hand's gone numb,' I said, staring at my fingers. I could move them, but I couldn't feel them at all. The old woman grunted.

'You're having a reaction to the venom. Happens sometimes.'

'What sort of reaction?'

'Only a little one. Try not to fall asleep.'

'Why?'

'Well, you might die.'

'Wonderful.' I clenched my hand, trying to force the numbness out. 'Who are you?'

'Name's Deshler. Not that anyone has called me that in a while. Not much use for names, out here.' She looked at us. 'And who might you be, traipsing around my swamp in eel-time? Couple of pilgrims, no doubt, on your way to Hightree Fane?'

Gint answered for me. 'I'm Gint, and this surly bugger is Blackwood.'

'I've been poisoned. I'm allowed to be surly.'

Deshler laughed. 'Too right. Don't sound like pilgrims, though.' She gave a knowing leer. 'Maybe you're escapees, eh? Got yourself free of the prison barges, maybe, and went looking for a place to hide in the swamp?'

'And if we were?' I said. Gint gave me a look, but I ignored him.

She reached down and lifted her crossbow. 'Well then, I might just turn you in for a reward, eh? How about that?' She sighted down the weapon's length, centring the bolt on my chest. I didn't blink.

'We're not escapees,' Gint burst out.

'Sounds like something escapees would say.'

'It does,' I said. 'You'd know all about that.'

She frowned. 'Would I, then?'

'That tattoo on your arm says you do.'

She glanced down at her forearm and then back up at me. A slow grin stretched across her wizened features. 'Know about the bilge-ink, do you?'

'Enough to know what that particular symbol means.' I glanced at Gint. 'A chained cannon. Sound familiar?'

He nodded. 'You were in Ironhole.' Ironhole was one of Greywater Fastness' nastiest prisons. A disused mineshaft made over into a dungeon deeper than any in Ghyran. The gaolers there often used transportation as a way of keeping the population in check.

Deshler spat over the side. 'You were in the Hole?'

'No. But I know quite a few who were.' I tried to flex my hand again, but found it unresponsive. The world was starting to spin. I heard the soft rustle of rain striking the leaves overhead – and something else. An undercurrent of laughter, hidden in the rustling.

Deshler laughed and set the crossbow down. 'Then it's your lucky day, I guess. Heading to town, were you? Sellswords, then. Looking for work with his lordship?'

'No,' I said, before Gint could reply. 'But we are looking to get to town. We were hoping to catch a ride with the cargo skiffs.'

Deshler peered up at the sky. 'No chance of that now. You'll have missed them.'

'How about you?' Gint asked. 'Care to give two unlucky travellers a ride?'

'What's in it for me?'

'A comet,' I said. I found my gaze drawn to the trees, where squat, quadrupedal shapes crouched, watching the skiff with eyes like dollops of rotten sap. They were dogs, but dogs with broken-bough legs and bodies shaggy with moss.

They watched in silence as we passed. Neither Gint nor Deshler gave any sign that they'd seen them, and I couldn't muster the words to ask them. My tongue felt thick, and there was something like threads of fire under my skin. I preferred the numbness.

'A comet apiece,' Deshler said.

'Fine.' I didn't feel like arguing. 'Pay her, Gint.'

'Me? But–'

'Pay her,' I hissed, gripping my forearm. It felt as if I were on fire. I wanted nothing more than to plunge my arm into the water, but something told me that would be a bad idea.

'Fine,' he groused. 'One now, one after we reach town.'

I didn't hear Deshler's reply. My head lolled, loose and heavy, as the dogs slid into the water without leaving a ripple. I leaned against the side of the skiff.

Gint nudged me. 'She said not to fall asleep.'

I shook my head, fighting against the need to collapse. Above me, the trees were like the roof of a cathedral, and suddenly it was as if I were back in Aqshy, kneeling before the grand altar in the great cathedral of Hammerhal, the scent of incense thick in my nose, and the droning prayers of the faithful ringing in my ears.

I looked up into the golden face of Sigmar, and saw that it was covered in a hairy mask of green. Vines crept down like serpents, and prayers became screams – and finally, laughter. Shrill and mad and ugly. Sigmar's face crumpled beneath its mask, bending and shrinking and becoming something other – something I could not bear to see.

I lifted my hammer to smash it. But there was no hammer in my hands, and my arms were like lead. The walls closed in around me, crumbling and twisting, as roots ran through the floor, shattering marble and creeping over the altar stone. I felt the devastation in my guts, and fought to keep my balance.

There was a sound, as of a great wind, and as I turned, I saw that the cathedral was a forest and the faithful were not who I'd thought they were. They wore faces of corn-husk and vine, and sang softly in voices like the tumbling of leaves. I heard what sounded like the wailing of an infant – more than one – and the moan of a wounded man. I saw vague blurs – the hints of shapes, of faces, wrapped in leathery greenery. Men and women. Children. All of them gathered together, like seeds in a pod.

A little girl wreathed in green half-turned towards me, as if struggling against whatever held her. Bloody lips moved in a silent plea as brambles dug into her chest. Her eyes were hollow black pits. I tried to reach for her – to help her, comfort her – but I still couldn't move. In moments, she was gone, ripped away, and other faces pressed forward in her place, eager and mocking.

They were maggot-pale, with eyes like knotholes and mouths of splintered bark. They crowded at the edges of my vision, murmuring in voices too low or too high for me to hear. Though I could not make out their words, I knew that they were pleased to see me. That they had been waiting for me. I could feel the thrashing of brambles as they tightened about me, cutting me. Digging into me.

I snapped awake. Gint yelped and fell backwards as my knife carved the air where his throat had been.

Deshler laughed. 'You're a tough son of bitch,' she said. 'Most men would've been unconscious for days.'

'How long?' I croaked, scrubbing at my face.

'Not long,' Gint said. 'How do you feel?'

'Like I need a drink.' I'd always had a brute vitality, even as a boy. I could shrug off the worst beatings, retreat to my lair to lick my wounds and emerge later like a bear from hibernation.

It was a gift that had stood me in good stead during both phases of my life.

'I don't recommend that,' Deshler said. 'Your stomach is going to be a touch sensitive for a bit. Trust me.' She grinned at me.

I grunted and tried to sit up. My arm still hurt, but it wasn't burning any more. A little pain was fine – it would keep me alert, if nothing else. 'Where are we?'

'Heading for town, like you wanted.' Deshler leaned into her pole. 'I was telling your friend here, don't blame me if you're disappointed. Wald isn't a pleasant sort of place. And I say that as someone who was in Ironhole for three years.'

I flexed my hand. 'You live there?'

She laughed. 'Gods, no. I live out in the swamp. Safer there, so long as you don't cut down any trees, and you leave out the occasional offering. There are quite a few of us, these days. We hunt eels and sell them in town, buy what we need and get out as quickly as possible. Not much of a life, but better than some.'

'Better than Ironhole, at least,' I said. The swamp didn't look any different to the last time I'd looked at it. More stones, perhaps. Weathered obelisks, covered in moss and reeds, and the tops of broken chimneys.

'That's truth you're speaking, and no two ways there,' Deshler cackled. She lifted her pole, letting it thud against stones and trees, manoeuvring us through narrow paths. I wondered how long she'd been out here, to keep us moving with such ease.

'Did you hear something?' Gint asked.

I looked at him. 'What?'

'I heard something – over there. Look.' He pointed towards a copse of trees. The mist thinned as we drew closer, and I could make out something lumbering towards us through the water. As we watched, it shouldered its way through the reeds, slipping and sinking. A low moan echoed over the water.

'What is it?' Gint murmured.

'None of our business,' Deshler said firmly. 'Ignore it.'

I waved her to silence. We were close enough to make out the thrashing shape now – woolly, with a pair of horns. It had become hung up, unable to free itself. 'Bramblehorn,' I said. But there was something wrong with the animal. It was hurt, and moving strangely. And the sounds it made weren't like any bramblehorn I'd ever heard. 'Get us closer.'

Deshler frowned. 'Why?'

I looked at her.

Deshler stared back. 'I'm not taking what doesn't belong to me,' she said flatly. 'That beast was probably left as a gift for the Lady of Leaves – a lot of folks do that, around here. I'll not earn her ire because you've got a soft heart...'

I drew my knife. 'Hold the skiff steady.' The animal's thrashing had increased in vigour as it tried to free itself from the brambles. Its movements were awkward – not like an animal's at all.

'Don't be a fool,' Deshler said. 'Sheathe that blade and sit down. I didn't just pull you out of an eel's jaws to watch you commit suicide.'

'Maybe she's right,' Gint said. 'Local customs and all that.'

'Fine. Stay here if you're scared.'

'Leave it,' Deshler shouted. Gint echoed her. I didn't listen to either of them. I was chest-deep in the water moments later, making my way towards the beast. I couldn't tell you why I did it – some buried germ of mercy, from my old life. Or maybe I was simply annoyed. I do stupid things when I get annoyed.

I wasn't really sure what I was going to do with the beast when I reached it. At the very least I could cut its throat, and end its suffering.

But as I drew closer, I realised why the beast had looked wrong from a distance. It wasn't a bramblehorn at all.

Rather, it was a man wearing the skin of a beast.

CHAPTER SEVEN

LORD WALD

'It's a man,' Gint called out. 'Harran, it's a man.'

'I see that,' I snarled, trying to silence him. I chopped at the brambles with my knife. The man struggled against me, moaning. He flapped at me with his hands, trying to push me away. When I'd freed him, he splashed forward, grunting.

He was bleeding, but not badly. I was no doctor, but I'd been on enough battlefields to know when a wound was superficial – even one I couldn't see. He trembled with exertion, as if he'd been running long and hard. Only desperation could push a man like that. 'Easy,' I said, as I reached for him. He made a low whining sound in his throat and tried to fling himself away from me. I retreated a few paces, hands raised. 'I don't mean any harm.'

He opened his mouth, as if to speak. His tongue was all but gone. Someone had cut it out. He gabbled nonsensically, and tore at the bramblehorn hide, trying to rid himself of it. But it was sewn on too tightly. I gestured with my knife. 'I can cut it off, if you let me.' He looked at me with wild eyes, and I knew that there was nothing left of him. Fear and exhaustion had eaten his mind, leaving him no more aware than the beast whose skin he wore.

Out in the mist, a horn sounded. A look of panic crossed his face. He grunted and shoved me aside. As he did so, I caught a look at his arm, and the tattoo there. Deshler wasn't the only survivor of Ironhole abroad in the swamp tonight. He stagger-splashed away, vanishing into the mist and reeds.

The horn sounded again, nearer this time. It was a hunting horn.

'Get back in the skiff, Blackwood!' Deshler called out. I turned to see her staring into the trees, face pinched and drawn. 'Hurry up. We need to go. *Now*.'

The horn blew again, and I heard the splash of heavy bodies coming through the trees.

'Harran, get back on the damn skiff,' Gint said, reaching out a hand.

'Something is coming,' I said, making my way back towards them before pulling myself into the boat.

'Yes, which is why we should bloody well be going,' Deshler snarled. 'I knew we shouldn't have stopped.' She threw her shoulder against her pole, and set the skiff into motion.

But too late.

The first of the riders burst out of the trees a moment later. Deshler cursed as the horse cut across her path. It was a tall brute, and heavy looking. Built for endurance, rather than speed. Its rider was naked but for a wealth of tattoos that marked his weathered flesh and a broad belt of tanned leather that held a variety of blades. He held a hunting spear in one hand, its narrow blade etched with strange patterns, and a horn hung from his saddle.

Silently, he urged his steed towards the skiff, his dark gaze sweeping over us. The animal squealed unpleasantly as it forced itself through the water. The rider was a tall man, raw-boned and worn to a sharp edge. His hair was swept back, greased and bound in a single braid, and he wore a bone amulet, carved to resemble a stag's skull.

Deshler dropped to her knees, causing the skiff to rock. 'Y-your lordship, a thousand apologies…'

The rider smiled thinly at her words and straightened in his saddle. I could make out a wealth of scars on his torso and arms. Whoever he was, he was no stranger to violence.

'None necessary, good woman,' he said, in honied tones. 'These swamps are not mine alone.' He turned in his saddle as more riders appeared, drifting out of the mist. 'Are they, brothers and sisters?' he called out.

The newcomers were as nude as he was. Some had daubed themselves in woad or ash, as if in accordance with some primitive rite. They surrounded us in moments. Some bore bows, others spears. Implements of the hunt, rather than proper weapons. The rider smiled and looked Gint and me over.

'I don't know either of you,' he said, after a moment. 'Strangers, then?'

'Who's asking?' I said. Deshler hissed a warning, but I ignored her.

A ripple of laughter spread through the riders. The man grinned.

'Hark at him. There's my answer, and no doubt.' He looked at me. 'I am Lord Wald, master of these demesnes, by the grace of the gods and the strength of my blood.'

'And a finer lord you'll not find,' Deshler said quickly, head still bowed.

I met Lord Wald's gaze, but only for a moment longer. Then I bowed as well. No sense antagonising him. 'My apologies, my lord. I spoke without thinking.'

'I find that is often the only way one hears the truth,' he said, eliciting another round of appreciative laughter. He looked down his nose at me, and I felt a sudden urge to commit an act of self-destructive violence. He had that sort of face, especially when he smiled. 'You are here perhaps to seek employment? Or maybe to celebrate the turning of the season, and the harvest?'

'Forgive me, my lord, but I can't see what there might be to harvest out here, save eels,' Gint said obsequiously. But he diverted the question well enough.

'The swamp provides us as great a bounty as any man deserves,' Lord Wald said. He set his spear across his saddle and scanned the trees with a visible impatience. 'Speaking of which, you didn't happen to see a beast come this way, did you?'

'I saw a man,' I said.

Lord Wald looked at me. 'They are one and the same. Man is as much an animal as my steed here. This one more so than most. A murderer. Which way did he go?'

Gint pointed in the opposite direction to the way their prey had gone. 'That way, your lordship. Running as if all the hounds of Sigmar were on his trail.'

Lord Wald frowned. 'Sigmar holds no sway here, man. You'd be wise to keep his name from your lips, lest certain parties take offence.' He jerked his steed's head about and thumped its flanks with his heels. The horse lurched into motion, and the other riders followed suit, slopping water onto the skiff in their haste. A few cast curious looks at us as they rode past, but none spoke.

Deshler let out a shaky breath. 'I should have left you to the damn eels,' she said, glaring at me. 'You can't speak to him that way – he's had men flogged for less!'

'I don't know about that. He seemed friendly enough, for an aristo,' Gint said, watching as the last of the horsemen vanished. 'Bit odd riding about in the nude, though.'

'Local customs.' I glanced at Deshler. 'Does your lord often hunt men for sport?'

She looked away. 'Only when it pleases him to do so.'

'His prey had an Ironhole tattoo, just like yours.'

She adjusted her shawl to hide her arms. 'So? Ironhole has thousands of prisoners. Tens of thousands. And we're not so far away from Greywater Fastness, whatever tricks the swamp might play.'

I looked at Gint, and he shrugged. I decided to drop it. We sat in silence for a time, listening to the hum of insects and the distant trill of eels. Once, I heard the winding of a horn, and I wondered if Lord Wald had caught his prey. I hoped not.

From the look on Gint's face, he'd heard the horn as well.

Gint leaned close. 'Is it me, or are you not overly concerned about what we just saw?' he hissed. 'I've seen some things in my time, but never anything like that.'

'Then you haven't been paying attention.' I looked out over the water. The swamp spread out around us, silent and green. Mist rose from the dark waters, obscuring all but the closest trees.

'You're not the least bit worried?'

'No. Why would I be? It's not my business. It's not yours either.' I looked at him. 'You'd be wise to forget you saw anything at all.'

Gint sat back. 'I had you pegged as a brave man, Harran. Looks like I was wrong.'

Deshler had been eavesdropping. 'He's smart, is what he is. You should listen to him.' She shook her head. 'Wald's not the sort of place that welcomes folks putting their oar in where it's not wanted. Take it from me – I've been here long enough to know.'

'Know what?' Gint asked.

'Everything,' she said, with a hint of pride.

'And everyone?' I asked.

She snorted. 'Near about. If I don't, I know someone who does.'

'Do you know a fellow by the name of Murn?' I asked.

Gint looked at me, perplexed, but said nothing. He settled back and turned away, apparently taking my advice to heart.

Deshler laughed. 'Have to narrow it down. There are – were – a lot of Murns hereabouts.'

I paused. I hadn't expected that. 'Evrek Murn,' I said.

She shook her head. 'Never heard of him.' Something about the way she said it made me smile. I'd heard that tone of voice before. Usually when I was asking someone where a debtor of their acquaintance had gone.

'No?'

She hesitated. A sly expression crept across her wizened features. 'I might be able to find out, though. Like I said, I know someone who knows something.'

'How much?'

'Another one of those comets would do it.' She flashed two fingers. 'Double if I find out something.'

'Good.' I fished a comet out of my coat and held it up. 'When we get to Wald, it's yours.' I put it back in my pocket before she could snatch it.

'Fair enough,' she said sourly.

'How far is it, out of curiosity?' Gint asked.

'Not far at all. We're passing through the old town now.' She pointed. Forlorn chimney stacks sprouted above the water's surface in places, and I could make out the murky shadows of sunken rooftops just beneath the surface of the water.

Deshler used her pole to push off of the ruins and the thick, serpentine roots that bound them all together. I realised she was following an old path – the old road. Even distorted in such a way, it was familiar – like an old ache. A pattern based on constellations few had ever seen in person.

Every village, every town, every city founded by the peoples of Azyr followed a similar pattern. First came the loggers, the miners, the builders... and then came the priests. To sanctify the ground, to spread the good word. To bring the light to the darkness. It was never that simple, though. Sometimes people were happier being in the dark.

I had done my share of spreading the light, before I realised that the cold stars cared nothing for any of us. Before I realised that we were all just grist for the mills of heaven. It was better now. At least Caspar Guno was an honest monster.

There were more than ruins among the trees. I saw what I took to be outlying farms as well, and fishing shacks, sitting well above the water on stilts of wood or brick. Almost all of the farms occupied small islands within thick copses. Scrubby clumps of black-stem and marsh-tomatoes floated inside make-shift nets. Elsewhere, splotchy stalks of green-corn rose from the water in stubborn, irregular patches.

'Surprised to see farms out here,' Gint said.

'Not really farms as such,' Deshler said, as we slid past a small shack, its roof all but collapsing under the weight of the moss that grew atop it. 'We learned how to make do. You can do a lot with reeds and grass, if you have to. And potatoes.' She spat into the water. 'I hate potatoes.'

'I suppose you've learned to love eel, as well?' Gint asked.

Deshler laughed. 'As much as they've learned to love us.' She peered about. 'Quietly now... we're near the keep.' She slowed the skiff. I followed her gaze.

A stone edifice rose out of the mist, and towered above the distant trees. I could make out few details thanks to the mist and the rain, but what I saw looked familiar enough.

Every canton I knew of was centred on its keep. The fortress was the spoke of the wheel, around which the rest of the community spread and grew. Most of the keeps were duardin-built – sturdy stone towers, with walls and barracks and storehouses. Even if the cantons fell, the keeps were relatively self-sufficient.

I spied the tops of sunken stone walls rising upwards, demar-
cating the outer limits of the keep. 'Used to be stables there, or
so I was told,' Deshler said. 'And gardens, where the first lord
would host parties and such. Now it's just more swamp.'

As we passed a gap in the ancient walls, I saw wooden walkways, stretching over rough-hewn palisades and running the
circumference of the keep's rear expanse. Men patrolled them,
their eyes on the surrounding trees.

'Guards are out early today,' Deshler muttered.

'Expecting trouble,' I said.

It wasn't a question, but Deshler took it as one. 'They always
expect it.' The old woman peered at me. 'You think you're the
first to come to Wald looking to cause trouble?'

'I'm not here to cause trouble.'

Deshler laughed.

Gint leaned forward. 'We only just got here. So what are they
worried about?'

'You ask a lot of questions,' she said.

'Just getting the lie of the land,' said Gint. He smiled. 'I like to
know who to avoid, and when to keep my head down.'

Deshler was silent for a moment. 'Things are changing,' she
said finally. 'More than some like. Lots of folks aren't happy with
his lordship, or the way he does things...'

'Like the way he hunts people through the swamps?' I said.

Deshler frowned. 'That might be part of it.'

Gint chuckled. 'Wonderful place you've brought me to, Harran.'

'I don't recall inviting you,' I said.

We fell silent as the skiff passed through the fields of shadow
that stretched beneath the trees. Deshler was adept at manoeuvring the flat-bottomed vessel through the swamp. She barely
seemed to move the pole at all, just rolling it every so often to
alter our course, however minutely. 'There it is,' she said, after
a time.

The mists had thinned enough for us to make out what lay ahead. Wald sat alone, surrounded by water, besieged by trees. It wasn't a single island, but rather several, linked by dirt causeways or bridges of crumbling stone or wood.

It had probably started small, like all villages out here. Azyrites had it down to an art. A few homesteads surrounding a watchtower or central edifice. But a century or so on, and it had grown up and out and around. People were adaptable. Give them less, and with time and need they inevitably did more. Wald was no different.

Trees were thick on either side of us, resembling the walls of a corridor. Old and gnarled, their branches hung low, weighed down by curtains of moss. Ahead of us was an old stone archway. Not duardin work this, but made by human masons. A small tree was growing from the apex, right over the carving of Sigendil. Its thin, tough roots wound down the sides of the archway and through the powdery mortar between the stones, seeking nourishment from the water below. The tumbled remains of what might once have been a stone wall extended through the water for several yards to either side, before vanishing entirely into the trees. Beyond the archway stood the entrance to Wald.

This side of the village was protected by a palisade of wooden stakes that had seen better decades. They were sunk deep into the water, and black rings of rot rose up their bases.

They were kept from total collapse by a skim of mud that had been shoved right up against the palisade in places, and packed between the stakes, as if to fill gaps. Grass and mould grew on the mud and stretched across the wood, making parts of the palisade look less like a wall than a hummock. A heavy gate, kept free of growth, occupied the centre of the palisade, and a line of skiffs and barges passed through to the quays beyond.

There were guards patrolling the walls above. Most were armed with spears, but a few had crossbows. A decrepit-looking cannon was positioned just above the gate, in a nest of sandbags and mud. The gunnery crew were a slovenly lot, their uniforms stained and patched. The other guards weren't much better.

'His lordship keeps the best men to see to his holdings,' Deshler said. 'The town gets the rest. Worst bunch of shirkers I've ever seen.'

'How big is the town?' I asked. I'd been expecting a farming hamlet, or a fishing village. From the height and expanse of the walls I was guessing that I'd underestimated the size by no small margin.

Deshler shrugged. 'Big enough. Used to be bigger, as I said.'

When we came to the gate, there were two men on duty. They were clad in homespun tunics and hauberks, with dingy leather caps covering their heads. They lounged near the postern to the left of the gate, atop a miniscule jetty. One of them sat on a stool, and was diligently weaving together what looked like corn-husks. A crossbow was propped against his stool. The other leaned on his spear, half-asleep. Neither of them paid much attention to the flow of traffic, save to wave on any stragglers with desultory gestures.

Deshler eyed them warily despite their seeming inattention. I followed her example and hunched my shoulders, kept my head bowed, and looked neither right nor left. Gint did the same. As we slid into line, I glanced up. Half a dozen rusty gibbets hung from the inside of the palisade, just above the gate. Half of them were occupied. Carrion birds perched on these, croaking and squabbling.

I didn't look too closely. It wasn't my business, so long as I didn't end up in one.

Hulls bumped and scraped noisily as the vessels passed through the gate. Bargemen yelled obscenities at one another as the smaller fishing skiffs edged between the bulkier flat-bottomed vessels. The air stank of fish, eel-soak and rot.

'Is it always this busy?' Gint asked, raising his voice to be heard over the hubbub.

Deshler shook her head. 'It's harvest season,' she said, as if that explained everything.

The rain, which had been slackening, picked up again. I decided not to take it as an omen. Looking around, I realised that the palisade was no defence against the swamp. Trees bowed shaggy branches over the rooftops, and roots broke the streets into irregular sections. Past the farthest buildings, I could see where parts of the village had slipped into the water over the years. Crumbled chimneys rose at intervals, the stones covered in cattails or full of reeds. Elsewhere, dykes of mud had been raised to hold back the encroaching water and keep streets and cul-de-sacs free of flooding.

The swamp-canal wound through the town like a great brown snake. To either side, jetties and duckboards extended from these new shores, sprouting like the feathers of a bird's wing. Barges were tied up at some of them, and fishing skiffs at others. Deshler shouted greetings to some of the fishermen as she poled past them. They responded in kind, or with torrents of obscenities. More of the latter than the former.

'You're popular,' Gint observed.

She grinned. 'I've been doing this for a while.'

'Where are you planning to let us off?' I asked.

She glanced at me. 'Not far from here. Figured you might want to avoid any prying eyes.'

I nodded and turned back. I'd seen worse places, but not by much. Clapboard buildings rose from the muddy dockside in irregular rows, stretching back and out of sight. The streets were serpentine streaks of brown, and the buildings were square, squalid things – cheaply made, decades ago. The sort of structures thrown up by newly arrived colonists, to get them through their first harvest season before more permanent habitations could be erected. Only, by the looks of things, that had never happened here.

The streets were still mud, where they weren't duckboards or sawn planks. The shacks were mostly rotting on their foundations, despite the years' worth of repairs that marked them all. And everywhere was overgrown. Thick grasses sprouted in the narrow alleys and passages, trees twisted upwards among and, in at least one case, *through* the older buildings. Moss-lamps hanging from posts and lintels cast a dull, ochre glow over the places where the faint natural light didn't reach.

A few shacks clung to the edges of the canal nearby, or sat on stilts further out in the hollows between the islands that made up the town's edges. They were connected to the main drag by badly maintained pontoon bridges or rickety planks.

'Not as quaint as I pictured it,' Gint said. 'Still, bigger than I feared. I might actually find a decent game or three in a slum like this.'

I didn't bother to reply. I had come to the conclusion that Gint talked mostly to hear himself spout off.

A flash of metal from beneath a jetty caught my attention. Several children had gathered in the shallows. As the skiff drew close, there was another flash as a knife passed over fingers and palms, drawing blood. I watched as the children dipped their bloody hands into the brambles and reeds growing about the jetty pylons. When they withdrew their fingers, the blood was gone. As if it had been licked clean.

I felt a chill as several of the children looked at the skiff, nothing in their eyes. No curiosity, no fear – nothing. 'What are they doing?' I asked.

'Celebrating the harvest,' Deshler said quietly. 'Best to ignore it.'

'Lot to ignore out here,' Gint said.

'Lot to ignore in the cities as well,' Deshler said. 'Just harder to do out here.' She turned as music crept across the air. She shook her head. 'Starting early this year.'

I saw people dancing, down among the shacks. Singing and celebrating. They danced among the reeds, awkward, graceless movements that reminded me of trees caught in a strong wind. They showed no interest in the skiff as it slid past. All of them were wearing masks made from corn-husks, vines and leaves.

The music was the sort of ribald clamouring that I'd come to associate with the wilds. Music with unfamiliar rhythms and wilder melodies than I preferred.

'I thought Taelya's playing was bad,' Gint murmured.

I didn't laugh.

Gint cleared his throat. 'His lordship mentioned a celebration, didn't he?'

Deshler frowned. 'It's the harvest. Happens whenever the waters drop and the eels start to sing.' She waved to a group of distant revellers as they sent up a whooping cry that carried through the trees. 'Lots of guests, oh my, yes. All of them come up from them downriver cantons at his lordship's behest. All to celebrate the coming harvest, and take part in his lordship's hunts.'

'Hunts like the one we just saw?'

Deshler didn't meet my eyes. 'No. Eels, mostly. Or troggoths. Deer, sometimes.'

'Hunts and harvests don't seem to go together,' Gint said.

'The harvest, the hunt, it's all the same,' Deshler said. 'Life feeds life. Something gets torn up and wolfed down, and them that eats goes on for another year. That's what it's all about. Especially here.' She sighed. 'Speaking of which...'

The skiff bumped up against a jetty. She tossed me a rope. 'Here, tie us up.'

Gingerly, I clambered out onto the slimy jetty and looped the rope about a mooring post. As I knotted it, I heard Deshler murmur a warning and straightened, my hand on my knife.

'Oi, you can't berth here,' a heavy voice growled. I turned.

He was big, with a labourer's muscles underneath his ill-fitting hauberk. A town guard. He had a sword belted at his waist. I stepped back, hands raised.

The big man glared at me, face twisted in a sneer of derision. 'Did you hear me, trash? Get that boat out of here.'

I frowned. 'My apologies, friend.' I could tell that he was spoiling for a fight, and smelled strongly of something alcoholic. 'We can moor elsewhere.'

'Stuff your apologies.' The sneer became a snarl. 'You think you're allowed to moor this leaky piece of shit anywhere you like? Is that it?' He reached for me, almost lazily. A bully, used to throwing smaller men around.

I easily avoided his grip and snatched my knife from its sheath. I pressed the tip to just above his belt, through a gap in his hauberk. The big man froze, his sneer slipping into an expression of fright.

'What's your name?' I asked softly.

'Buell,' he said, after a moment's hesitation.

'Buell, do you want me to spill your guts on the dock here?'

Buell shook his head.

I smiled. 'No, I didn't think so. But I will, unless you close your fat mouth, turn around and pretend this never happened. Do you understand?'

Buell licked his lips. I could read the indecision in his eyes. Humiliation would eat at him like acid, even if it was private. His gaze flicked to the hilt of his sword.

I leaned close, just short of sliding the knife in. 'Decide quickly, Buell.'

The big man relaxed and stepped back, hands spread slightly. 'Next time,' he muttered, before turning on his heel and sloping off. I heard Gint whistle, and Deshler release a pent-up breath.

'Sigmar's balls, I thought he was going to go for his sword,' she said. 'Never seen big Buell run off with his tail between his legs before.'

'You know him?' I asked, watching the guard vanish into the rain.

'Everyone knows him. He likes to roust the fishermen.' She climbed up onto the dock and held out her hand. 'Coin.'

I handed over the comet and it vanished into her robes.

She grinned. 'Pleasure doing business with you. Now if you'll excuse me, I have eels to unload.'

I started walking as Gint climbed up onto the dock. 'Wait up,' he shouted.

I didn't.

CHAPTER EIGHT

WALD

'Think she'll do as she promised?' Gint asked, after he caught up with me.

We strode through the streets, side by side. The rain fell in sheets over the town, and every roof-edge was a waterfall. It didn't seem to dampen the celebratory spirit of the inhabitants, however. Music echoed through the narrow streets.

I grunted. 'Whether she does or not, she'll talk'

'And that's what you want?'

I nodded.

Gint grinned. 'Clever. I mean, dangerous, but clever.' He paused. 'So who's Murn?'

'None of your business.'

'Fair enough. But I might be able to help. Two heads are better than one, and all that.'

'I thought you were here looking for a wife.'

'Until then, I need something to keep me occupied.'

I snorted. 'He owes someone money. I'm here to collect.'

Gint paused briefly. 'Somehow, I think you're leaving something out.'

I didn't reply. I was somewhere else. The music had put me in mind of another place, another time. I recalled the taste of dust at the back of my throat, and could feel the heat beating down, despite the rain.

Tenth Cohort had mustered in the shadow of Baraat, the sky-city, preparing for the long march back to Hammerhal Aqsha, after the Third Darezi War. The locals were celebrating – playing their weird bone-flutes and beating their salamander-hide drums.

I'd never seen an army ready itself for march before, not up-close, and the noise – the confusion of it all – had been overwhelming. Tents falling like waves breaking against the shore, the sound of thousands of voices raised in command, in protest, in laughter. The rattle of weapons, the boom of cannons as excess powder was expended to lighten wagon loads. Despite the noise and dust, it was efficient. The Gold Gryphons were masters of their craft, and a camp of thousands could be made ready to march in a day or less.

They were among the largest of the Freeguild regiments out of Azyrheim. If there was a battlefield, soldiers bearing the heraldry of the Gold Gryphons had likely shed blood on it. They'd fought in Chamon, in Aqshy and Ghyran. Even in Shyish. I remembered my father telling me what a great honour it was to serve with such a regiment.

Then, my father told me a lot of things.

I'd been barely more than a boy, wrapped in gold and azure, clutching a hammer I had yet to swing at anything more threatening than a few wolf rats. It was my first posting – a favour to my father, by an old friend. Of course, the Gold Gryphons had had little use for priests, and Arch Lector Cassian had even less.

He'd been a holy terror – a bellicose warrior, with less interest in men's souls than in how well they wielded a blade in Sigmar's name. Gruff, impassive and loud. I'd liked him, though I doubted the feeling had been mutual.

I recalled looking up, seeing the underside of Baraat for the first time – the sheer, aching expanse of a city in the sky. Strange towers hung like stalactites from the city's belly, amid great mechanism-bastions and aether-drifts. Innumerable bridges and skyways were strung like garlands, and if I squinted, I could almost make out people crossing them. I'd stared upwards for what felt like hours. In reality, it had only been a few moments, until Cassian had slapped me on the back of the head, breaking the spell.

I missed him, sometimes. Until I remembered why I'd killed him.

'We're being watched.' Gint's voice shook me from my reverie.

'What?'

He jerked his chin. I glanced around. There were guards patrolling the back streets. More than I expected for such a place. I could feel a tension on the air – familiar to any city dweller. Some of the guards eyed us more closely than I liked. I kept my head down and tried not to attract attention.

'We're strangers,' I said. We passed an old statue of Sigmar the Redeemer, kneeling on a cracked and crumbling plinth. The statue had been beaten into submission by the weather and the moss that clung to Sigmar's face like a second beard. I glanced at it, wondering how the God-King felt about such desecration.

I supposed if Sigmar cared, he'd have done something about it. About all of it.

'This town isn't very welcoming, at first glance,' Gint continued.

'I've seen worse,' I said. Around us, the shops were open, and the smell of baking bread and spilled beer filled the damp air.

Walkways and balconies formed a creaking canopy overhead, and weak waterfalls of rain splashed down through them to spill across the cobbles. Jade-feathered swamp-birds nested in the high gutters, and piebald mongrels stalked the cul-de-sacs, hunting rats.

I caught a flash of something black out of the corner of my eye and turned, a hand on my knife. Something that might have been a dog scuttled away from me. The beast had been following us, perhaps hoping for a meal. Something about it unsettled me, though I couldn't say why. Something about the way it had moved – awkward and stiff. It reminded me of the beasts I'd seen in the swamp.

'What is it? What did you see?' Gint asked.

'Nothing.'

Gint frowned, but didn't ask any more questions. I pressed on, and he followed. This far from the palisade, the streets were crowded. Smoke hung on the wet air, and the growl of commerce squeezed out all other sound. Vendors rang bells or bellowed their prices, wagon wheels clattered. Strangest of all, an eel made from paper and wood curled between the buildings, creeping along on a dozen stamping feet.

We were forced to stop as the procession crossed the street ahead of us. It spilled into a nearby square, and the eel spun and writhed, feet splashing in the mud. People laughed and clapped, and the music grew wilder and louder. Many of them wore those crude vine and corn-husk masks, and clashed knives and sickles.

'Tools of the hunt and harvest,' Gint murmured.

I looked at him. 'What?'

'Nothing. So are we just going to wander around forever, or...?'

'Quiet,' I said.

'Answer the question and I'll consider it.'

'Fine. Ever played injured bird?' It was an old game, in the Fastness. You played at being lost or stupid or drunk, and waited to see who was stupid enough to take the bait.

'Maybe.' Gint frowned. 'Is that what we're doing? Why?'

'I'll tell you in a moment.' I'd felt the fingers on my coat a moment before I'd replied. Quick, but clumsy. Then, it wasn't the sort of art that required finesse out here. I clamped my hand around the offending digits and squeezed. Someone yelped and I turned. The pickpocket tried to pull away, but he wasn't strong enough or fast enough.

He was a little fellow, wiry and lean. Malnourished, with pox-scars on his face, and wearing rough homespun clothes. But he was armed. I snatched the knife from his belt and tossed it to Gint. 'Hold this.' Then I hit the pickpocket low, and lifted him slightly off his feet. He stumbled, but I didn't release him. I hit him again, barely more than a tap, just to assert my position, and propelled him into a nearby alleyway and away from the crowd.

Gint followed, a startled look on his face. I waved him back as I deposited the pickpocket into a trough of rainwater. No one paid any attention to us – or if they did, they knew better than to interfere.

'What are you doing?' Gint demanded.

'Shut up and keep a look out.' I shoved the struggling, cursing pickpocket's head beneath the water, and counted to five. 'I want to talk to whoever is in charge,' I said as I dragged the pickpocket out of the trough. 'Point me in the right direction or I'll start cutting pieces off.'

He stammered a curse and I thrust him back under the water. Gint caught at my shoulder. 'Don't kill him,' he hissed.

'I thought I told you to shut up and keep an eye out for the guards.' I hauled the spluttering man up. 'Ready to tell me what I want to know?'

'What do you want?' he gasped.

'I told you… I want to talk to whoever is in charge. Look at my face – think you'll remember it?' He nodded and I dragged him out of the trough. 'Good. Now go tell somebody who matters.' I shoved him towards the mouth of the alleyway, and gave him a kick to encourage him.

'That wasn't smart,' Gint said. 'I can't imagine the criminals around here are the refined sort. They'll come looking.'

'That's the idea.'

'So?'

'Murn liked to gamble,' I said. 'I doubt that's changed.'

'I don't understand.'

'If Murn owes money, his debtors may know where he is.'

'How do you know?'

'Because I would.'

'And you think they'll just – what? Share information in the spirit of cooperation?'

'No, I think they'll send someone after me. Then, after I hurt them, the boss will talk to me. Might even try and hire me.'

'And then…?' Gint prodded.

'And then I'll find out what I need to find out.'

Gint shook his head. 'All very simple, except for the bits involving violence.'

I shrugged. 'I've never had a problem with violence.' I'd always been very good at it, in fact. The priest part had always been less appealing than the warrior part. That was one of the reasons I'd taken Caspar Guno up on his offer, that day, rather than joining another regiment under an assumed name.

When I was hitting something, or being hit, I wasn't thinking. And when I wasn't hitting, I could be drinking or whoring or any number of other more pleasant activities than thinking. Being a blunt object wasn't as bad as it sounded. Besides which, it was thinking that had got me in trouble in the first place.

Someone blew a winding horn, and four men clad in a wooden mock-up of a giant stag tromped down the street to meet the eel in what I thought was either fierce battle, or an amorous encounter. Maybe both. I watched it, and felt something grate inside me. My mind kept trying to go back to that night in the swamp, and I fought it with every bit of will I had.

In the Fastness, you learned quick not to see things. If it wasn't your business, you kept your nose out of it. This wasn't my business. This wasn't my place. I had one thing to do and one thing only, and once it was done I was leaving and never looking back. Wald could keep its secrets. I had plenty of my own.

Dancers clad in bells and bark spun and yelped in time to the sawing rhythm of a fiddler as she led them past the battle, trailed by laughing children. The eel burst away from its opponent in a flurry of undulations and crimson paper and slithered towards us, paper jaws agape, as bystanders struck out at it with their knives and sickles. I stepped aside at the last moment, letting the false beast wobble past.

'I don't know what's scarier – the real thing or that monstrosity,' Gint said, as we stepped to the side of the street to allow the procession to stream past. He took in the revellers that paraded past us, splashing along the street. 'They're all wearing masks.'

'So they are.'

'Doesn't look like any celebration I've ever seen'

I looked at him. 'Seen many, then?'

Gint shrugged. 'Better to say, seen one you've seen them all.' He looked at me. 'So what's the plan now? Wait for someone to come looking for you?'

'No. My plan is to find the local road agent post. You can do what you like.'

'Why do you need a road agent? Sending money home to mother?' He laughed. I didn't. When he realised I wasn't joining in, he fell silent.

'None of your business.'

'Well, I'm not doing anything else. Might as well go with you.'

I didn't argue. As long as he stayed quiet, I didn't care.

Messages were delivered in myriad ways, in Ghyran. Official documentation was the province of the Swifthawk Agents, or private couriers. Everyone else used the road agents. They were a loose confederation of couriers and gossipmongers, often paid by local lords or conclaves to act as despatch riders for the populace.

Murn hadn't sent the coin by private courier. It had come by rider, wrapped in a book of catechisms. A sort of joke. Murn's sense of humour had always been hard-edged. Regardless, it meant there might be a record of who'd sent it. Murn himself, maybe, or someone who knew him. That was the place to start.

I'd become good at finding people in the past few years. No one disappeared more quickly than a debtor – especially when they owed money to someone like Caspar Guno.

The road agent post was located in a central square. It was a narrow shack squeezed between two larger, older stone buildings. A sign marked with the sigil of a bird in flight hung over the entrance.

'Wait out here,' I said.

Gint didn't argue. He saluted lazily and took up a position beside the doorway. The door was unlocked, so I didn't bother to knock. When I stepped inside, the first thing I saw was the aelf on the table. She groaned softly, so I knew she was alive.

I'd never seen an aelf with a hangover before. I hadn't even been aware that they could get drunk. She lay back on the table, one foot resting on the back of a chair, her hand over her eyes. I knocked on the doorframe.

'Go away.'

'I need to ask a question.'

'Ask someone else.'

'Are you in charge?'

'No. There. You asked. I answered. Go away.'

'No.' I yanked the chair out from under her foot, and kicked the table. She was on her feet in moments, a knife in her hand. I twisted aside, and the blade gouged the doorframe.

'Who in the seven hells do you think you are?' she hissed, eyes bleary. She was pretty, in the way aelves are pretty – like a snake or a wolf. Like something best observed from a distance.

'Someone who's not inclined to give you more than one chance with that pig-sticker.' I fell into a crouch, arms spread, ready to deflect or snatch as the occasion warranted. 'Settle down, or I'll take it from you.'

She shook her head. 'I'd like to see you try.' Despite her words, she straightened and sheathed the blade. 'What do you want?'

'Are you the road agent for this canton?'

'For my sins.' She went to the corner, where a bucket of water rested on a stand. She bent and splashed some onto her face. She ran her hands through her hair, dragging it back and swiftly knotting it with a leather strap. 'I ask again – what do you want?'

'I need to know who sent me this.' I set the coin down on the table.

She sneered. 'How am I supposed to know that?'

'It was delivered by one of your road agents. Or someone wearing their livery.'

She frowned and picked up the coin. After a moment, she tossed it back to me. 'When did you receive it?' I told her, and she sighed. 'That was Pulo. He isn't back yet.'

'Do you have a record of who wanted it delivered?'

'Pulo would know, but he's not back yet. Like I said.'

I looked around. There were papers everywhere, and logbooks mouldering in tottering piles. Notices mildewed on the walls. 'You don't keep records, then?'

'I told you, Pulo would know, but...'

'He's not back yet, yes, I know.' I looked at her. 'When do you expect him back?'

'Yesterday.'

I was careful not to let my annoyance show. 'When he returns, let him know someone wants to talk to him.'

She went to a cabinet and pulled down a clay bottle and a cup. 'I'll make a note. Name and address?'

'Blackwood. Harran Blackwood. As for an address... care to make a recommendation?'

She emptied her cup and refilled it. 'The Stag's Head, over on Eelmonger Lane.'

'They have rooms available?'

'No clue. But the wine is good.' She turned away. 'Close the door behind you.'

I didn't. Gint was waiting for me where I'd left him, an apple in his hand. 'Anything?' he asked, as he fell into step with me.

'Yes.' I pointed to the apple. 'Where'd you get that?'

'Orchard,' Gint said. He gestured vaguely. 'Found it while you were busy in there.' He shined the apple on his sleeve. 'Sour apples are better than none. I gathered from the tenders that there are similar communal gardens scattered across town. The harvest Deshler was talking about refers to them, mostly. And the corn and potatoes.' He took a bite of the apple and frowned. Carefully, he spat the bite out.

'Too sour?'

He wiped his mouth with his hand and flung the apple into a night-soil cart. 'It tastes like eel,' he said.

'They must use them as fertiliser.' I turned. 'Look for Eelmonger Lane.'

'What's on Eelmonger Lane?'

'Somewhere to get out of the rain, hopefully.' I glanced back at the post, and saw the aelf watching us from the doorway. She didn't look as hung-over as I'd first thought. When she realised she'd been noticed, she stepped back and shut the door.

When I turned back, Gint was looking at me. 'Something wrong?' he asked.

'No,' I said. 'Not that I can see.'

CHAPTER NINE

THE STAG'S HEAD

Dusk was coming on by the time we found Eelmonger Lane. The village was like a miniature labyrinth – small, but convoluted. It had seemed to contract about us with every passing moment. Like a trap, with no way out.

The Stag's Head sat back along a narrow side street, its rear hanging over the waters of the canal. Skiffs and small boats were moored to the jetty that extended from its back wall like an animal's tail. Smoke seeped from the slanted chimney, and the windows were shuttered against the weather. From the sound of it, it was full of customers – bargemen and drunks, eager to spend their wages.

Standing outside the grimy, wood-frame building in the spitting rain, I hesitated.

Gint looked at me. 'Are we going in, or...?'

'After you,' I said. The door was little more than a curtain of tanned hide, and I swept it back. Noise and stink struck us like physical blows.

The common room of the grog-house echoed with the sounds of laughter and wagers being placed. The air smelled of burning fat, woodsmoke and sweat. Like a tavern, in other words. Tables and chairs surrounded a central firepit. The bar, such as it was, stretched along the far wall. There was a second room near the bar, and it stank of grease and eel – the kitchen, I suspected. At least I hoped it was the kitchen.

Most of the tables closest to the firepit were occupied. None of them looked friendly. Fishermen, milkweed harvesters and others. Men and women both, with hard eyes and hard faces, blistered hands and scarred fingers. They nursed clay mugs of harsh cider or sipped at bowls of soup.

Something snarled, and the floor shook as a heavy weight struck the supports below. Tables rattled as hands steadied mugs and bowls. A shout of laughter went up from the rear of the common room.

'What's that racket?' Gint asked.

'Over there.' I pointed. A crowd of boatmen and loafers surrounded a hole in the floor. We pushed through the crowd, ignoring the angry looks tossed in our direction. I could hear wagers being made as we reached the edge of the pit.

Slabs of bronze had been sunk deep into the water below, creating a makeshift cistern. Within the circle, an adolescent troggoth slammed warty fists against the bronze, and bellowed. Abattoir leavings floated on the surface of the water, slopping against the bronze or slipping out into the canal.

The troggoth resembled a human, but only in basic outline – it was an overgrown, hunched shape, with wide, bat-like ears and a face that was twisted all out of proportion. Jaws full of outsize teeth champed and gnawed the air with mindless ferocity. A mane of kelp-like hair hung from the creature's scalp, and crept down its scaly back.

Broken claws scraped at the bronze, as the creature tried and failed to haul itself out of the pit. A collar of iron bit into its wattle neck, and a heavy anchor-chain was attached to it. The chain was hooked to something below the waterline, preventing the beast from going very far.

'It's only a pup,' Gint said.

I laughed. 'Don't tell me you feel sorry for the brute.' I'd fought too many troggoths to feel sympathetic to the creature's plight.

'And what if I do?' he said.

I shrugged and stepped back as someone dragged a heavy, twitching sack towards the pit. Patrons leapt aside as the sack twisted towards them. Something inside it hissed gutturally. It took several men to upend the sack over the mouth of the pit. A massive, serpentine shape slipped out and fell towards the water.

The leopard eel shrilled audibly as it struck the surface. It rose immediately and began to circle the troggoth. The troggoth roared and caught at its attacker, eliciting a spray of venom. The two creatures reeled back and forth, bouncing off the bronze slabs. Their blood mingled, turning the water the colour of tar. Gint turned away, grimacing.

'What's the matter? Don't feel like wagering a few motes?'

'I only wager on games of skill,' he said flatly. 'Let's find a table.'

We claimed one in the corner and sat, watching the other patrons pretend to pay us no attention. I wondered if any of them knew Murn. If they did, he probably owed them money. That was usually the way of it. Murn had debts the way a crow had feathers.

He'd lived well, in the regiment. Too well. Beyond his means. He'd always had a fancy for comets and the things they could buy. Never save tomorrow what you could spend today, that had been Murn's motto.

I'd found it amusing at first. Only later had it become concerning. 'And now here I am again,' I murmured. I drew Murn's coin from my coat without thinking about it. I turned it slowly. 'One more time.'

For the last time.

'Lucky coin?' Gint asked, watching me. I dropped the coin back into my pocket.

'No. I'm hungry.' I stood.

Gint smiled. 'I thought you'd never ask. Bowl of soup, please. And a mug of the local cider.'

I considered telling him to buy his own, but decided not to waste my breath. Instead, I made my way to the bar, careful not to make eye contact with anyone. In a place like this, a wrong look could get you a fish-knife in the guts. Eyes followed me regardless, and whispers as well. Strangers were always of interest in places like this.

At the bar a surly, silver-haired woman greeted me with hostility. 'What do you want?' she asked. I could hear the unspoken imprecation. I smiled in as friendly a way as I could manage.

'Some food and something to drink for my friend and I.' Before she could reply, I put a few coins on the bar. 'If you have any left.'

She gazed at me sourly. Then, almost reluctantly, she pulled the coins towards her. She bit one. Her eyes widened slightly, and she quickly thrust the coins into her apron. 'Sit down,' she said. 'I'll bring some bowls.'

'And some bread, if it pleases you,' I said, as she turned away. I made my way back to our table. There was a shout from the troggoth-pit, and a high, shrill screech. One of the combatants had finally succumbed. Gint was watching the crowd, a rueful look on his face.

'Maybe I should have made a bet after all.'

'You'll get your chance. I'm sure they'll drag in another eel before too long.'

He laughed. 'You're probably right.' He eyed me speculatively. 'I couldn't interest you in a game, could I?'

'No.'

He sighed and nodded. After a few moments, he said, 'You know, you don't seem like a bad fellow, Harran. Despite the many rough edges. How'd you come to work for a man like Caspar Guno?'

'That's my business.'

'And I'm asking.'

I was silent for a moment. Then, 'I needed a job.'

'Easier jobs to be had.'

'Maybe. Maybe I just like it.'

The soup arrived then. Suddenly ravenous, I fell to eating. It tasted the way it smelled, but it was warm and I was hungry. The bread was tough, but chewable. The drink was bitter, and pleasingly alcoholic. It steadied me more than I liked to admit.

'I find it's easier to think with a drink or two in me,' Gint said, around a mouthful of bread. 'If I'm sober for too long, I start making risky choices.'

'Explains why you followed me,' I said, as I observed our fellow patrons and they observed us in turn. Hurried glances and lingering ones. Calculation, assumption and dismissal.

'I followed you because I'm allergic to boredom.'

I nearly choked on a chunk of bread. 'Well, it hasn't been boring, I guess.'

Gint's smile was broad. 'Not so far.' He dipped his bread in the soup and chewed thoughtfully. 'So what happens when you find him?'

'What do you mean?'

'Planning to beat him up, or... what?' He studied me, and for a moment, I saw something in his eyes. A calculation at odds with his normal cheer.

I turned my attentions back to my soup. 'You ask a lot of questions.'

'Like I said, you seem like a nice enough fellow. I can't imagine you're going to kill this... Murn, was it?'

'What I do, or don't do, is no concern of yours.'

He nodded, and went back to his food. As I bent back to my own, he said, 'Only, it seems to me that you've come a long way just to kill a man.'

I put my spoon down. 'Who said I'm going to kill him?'

Gint gestured with a chunk of bread. 'I'm not stupid. Collecting debts is all well and good, but this is a trifle too far from the city for anything but bloody murder. And even then, I've never known a leg-breaker to come so far off his patch just to kill one man.' He took a bite. 'That's the sort of thing you hire a paid killer for.'

'Caspar Guno prefers the personal touch.'

'So I hear. But do you want to know what I think?'

'No.'

He told me anyway, leaning close as if we were friends. 'I think this is personal.'

I didn't reply. Someone was watching us, and I was watching them. The old man sat near the firepit, regarding us openly. Unafraid, or maybe simply unused to being observed in turn. I considered doing him the courtesy of pretending I hadn't noticed, but decided against it. I met his gaze and held it. If he wanted to start something, I welcomed it.

It was clear from the number of heads bending towards the old man, and the intensity of the whispered conversation at his table, that he was someone of standing. I sipped my drink and waited.

I'd seen cults before. I knew the signs. A place like this – isolated, deprived – was fertile ground for sour fruit. But I was no witch hunter. Once, I might've cared enough to investigate further. At the moment, I just wanted to find Murn and go home. I swallowed a spoonful of soup. Of course, Murn's trouble might well have to do with whatever was going on here. I hoped not. I wasn't in the business of faith, these days.

There were gheists in the common room. Just little things – wisps of bad feeling. Ragged and small, barely strong enough to exist, let alone hurt anyone. Children, maybe.

One of them stared at me with a face like a sheet of crumpled linen, with three black holes for eyes and a mouth torn in it. It made as if to speak. A moment later, it was gone.

Suddenly, the soup wasn't sitting right. I leaned back. A warning, perhaps.

Gint coughed, and I looked up. The old man was making his way towards our table. Gint made to speak, but I stamped on his foot, silencing him.

The old man caught a chair, dragged it over, and sat, without waiting for an invitation. 'Don't know you,' he said, without preamble. His voice was soft, and creaky. Like branches in a windstorm.

'I don't know you either.' I glanced around. We were the centre of attention, though most were trying to pretend otherwise. I wondered if this was one of those quaint local customs, like hunting men or riding a horse naked.

'You're not from here,' the old man said.

'No.' I dipped the last of my bread into my bowl and took a bite.

'I know everyone from around here. Every face. Every voice. Don't know yours, though.' The old man peered at me sidelong, as if trying to memorise my features. 'You a merchant? No. Not got the look, you. Sellsword, then. No business for sellswords here. We defend our own, happy to say.'

'I've heard different,' I said.

'You heard wrong.' There was a bit of heat there. He didn't like being argued with.

'Good thing I'm not a sellsword, then.'

'No? What are you selling, if not steel?'

'I'm not selling anything.' I paused. 'I'm buying.'

The old man sniffed, and looked at the firepit. 'Not much to

buy, here. We make what we need. Not for selling, but for having. That's always been the way of it.'

'Does that include information?'

The old man grunted. 'None of that here. I'm not a gossip,
me. We don't gossip.' Eyes slid away from us and chairs turned
away, as if that had been a signal. I had the feeling that this was
a test – one I was failing. I didn't like that. But I kept my temper
in check. I'd had practice dealing with men like this.

'But you do know everyone in this village?' I pressed, gently.

'You're looking for someone, then?'

'A man named Murn. Evrek Murn.'

'Funny sort of name, that.'

'You know him?'

'I knew a Murn or two.' The old man leaned back, and the
barkeep appeared, drink in hand. She set it down and scurried
off, all but genuflecting the whole while. The old man took a
sip and smacked his lips appreciatively. 'Lots of Murns around
here, once. Not so many now.'

'No?'

'No. They all died. Sickness, some of them. One or two drowned,
when they were out where they ought not to have been, when
the waters rose. Swamp took the rest, as it takes most. Not a
soft sort of place, the swamp.' The last was said with a meaningful look at us. Gint said nothing, but I could feel him tense.

It was a threat, and not a subtle one. I almost laughed. I'd
been threatened by more frightening men in my time. And a few
things that weren't men at all.

'So I hear.'

'You smell like stone and fire. City lad. What do you know
about the swamp, save what old men like me tell you? Nothing, that's what. If you did, you'd know better than to sit here,
smelling of the city, asking questions.' The old man was smiling,
but there was nothing friendly in the expression.

'Speaking of which, you never said whether you knew Evrek Murn or not.' I was pushing it, but I didn't think it was going to come to violence. Not yet. Not here. This was just a scouting foray – he was feeling us out.

'You ought to leave this place. There's nothing for you here.'

'I'll be the judge of that, I think. Thank you for the advice, though.'

The old man's expression became mulish. He was clearly a man not used to hearing the word no. Chairs scraped back throughout the common room. Gint grabbed my arm, but I ignored him.

'Now, about Murn...' I raised my voice. 'I'll pay for the information. I know times are hard. Even with the harvest.'

I looked around the room, but no eyes met mine, save those of a heavyset man sitting near the entrance. The big man surreptitiously indicated the doorway, rose and left. I looked back at the old man. I smiled.

'What about you? A few coins always come in handy.'

'Don't need your filthy money, city dweller,' the old man said. 'Me nor anyone else. You'll find no succour here. Go on and go. Leave us to our business.' He leaned forward, suddenly more menacing than he'd seemed at first. I revised my estimation of him. 'You only get one warning from me.'

'Then perhaps I'd best take it, eh?' I pushed my chair back unhurriedly, my hand resting on the hilt of my knife. 'Of course, I'm not the sort of man to take kindly to warnings... or threats, for that matter.'

The old man's gaze sharpened, and I was reminded of the knives and sickles the celebrants carried. He rose abruptly, turned and went back to his seat without a backward glance.

Gint released a slow breath as patrons turned away from us. 'That was stupid.'

'Depends on what happens next,' I said.

He shook his head. 'Is this how you make friends?'

'Wouldn't know. Don't have any.'

He leaned close. 'The man who left... you think he knows something?'

'Only one way to find out.' I made to rise.

Gint caught my arm. 'You sure?' he asked, in a low voice.

I shook him off. 'No. But I might as well. Stay here.'

'You don't have to tell me twice.' He pulled out his deck of cards and shuffled them. He looked around, frowning. 'Maybe I'll see if anyone is interested in a game.'

'You do that,' I said, as I headed for the door. No one tried to stop me.

Outside it was still raining. I heard a whistle, and turned. The big man stood between two buildings, just out of sight. I looked around, and then hurried towards him.

'You really got coin?' the big man growled. He stank of salt and eel.

'Depends. Do you have something for me?'

The big man sniffed, and looked at the tavern. 'Come with me. Don't want them to see us talking. Don't need any trouble.'

I glanced back and saw the old man standing in the tavern doorway. But I didn't say anything. No sense spooking my new friend.

'Lead the way.'

CHAPTER TEN

FULDER

The big man led me down a crooked side street, across a board-walk square to a small shop sitting diagonally to the rest of the buildings. 'My shop,' he grunted. His accent was rough and foreign. Harsh. Like me, he wasn't from around here. I guessed that was why he was willing to talk.

He shut the door behind us and latched it. He peered out the window and then turned back to light a candle. 'Show me the money. Hurry up.'

'What are you worried about?'

The big man smiled nastily. 'You really aren't from around here, otherwise you wouldn't ask that.' In the candlelight, I saw that the shop was small – a counter, and a back room hidden behind a tatty curtain. Sacks of dead eels sat on the floor, and dried and salted strips of meat hung from racks on the wall.

'Eelmonger,' I said.

'What of it?'

'Business good?'

'We're not here to talk about my business.' Something clattered in the back room. My hand went to my knife, and the eelmonger jerked back, eyes wide.

'What was that?'

'Nothing – *nothing*,' the big man said, in a low voice. 'Keep your voice down.'

I stared at him for a moment, and then stepped quickly behind the counter and headed for the curtain.

'Hey,' he said. 'Hey! No!'

I swept the curtain aside. A boy – barely eleven seasons – jerked back, nearly dropping his basket. It was full of eels, some of them still twitching. The boy was grubby, dressed in home-spun clothes, but well fed.

'Hello,' I said. The boy stared up at me, mouth slightly agape.

'Leave him be,' the big man growled. 'Get to the back, and strip the rest of those bones,' he added, nudging the boy. The boy nodded jerkily and hurried out of sight, dragging the basket with him. The man watched him go, and then turned to me.

'Your son?'

'Yes,' the man said. 'Money.'

I took out a handful of coins and spread them across the counter. The eelmonger licked his lips. Rather than taking the coins, he retrieved an eel from a sack behind the counter and slapped it down on his chopping block. It was a small thing, barely as long as a man's forearm and slick looking. It had a vicious mouth full of teeth, and eyes like dollops of jade. I had seen similar eels cut up and fried at street stalls in the Fastness. They were decent, with enough Aqshian spice to cover the taste.

'That buys you two. How do you want them?' The eelmonger drew his cleaver from his apron.

'Fillet them. Take your time.'

The eelmonger gave a harsh laugh and brought the cleaver down, chopping the creature's head off. A flick of his wrist was enough to scrape the snapping jaws off the block and into a waiting basket. 'Cur-eels,' he said. 'Bite you even after they're dead. Got to remove the head first, just to be safe.' He began to fillet the eel with the edge of his cleaver. 'They're a gift, you know.'

'The eels.'

He nodded, not looking up from his work. 'That's what the locals say. The jade-bloods, I mean. A gift from their god.' He plied his cleaver deftly. 'I thought all of them worshipped the Everqueen. These don't, though. Not really.'

'Who do they worship?'

'Something else.' He paused. 'It's got a fair few names. It's a little god, I think. Some spirit of the swamp. They used to bend their kin over wooden altars and spill their guts with knives of eel-bone to appease it.'

'They don't any more?'

He paused, as if uncertain how to reply. 'Not that I've seen,' he said, finally. 'Others you could ask, if you were of a mind. Like Fulder.' He looked at me. 'Friend of his?'

'The old man, you mean? No. Was that his name?'

The eelmonger grinned, showing gapped teeth. 'Honest man.'

'What?'

'Fulder doesn't have any friends. At least, none from outside Wald. If you'd said yes, I'd have known you were trouble.' The eelmonger eyed me up and down. 'Might still be, at that.'

'Only one way to find out,' I said. 'I'm looking for someone.'

'So I heard. Why here?'

I made a show of looking around. 'Why not here?'

'Folk in Wald don't often have business outside of the village.'

'You do seem quite isolated.'

'Backwater, you mean.' The eelmonger gestured with his cleaver. 'I'm not from Wald, you know. Not originally. That's why I'll talk

to you. And I'll tell you straight – whoever you're looking for…
don't. Go home. Let Wald keep its own.'

'I'll take it under advisement.' I looked down. The heads of
the cur-eels were bouncing and snapping in their basket. Needle
fangs clicked as the last vestiges of animal malice fled the cool-
ing meat. 'What do you know about Evrek Murn?'

The eelmonger hesitated, mid-blow. It was a little thing. I only
noticed because I'd been expecting it. I also noticed the tattoo
on his forearm – a cannon, wrapped in chains. Another Ironhole
alumnus. 'And why are you looking for him?'

'That's my business.'

The eelmonger grunted. 'Fair enough.' He scraped another
head into the basket, and began filleting the still-wriggling body.
'There's no one by that name here.'

'That's not what I asked.'

The eelmonger nodded. 'But that's my answer, regardless.' He
paused in his work. 'Take my advice, friend. Wald's no place for
a fellow like you.'

'And what sort of fellow am I?'

He snorted. 'You're a debt-collector or I'm a Sister of Charity.
Got that look that says you know what a breaking bone sounds
like.'

'You've got a good eye.'

'And you don't belong here.'

I smiled. 'So people keep saying. I'm not planning to set up
shop. I'm just looking for Evrek Murn. Is he dead, or is he alive?'

'If he's dead, will you leave?'

I paused, considering the question. 'That depends… Is he?'

The eelmonger finished his task and reached for another eel.
'I'm tired of all the damn Ghyranites. Of being wet all the time.'
He sank his cleaver into the eel's neck. 'But mostly, I'm tired of
eels. I want to leave here. Need money for that. And more than
just a handful of comets.'

I pulled out the pouch I'd taken from Gint. 'I have more.'

The eelmonger looked at me. He licked his lips. 'He's not dead.'

'Good to know. Where is he?'

'I don't know, but you're not the only one looking for him.'

'Who else?'

He gave a meaningful glance to the pouch. I started setting out coins. When I got to five, I stopped. He frowned, but said, 'The guards are after him.'

'Why?'

He didn't reply. I set another coin down. A baron's ransom. I didn't care. Money was just a means to an end for me. If I couldn't buy something, I'd just take it. He smiled thinly, as if reading my mind. 'Rumour has it he tried to kill his lordship.'

'What?'

He nodded. 'That was my reaction. Not like him at all, frankly.'

'You knew him, then?' Despite myself, I was curious. Had Murn changed in the years since we'd last seen one another?

He made to speak, and stopped. Froze, rather. I turned and saw Fulder standing at the entrance. The door hung open, unlatched. The old man stared at us and then, very deliberately, turned and strode away.

'Get out,' the eelmonger said, all former amiability drained from his voice.

I looked at him. 'What?'

'*Get out,*' the eelmonger hissed. He came around the counter, cleaver raised threateningly. 'Get out of here. I can't speak to you any more! Get out, *get out!*'

I backed away in haste, retreating into the street. The eelmonger didn't follow. He slammed the door behind me and latched it.

Fulder was waiting for me, and he wasn't alone. He had three friends with him. I recognised them as the old man's hangers-on from the tavern.

'I thought you were taking my advice,' Fulder said.

'Did I say that?' I kept my hands away from my knife. None of Fulder's friends appeared to be armed, and I didn't want to commit murder if I didn't have to. It would only make things more difficult.

'It's time for you to leave. Now.'

'I'm not looking for trouble.'

'You found it anyway,' he said. 'The god has marked you, boy. I can smell it on you.'

That brought me up short. 'What god do you serve?'

Fulder laughed. 'The Huntsman,' he said. 'Red Kern. The Old Stag. The bramble-crowned black-shanked god of dark shadows and tall trees. He's marked you, boy, and no two ways about it. I smelled it on you the moment I sat down.'

'Marked me?' I felt a chill, and not from the rain.

Fulder nodded, baring gap-teeth in an animal grin. 'I can smell his musk on you. He's pissed in the hollows of your soul.' He leaned forward. 'I'd leave, if I were you. He might let you go. Might let you escape, if he's feeling merciful. Sometimes the prey lives to fight another day.'

'I'm no one's prey.'

Fulder licked his lips. 'No?' The way he said it made me think he was laughing at me. Fulder struck me as a man who'd seen too much to believe anything that came out of anyone's mouth. He reached into his coat and produced a knife. 'We should see about that, maybe.' He glanced at his companions. 'Hold him.'

His three companions moved forward. I considered running – three on one was bad odds. But there was nowhere to go. Better to make a stand.

I set my feet, and when the first of them drew close enough, I struck. They hadn't expected that, and the first man went down easily enough – a strong jab to the midsection and he was on his knees, wheezing and heaving. The other two came in hard and close after that. They were brawlers, built for tavern scuffles.

They hemmed me in, and pushed me back, cornering me against the eelmonger's shop. Their punches were slow, but strong. I weathered them, taking the pain the way I'd been taught.

Once you learn how to take it, pain is just fuel for the fire. I caught a blow on my forearm and swept it aside, even as I slammed my foot down on the side of my opponent's knee. There was an ugly crack, and the man leaned forward, right into my palm. The blow was quick, and one broken jaw later he was down.

The remaining one took a wild swing, nearly catching me on the side of the head. I twitched aside, caught his arm, twisted and dislocated it. It made a nice pop, and his scream was music to my ears.

I stepped over the whimpering man and advanced on Fulder. The old man had a look of consternation on his face, and he backed away. This wasn't going the way he'd foreseen.

'You can fight,' he said. 'You'll wish you hadn't, before they're done with you.'

'Who?' I said, reaching for him.

'Who do you think?'

The whinny of a horse caused us to turn, and I saw a coach rattle into the square. There were guards sitting atop it, hooded against the pelting rain. Fulder took the opportunity to scuttle away, and I let him go. The coach rolled to a stop, as the horse pulling it reared. The door opened, and a slim figure climbed down.

She was tall and lean. Dark, with curling, vine-like tattoos that marked her cheeks and chin. She wasn't dressed like a farmer. Farmers didn't wear hauberks, or carry swords.

From what I could see, the blade was cheap – forged locally, I suspected – but it was probably sharp enough. She wore heavy gloves with iron bracers, and had thick, hobnailed boots. Good for grabbing and stomping. A cloak was thrown over one shoulder. She tapped the pommel of her sword.

'Well then. What have we here?'

As she spoke, the guards atop the coach stood, raising cross-bows. She strode towards me. 'Disturbing the peace? Public intoxication? Pick your poison, stranger.'

'None of the above.' I raised my hands and stepped back.

She laughed, and looked down at the men I'd despatched. She whistled softly. The guards climbed down from the coach and started towards the groaning men.

'New to the village, then?' she said. 'We don't get many visitors.' She smiled. 'Might I ask your business in Wald?'

'Are you the sheriff?'

'Close enough,' she said. 'Answer my question.'

'Am I breaking some law by defending myself?'

'Is that what it was?' She scratched her chin. Still friendly. On the surface, at least. 'Answer my question. What's your business here? Other than crippling the locals?'

'I'm looking for someone.' I glanced at the guards as they hauled my opponents to their feet. 'May I lower my hands?'

'No. Who are you looking for?'

'That's my business, I think. A private matter.'

'No such thing in a place like this.' She looked around, and grimaced. 'Seen bigger privies. Nicer, too.' She looked back at me. 'It'll save time if you just tell me. Maybe I can be of help. Quicker you settle your business, quicker you can be on your way.' She peered at me. 'What's your name?'

'Blackwood.'

'Funny name.'

'Is it?'

'Around here? It's hilarious. I'm Sepesh. I'm what passes for the law in Wald.'

'Much call for that?'

'I break up fights, mostly.' She looked pointedly at me. 'And encourage uninvited elements to be about their business. The realm is vast, and there are other places to go.'

'Better places?'

'For you.' Her smile widened. She was enjoying herself. 'We can keep dancing if you like, or you can be sensible. Who are you here for?'

I looked at the guards. Sepesh looked dangerous enough – the guards weren't local either. Mercenaries, then. 'Murn. Evrek Murn.'

She raised an eyebrow. 'Well, isn't that interesting.'

'Oh?'

'I'm looking for him too.'

'So I hear.'

'Oh? From whom?'

'A little eel whispered it to me.'

'Is that so?' Her fingers tightened around the hilt of her sword. 'It might be for the best if you come with me now, Blackwood. Just so we can get this all cleared up.'

I considered my options. I could feel people watching from behind barred doors and windows. I could read the fear in the eyes of Fulder's compatriots as the guards bound their hands and shoved them roughly to the ground. Whatever they were expecting to happen now, it wasn't good.

'What about them?' I asked.

Sepesh shrugged. 'We'll lock 'em up. Teach them the error of their ways. Hear me, boys – teach them thoroughly, huh?'

The guards laughed and nodded. One of them kicked one of his captives in the hip, causing the man to groan. 'Yeah, we'll teach them, captain.'

She looked at me. 'See? Law and order.' She indicated the coach. 'Let's go.'

'Lead the way.'

'Hoped you'd say that.' She winked. 'Always nice when people are sensible about things, don't you agree?'

The coach was old-fashioned. A box on narrow wheels, the gilt tarnished and the canvas blotched with age and damp. The horses were restive, and the wrong sort for pulling coaches. As if they'd been recently pressed into service. The guard sitting atop the wagon was a familiar face – Buell.

I smiled thinly as the big man glowered down at me from beneath his cloak. Sepesh caught the exchange and grinned. 'You two friends?'

'We're acquainted, yes.'

'Bastard,' Buell spat, and turned away.

Sepesh chuckled. She gestured.

'Up you get.'

CHAPTER ELEVEN

THE MANOR

I watched the town stretch past in streamers of brown and grey.

The coach wasn't moving fast, but even so, most of the buildings blurred. When I judged that enough time had passed, I asked the obvious question.

'Where are we going?'

Sepesh gave me a lazy glance. 'To see his lordship.'

'And why does he want to see me?' I wanted to ask if he'd be fully clothed this time, but I kept my comment to myself.

'He doesn't, particularly. But he's also interested in your friend Murn. So I expect that he'll want to talk to you.' Sepesh stretched slightly and interlaced her fingers behind her head. 'Your friend has caused a lot of trouble.'

'A bit of trouble can liven a place up.'

'And it does. But trouble has its place. It comes and it goes, and things go back to being quiet. That's the way of it. You understand?'

'All too well.'

'Care to tell me why you're looking for him?'

'Maybe later.'

She grinned at me. 'Careful you don't wait too long. I'm not a patient woman.' She leaned forward. 'There it is. Impressive, no?'

I craned my neck and peered out the window. From a distance, the keep resembled a headstone rising from the murk. Squat, grey and lacking in all character save a dour malignity. It had seen better days, and was a faded echo of what it once had been. Recent additions and extensions cluttered about its base like barnacles on a ship's hull. It looked like it had been a watch-keep once. Now it was a manor house – or the closest thing Wald had to one. A pontoon bridge, larger and sturdier than the others, stretched from the island to the main track, and there were guards patrolling its length.

The bridge was protected by a simple portcullis of wooden logs lashed together, which was controlled by a winch on the other side. As the coach approached, the portcullis swung upwards with a groan of wood. Rainwater sluiced down from the logs, slapping the roof of the coach. I heard Buell curse as he got even wetter, and allowed myself a small smile.

'I sense some tension there,' Sepesh said, indicating the roof. 'Best be careful. Buell nurtures his grudges as if they were children.'

'So do I.'

She laughed. 'I like you, Blackwood. I hope his lordship doesn't order me to kill you.'

The coach rattled as it crossed the swaying bridge. Trees rose in clumps and groves from the murky waters. I spied the crumbling remains of an old lumber mill on one of the outlying islands. It was all but swallowed by the thick copse of crooked trees that had grown up around it. Even the bridge that had once connected it to the town was all but gone, slowly disintegrating from neglect and the elements.

'I take it that's of little use, these days.'

'What?'

'The lumber mill.'

Sepesh stirred. 'Not for a century, as I recall. There's a few of them scattered about. Not much logging out here, these days. Not much farming either.' She smiled. 'Fishing, mostly.'

'Eels,' I said.

'Famous for our eels,' she said. 'Like eels, Blackwood?'

'Depends on the seasoning.' I studied the keep as it drew closer. The faint strains of music were audible now, and I saw lights bobbing on the water. 'Is there a celebration of some sort going on?'

'There's always a celebration going on this time of year,' Sepesh said. 'His lordship likes a party, and his friends get so easily bored, out here. Not much to do but drink and hunt.'

'I'd hate to interrupt. I can come back later.'

'Not to worry. He asked me to find you.'

I tensed. 'Fair warning – I'm not going to put on a bramble-horn hide. I don't care how much he's offering.'

She looked at me. 'What?'

'Does his lordship sew it onto his prey himself, or does someone do it for him?'

She frowned. 'Best keep those clever comments to yourself, Blackwood. His lordship isn't a man to be disrespected.'

'Also not a man for trousers, going by what I saw.'

She snorted. 'His lordship is a traditionalist.'

'And what tradition is that, exactly?'

'Do you always ask so many questions?'

'Only when I expect an answer.'

Sepesh shook her head, but didn't reply. There were more guards at the other end of the bridge. They were hard-looking men – not local bully boys, these. They were better armed as well, and carried themselves like professionals.

'Expecting trouble?' I asked, as they waved the coach on.

'Better to expect and never see than otherwise,' Sepesh said. 'Never know what might happen out here.' She straightened as the coach rolled to a halt in the muddy courtyard before the keep's entrance. A handful of guards waited on the steps, leaning on halberds. They studied me with disinterest as I followed Sepesh up the steps to the main entrance.

The interior of the structure held only the barest hint of what it had once been. Effort had been made to hide its origins – no longer a fortress, but still a seat of power. A wide set of steps stretched up and back to a landing that ran the width of the entryway. Windows dotted its length, and trophies decorated the walls – bog-grot headdresses, ghyrlion pelts, weapons scavenged from battlefields, tattered banners from forgotten campaigns and bits of war-plate. Too much of it to count.

Sepesh led me upstairs. At either end of the landing, steps rose to meet double-doors, which led into the manor proper. The reflection of many lights streaked the windows and painted the stones of the landing a pale brown, like dried blood. I heard muffled singing, and shouts. I paused at an open window.

It overlooked a walled garden. Below me, I saw men and women dancing beneath a canopy of lanterns. Not one of the stately dances of High Azyr or even the exaggerated gavottes of Verdia or Lyria This was wilder by far – tribal. One of the partygoers blew on a flute of lacquered ivory, made from a beast's tusk. As I watched, the flautist danced and gyrated, piping out a sinuous tune as he capered.

Others joined him with lutes and reed pipes, creating a shrill cacophony which evened out into a primitive rhythm that pulled at me in ways I found unnerving. It stirred a heat in me, and then doused it just as swiftly.

The tempo increased and a squealing bramblehorn was dragged into the middle of the celebration by a pair of servants. When the first of the dancers drew a knife, I turned away from the window. I didn't need to see what came next.

'Harvest celebration,' Sepesh said, watching me, a half-smile on her face. 'What's wrong? Surely a little blood doesn't bother you. The gods ask for so little, and we're obliged to give it to them. Harvest and hunt alike.'

'Blood's never bothered me. It's the religion I've got a problem with.'

Her eyes widened slightly. 'That's a new one on me. I had you pegged as a Sigmarite, if I'm being honest.'

'I used to be.'

'And now?'

'I don't concern myself with gods or their doings.'

'Probably wise. Come on. This way.'

I followed Sepesh up the steps at the far end of the landing as the animal's squeals rose to a febrile pitch, and then were abruptly silenced. The music swelled, discordant and lustful. It reminded me of a stag's call.

Past the double-doors, the corridor was a narrow scoop of stone, lit by candles set in small glass-plated alcoves. The reflected light filled the passage, making it seem larger than it really was. Oil paintings in gilded frames lined the walls – hunting scenes, or bucolic pastorals. None of it to my taste. I studied a few of them as we walked, and found something amiss about all of them, though I couldn't identify what. I was left with a vague sense that whatever I thought I'd seen was wrong – as if the artist were playing some trick.

Sepesh led me past doors and offshoots, to the end of the passage, where another set of double-doors awaited. She gestured to a small bench. 'Wait here.'

I sat without argument. It was all for show. I recognised the signs. I suspected that there was no purpose to this meeting other than entertainment, and the more patience I showed, the sooner it would be over. I leaned back, not quite relaxing.

I could feel the music echoing through the stones. It tugged at the edges of my perception like moth-wings, whispering and plucking at me – trying to get my attention. But the more I tried to ignore it, the more persistent it became.

I also thought I could hear something moving in the walls. Rats, maybe. It was beginning to get on my nerves when the doors opened. I looked up, and Sepesh gestured.

'Come in. Lord Wald will see you now.'

The chamber beyond was brightly lit, by both a crackling fire and several lanterns hanging from hooks strewn about in almost haphazard fashion. Tall shelves lined the walls, and several cushioned benches were arrayed about the fire. A desk sat near the towering windows, and a man stood beside it, looking out into the gloaming. Sepesh coughed politely.

'Your name is Blackwood.' He laughed. It was a low, throaty sound. Like the rumble of a ghyrlion. 'A good name.'

'I've always thought so.'

'Unusual, as well. Verdian?'

'No.'

He frowned slightly. 'You are not from Ghyran, then?'

'No.'

'Ah well. No matter. We are none of us perfect.' He looked at Sepesh. 'You may go, dear Sepesh. But await my call.'

Sepesh bowed, a mocking half-smile on her face, and backed out of the library. She closed the doors behind her as she went.

I looked around. I'd seen larger libraries, but it was big enough to be impressive, if you found quantity imposing. There were books everywhere, crammed onto the rough-hewn shelves in haphazard fashion. The air smelled faintly of mildew and neglect. The books were for show, and probably weren't moved much. Lord Wald didn't strike me as the scholarly type – more an outdoorsman. I cleared my throat.

'Have I done something wrong, then, my lord?'

'I don't know. Have you?' Lord Wald said, smiling slightly.

'Forgive me. A little joke. You are a stranger here, in a place where we do not often see new faces. I was curious, earlier, when we met. But otherwise occupied. Now I am not. You understand?'

'I do, my lord.'

'Good, good. You are from the city?' Lord Wald asked. 'The Fastness?'

'Yes, my lord.' Outside, the music swelled. I could hear the celebrants shouting something that might have been a name. Only it wasn't the name I expected.

Then, maybe I hadn't been paying close enough attention.

My eyes strayed to the corner near the fireplace, where there sat a statue carved from bone. It reminded me of a crouching ghyrlion, with the head of a man and the antlers of a stag. One of the first things you learned when you took the azure were the names of the Known Gods. Some of them were easier to remember than others. This was one of them. Kurnoth, the Hunter.

If the Lady of Leaves was the queen of Ghyran, then Kurnoth was its king – or at least a prince of no small standing. He was also a god of bloody hunts and black forests. The Lady of Leaves was the mistress of life in all its forms. Her paramour was more restrained; he was master of all that was red in tooth and claw – of life that preyed on other life.

Lord Wald followed my gaze. 'Kurnoth. The Huntsman. The Old Stag.' That last name sent a spike of something through me. Fulder had mentioned that name. And the sylvaneth.

If Lord Wald noticed my sudden discomfort, he said nothing. 'He was worshipped across Ghyran, in the days before the Everqueen awoke from her bower and tamed the Jade Kingdoms. Another old god, discarded in favour of the new.'

'Not entirely, it seems.'

He smirked. 'No. Some of us remember our debts.'

I wasn't in the mood for this. 'Why am I here, my lord?'

He laughed. 'Right to the point, then?' He pointed to the table.

There was a pouch there, and it looked like it was full of comets. 'You are a sellsword. There is your retainer. You work for me now.'

I looked at the pouch but didn't touch it. 'I think I'd recall agreeing to that.'

Lord Wald's smile widened. It wasn't a friendly expression at all. More like a ghyrwolf's snarl. 'Everyone in this canton serves me, one way or another.'

'I'm not here looking for work... just an old friend.'

He nodded in a way that said he didn't believe me in the least. 'And does this friend have a name? I know everyone in my fiefdom. I am very meticulous that way.' His smile thinned, and I could tell he was losing patience.

I decided to play it straight. 'Murn. Evrek Murn.'

The smile vanished. 'I know Murn,' he said slowly. 'I know him very well indeed.'

'No one else seems to,' I said.

Lord Wald laughed. 'No. They wouldn't, if they know what's good for them.' He turned back to the window. 'As far as they're concerned, he's dead.'

'Is he?'

'I'm not certain, but I'd dearly love to know.'

'Why?'

He didn't turn around. 'Because he tried to kill me.'

That brought me up short. It was confirmation of what the eelmonger had told me and though the Murn I remembered was a lot of things, he wasn't the sort to try and kill a landed lord. Not without good cause. But I didn't say that. What I said was, 'What happened?'

He pushed back the edge of his robes and scratched his bare stomach. For the first time I noticed the weal of pink scar tissue stretching across his abdomen. Someone had tried to open his lordship's belly, but hadn't finished the job. That was more like Murn. Sloppy.

'Context is unnecessary. All that matters is that he tried to kill me, and I would like to see him hang. I have that right, I think.' Now he looked at me. 'I might also hang you.'

There was a wild light in his eye that I didn't like. Lord Wald wasn't the sort to make idle threats. He was really considering it.

I met his gaze. 'That'd be a mistake,' I said, carefully. I had to play it smart, or I'd be meeting my maker much sooner than I hoped.

'Why?'

'I didn't come to renew old bonds.' My hand fell to my knife. 'I came to sever them.'

His smile came creeping back, slow and sharp. 'How fortuitous.'

'For both of us,' I replied.

He laughed, like I'd said something funny. 'Yes.' He went to the table and scooped up the pouch. 'Sepesh is a killer, not a hunter. And she's an outsider. She has no experience with the common folk, being of royal blood.'

'I'm an outsider as well.'

'But they're frightened of her. Not of you.' He tossed me the pouch, and I caught it without thinking. 'As I said... a retainer. You will be my huntsman. Find Murn. Bring him to me. If you can bring him in alive, I will double what is in that pouch.'

'And if I can't?'

'Then bring me his head.'

The pouch was heavier than I'd thought. Enough to see me through a few months in the Fastness, at least. At that moment, it didn't even matter to me that I had only Lord Wald's word that Murn had tried to kill him.

I put the pouch away and nodded. 'I can do that.'

'Excellent,' said Lord Wald. His smile was back to its former width. 'You will find me a considerate master, Blackwood. I reward my followers generously.'

He turned back to the fire.

'You may go.'

It took me a moment to realise I'd been dismissed. When I closed the doors behind me, I found Sepesh waiting for me in the corridor. 'Staying for dinner?' she asked.

'Not tonight. Take me back to the village.'

'Do I look like a coachman?'

I shrugged. 'Then point me in the right direction. I'll walk.'

She frowned. 'Not safe to be walking around here after dark.'

'Neither is the city. I think I can handle myself.'

It was her turn to shrug. 'Your life, your choice. But don't say I didn't warn you.'

CHAPTER TWELVE

THE OLD MILL

The guards who opened the inner gate watched me as I drew close without so much as a stern glance. Sepesh had ensured that they'd give me no trouble as I crossed the pontoon bridge. Or so she'd claimed.

Even so, one of them stopped me. He was an older man, craggy and lantern-jawed. 'You sure about walking back?' he asked in a rusty voice.

'Unless you're planning to carry me.'

He frowned. He looked nervous. They all did. Like they'd seen something, or heard something. 'There's treekin abroad tonight. Keep to the path, and they'll leave you be.'

'It's a bridge. It's not like there's many places to go.'

'Even so,' he said. 'We're not opening this gate again until morning.'

'Just so long as you open it now.'

They did, cranking the winch and causing the palisade gate to swing wide. I walked through and onto the bridge. It swayed slightly and I pulled my coat tighter about me as I pressed into the teeth of the rain. I could hear the timbers groaning beneath my feet. Like a heartbeat – creak-thump, creak-thump.

The gate slammed shut behind me, and the only light was from the lanterns strung along the support beams. Their glow was weak and watery, but it was enough to make my way along. To either side of me the swamp crouched in silence, observant and patient. I met the blind glare of the trees with one of my own.

Hunting horns sounded somewhere close by. The mist was rising, but I could see the dim, bobbing glow of lanterns and hear the whinnying of horses. His lordship was off on another hunt. I didn't know whether to wish him success or not.

The walk was long. I could see the lights of the town in the distance, despite the rain in my eyes. I thought about the warm tavern, and wondered whether there were rooms. If not, it wouldn't be the first time I'd slept in a stable.

The bridge creaked and groaned. I didn't hear the sound until I was almost halfway across. It was a steady *thud – thud – thud*. The sound of great hooves striking the muddy timbers. I couldn't say how long they'd been following me, but they were closer than I liked.

My hand fell to my knife, and I wanted to draw it, to turn – to face whatever was coming towards me across that narrow expanse. But I didn't. That same beast-urge that wanted to fight kept me moving. Fight or flight. Hunter or hunted.

It had kept me alive for longer than I could remember, that urge. Kept me fighting, kept me in motion when other men might've dropped dead. But I didn't run, either. Running just meant I'd probably die tired. So I started walking again, through the rain, and it followed, only a few steps behind. I could feel

its breath wash across me, like a hot, wet wind. It wanted me
to turn around, so I didn't.

Harran...

I didn't stop. My name – the name I'd given myself – quiv-
ered through me like a drumbeat.

Harran...

I bowed my head and hunched my shoulders. It plodded along
in my wake, and I could see its shadow in the glow of the lanterns hung from the struts of the bridge. Two great spiked arcs
stretched before me, surmounting my own shadow-head like a
crown.

Harran...

Suddenly, running seemed like a good idea.

I broke into a sprint, aiming myself at the distant gate and
the torches that burned there. If I could reach it, well, I didn't
know. Maybe nothing. Maybe the guards would just watch as
whatever it was tore me to pieces, or maybe they'd help me. At
least I'd be in the light. For the moment, that was all the motivation I needed.

It galloped after me, shaking the bridge, causing the timbers
to bow and flex. It let loose an awful bellow – a bugling cry, at
once as shrill as cracking ice and as deep as the rumble of an
avalanche. The force of it sent me skidding and tumbling like
a leaf in the wind, and I found myself sliding towards the edge
of the bridge.

I snatched my knife loose and stabbed it down, trying to anchor
myself as something dark and as vast as the peaks of Aqshy
barrelled after me. Something – a hoof, maybe – slammed down
and the timbers burst and I fell away, into the cold waters below.

I went under, just for a moment. Through the water's haze, I
saw my pursuer backlit by the lantern-light. It was too big to be
a stag, and its head was the wrong shape. I struck out, swimming away from the apparition. It was big enough to simply step

off the bridge and into the water, and I didn't intend to wait around for it to do so.

But where to go? Panic gripped me. There were lights in the swamp. Maybe lanterns – maybe a barge or a skiff. I started towards them, swimming for all I was worth. It wasn't easy. I'd never been a natural swimmer and the water felt like it was mostly mud. When I finally floundered onto semi-solid ground, panting and half-drowned, I found myself near the old lumber mill I'd spied earlier.

I realised that the lights I'd seen weren't lanterns at all, but hag-lights, dancing across the hummocks and low boughs. Twisting and turning like spores in the breeze. They drew close, their sickly radiance washing over everything, revealing that my sanctuary was not the only one of its kind. Drowned remnants stretched in all directions around me.

The old mill slumped in an untrustworthy fashion and was half-sunk, but it was better than nothing. I waded towards it through the reeds, carefully navigating the detritus of the old timber stacks left to rot in the rising waters. I felt unidentifiable objects roll beneath my feet, and thought of skulls browning in the muck.

The bugling call came again, echoing over the swamp. It sounded angry. Frustrated. Night-birds took flight, shrieking. I reached out, grabbed a broken board and hauled myself up onto the creaking floor of the mill. The building was mostly moss and rot, but it would serve long enough for me to catch my breath.

The bridge was empty when I looked back. I leaned against a broken timber, breathing heavily. Trying to think, but failing. I was content with survival, for the moment. I was tired, as well as wet and cold. I realised that I hadn't slept since I'd passed out aboard Deshler's skiff. I looked around.

There was a tree growing through the floor and slowly shoving the walls and ceiling aside. It was an old thing, fat and heavy with swollen boughs and serpentine roots. It had burst through the back and filled the rear of the mill. I bit back a laugh. A tree growing in a lumber mill – it was like a joke.

I wasn't the only one to think so. Outside the shack, something tittered. I saw nothing, but I could hear the scrape of brambles and branches across the outside of the structure, too deliberate to be the wind. Something pale flashed past me, moving swiftly through the waters outside. I jerked back. Again, the soft tittering. Like sharp rain on metal. I heard them moving through the water now, all around.

Stay on the path. That was what the guard had said. Well, too late for that now. I reached for my knife. I wondered if I could make it to town from here. I wondered if they'd let me. I didn't think so. The warped boards beneath me began to twitch. Water burbled up between the cracks. It was hard to see in the gloom, but I thought something was trying to reach up through the floor.

'You left the path.'

I looked around, trying to find the owner of the voice. 'Who's there?' I stumbled, as a board cracked. The shack swayed in an alarming fashion. It wasn't stable, and the movement beneath it was making things worse.

'You shouldn't have left the path,' the voice croaked. 'That is the first rule. The oldest rule. You shouldn't have left the path.'

'Tell me something I don't know.' I turned, knife in hand, squinting into the gloom. 'Better yet, come out and do it face-to-face.'

'He said you'd come. Sent your name a-whispering down the roots and along the boughs. Said "don't you hurt him – he's mine".' A rattling laugh. 'Some of us don't listen well, though. Especially to him. Old beast. Old broken thing. Why should he have you all to himself?'

'Come out where I can see you, and we'll discuss it.' It was a woman's voice, I thought. Only no woman had ever sounded like that without swallowing a throatful of broken glass first. 'I promise I'm friendly.'

'If you were friendly, you wouldn't be here.'

That brought me up short. 'Should I come to you, then?' I said. 'You might not like it if I do.' I'd never cut a woman who wasn't trying to cut me first. In the church, you learned quickly that a determined woman will kill you just as dead as a man, and it was one of the few lessons I'd retained. I took a step, and the boards flexed like something alive.

That rattling laugh came again, slip-sliding over the air. Something else came with it, like the scrape of broken branches over rocks. The creak of a falling tree. Water shifted, splashed and dripped as something stretched up out of the dark and leaned towards me.

She was old, I think. Hard to tell with her sort. As she stretched into the light, I saw why she'd been so slow to move – she'd grown into the body of the mill. Her roots threaded through the walls and the floor, and stretched up to the sagging roof. She – the she who was talking – was just an extension, like the figurehead of a ship's prow, jutting from the body of the great tree that was slowly subsuming the structure. She undulated through the air towards me with much crackling and popping, bark-face twisting into what might have been a smile. But all I saw was a slash of splinters and the sap that leaked out as she spoke.

'I'll take my chances,' she said. She circled me, branches and root-feelers running with mock-gentleness across my arms and shoulders. I wanted to move, to run, but I stayed still. If she wanted to talk, fine. It was preferable to the alternative.

'What do you want?' I asked.

'You killed one of us,' she murmured. Her voice was rough and soft all at the same time. A parody of a mother's coo. 'How did it feel to end the life of something old when you were not yet born? Did you enjoy it?'

'A bit. Given that it was trying to kill me I think I'm allowed.'

She laughed and the sound made me flinch. 'I enjoy it as well. The scream and squirm of meat in our boughs and brambles, as we squeeze and twist. It is a shame you belong to another, or I might indulge myself. It has been so long since I have watered my roots in blood. I grow stiff in this place.'

'Maybe you should leave.'

Claws of bark settled on my shoulders in a matronly gesture. 'Maybe. Or maybe you should go. This place is not for you.' She leaned close, so close I could smell the sap. It had a curdled sweetness to it that made my guts give an agonised lurch. 'It has never been for you.' Her splinter-teeth clicked just beside my ear.

An old story. The oldest in Ghyran. Men went where they were not wanted, and cast down the first inhabitants – the trees. They cut and pulled and uprooted, scourging the land with iron and fire, and the land fought back with tremors and water.

'But you let them stay,' I said.

'They used to offer up their young to us, as a sign of good faith. Sweet, soft blood to nourish our seeds and pods in their sleep of seasons. How could we refuse? Blood to keep the water at bay. Blood to buy peace.' A claw traced my cheek, scratching it. 'Blood for the harvest. Blood for the hunt.' I clapped a hand to my face and stepped forward. 'What will you give us, to help you escape?'

'Escape what?' I growled. My hand was sticky and my jaw hurt. I wondered if she'd cut me to the bone. She laughed again. It sounded less like a person's laugh every time. She was putting on a good show, but it wouldn't last long.

'Him, of course. The one who marked you. He thinks like meat, that one. Old and wild and savage. We are fierce, but he is fiercer still, even diminished. He circles you, just beyond the gleam of your fire. Waiting. Watching.' She swayed towards me, a serpentine shape in the gloom. 'We could help you, if you like. If you ask us.'

'Why?'

'Because it amuses us. Because he is a demanding old beast, and refuses to keep to his place. She planted him here so that he might slumber, and what did your kind do but wake him up, and feed him, and make him think that he could again be what he was.'

I didn't understand any of it, but I could tell she was getting agitated. 'Who is he?'

Her face drew close to mine, too close, and the sickly-sweet stink of her enveloped me. 'The Old Stag of the Woods. Can you smell him, meat? Can you smell his musk on this place? With every drop of red, he grows stronger. Soon, he might burst the bonds she set on him, and gallop free of his bower to rut and ravage as he did in time out of mind. Then you will know true fear. We merely hate you... but he *loves you*. And that is infinitely worse.'

Outside, the sylvaneth began to laugh and hiss. Her claws traced sap across my face and chest, and my stomach heaved, giving up the fight even as it began. I suddenly felt as if someone had taken a scour-brush to my insides, and I vomited up the contents of my stomach onto the rotting boards. I wondered if Deshler had been right about the venom. I wiped my mouth, feeling shakier than I liked.

I hauled myself to my feet, conscious of the weak boards beneath me, and the water tugging at my ankles. 'Is this supposed to impress me?' I said hoarsely. I gripped my knife, and wondered if I could get it into her before she tore me apart. 'What do you want?'

Clawed hands burst through the floorboards before she could answer. They caught at my legs and coat, and I was wrenched downwards with convulsive force. Water surged up around me. I flailed about with my knife, hacking and chopping at the woody talons as the water rose up and subsumed me. Bubbles burst from my lips, carrying my screams to the surface as they dragged me down into the shadows and mud beneath the old mill.

I could barely make out the forms of my attackers in the murk. They were everywhere, clawing, biting, striking. I stabbed and cut as we roiled in the dark, even when my vision started to go black. I'd killed one sylvaneth – I could kill others. But there were too many of them and they didn't need to breathe. I was pummelled into the mud, straining for breath, set to be buried among the rotting support beams, when something reached down and snatched me loose of my attackers.

I hit the air so hard my lungs almost collapsed, and then I was rolling across the floor, gasping and heaving. My knife was still in my hand, heavy with sap. The old woman in the tree leaned down, eyes gleaming like hag-lights.

'Apologies. They could not contain their exuberance. They are still but infants, and new to the song.'

I spat swamp water and tried to speak, but only a hoarse growl emerged.

She tittered and prodded me with a branch-claw. 'You are resilient. That is good. He likes prey that fights most of all. Not like us. We prefer you to be still and silent when we make mulch of you. Too much struggling only damages the roots.'

I rose to my feet, knife flashing. She caught my hand easily. Held it. Began to squeeze. I felt the bones of my hand creak as she looked me over.

'You are not ready to receive our mercy, I think. You do not understand what awaits you, yet. When you do – you will come back. And then...'

I heard the bugling call of a stag – or something mimicking it. The call echoed over the swamp. She fell silent, as faces-that-were-not turned away, and trills of disappointment quavered on the air. She released me.

'And then what?' I said, as I tried to rub some feeling back into my hand. But there was no answer. The treekin had vanished, and so had she. Thankful as I was, I didn't think I'd scared them off. No, I knew in my gut that whatever had pursued me from the manor had also sent the sylvaneth fleeing. Just like the last time. Just like Fulder had said.

I didn't know what it meant.

But I intended to find out.

CHAPTER THIRTEEN

FESTIVAL

The celebration was still going on by the time I reached town, sopping wet and wrung out. I wanted nothing more than to sleep, but I wasn't planning on doing so on the street or in a stable. I wanted to be inside and out of the rain. Somewhere warm. I hadn't been really warm in days, and it was my driving motivation at that moment. I didn't know whether the Stag's Head had rooms, but I intended to find out.

I passed the paper eel, abandoned, crushed and stamped into fluttering ruin. Strange decorations hung from roof-edges and doorways – corn-husks and brambles twisted up into an approximation of a pair of what I thought were antlers. They weren't everywhere, but those places that did not have them were dark and shuttered.

Moss-lanterns dangled by chains from the edges of nearby roof-tops, and their flickering radiance made the shadows dance and the rain glisten jade. The smell of freshly butchered eel stank up the narrow streets, and I saw children streaking their faces with hunt-masks made from mud and ash.

Wooden cages containing leopard eels, wolf rats and other verminous beasts sat on the backs of carts and wagons, surrounded by masked men and women. The creatures hissed, shrieked and howled as their captors tormented them with barbed poles or torches. Stoking their fury.

A masked man, stinking of booze, caught me by the shoulders. I nearly gutted him. He didn't notice. 'Come to join the hunt, brother?' he said, in slurred tones. 'We've got a bounty this night! Beasts aplenty for the Huntsman's Bower.'

I extricated myself with mumbled apologies. The animals in their cages glared at me, their eyes mad and savage – and resigned. I didn't like that look. It reminded me too much of what I saw in the mirror, sometimes.

As I trudged away through muddy streets, I wondered what the Huntsman's Bower was. A place? A turn of phrase? There was an itch of fury under my exhaustion. I didn't like being chased. Being made a fool of.

The sylvaneth were obviously holding a grudge. The treekin were famous for it. Whatever nonsense they'd spouted, this was about the one I'd killed. They would torment me, and then move in to finish things.

I wasn't scared. I didn't get scared. Not really. Moments of animal panic, perhaps – like what I'd felt on the bridge. But fear wasn't really in me, these days. If they wanted me, they could come and get me.

Even as I thought about it, I knew was lying to myself. Telling myself what I wanted to hear, rather than what was. It wasn't just the sylvaneth, whatever I wanted to think. A part of me wanted to run. To leave Wald, leave Murn – leave it all. To go back to the Fastness, back to the life I'd made for myself.

But I didn't like running. I never had. Cowards don't last, wearing the azure. If you pick up the hammer, best be willing to swing it – one of Cassian's favourite sayings. I'd never been afraid to swing a hammer or bust skulls in the God-King's name.

More than that, I *enjoyed* it.

I had always enjoyed it.

A hard truth, and one I'd come to understand more in the years since I'd cast the hammer aside. I'd made grist of Sigmar's enemies for the mills of heaven. I had burned towns like Wald to the ground, in the name of Azyr, in the name of Order, and of justice. But what justice was there in this world?

There is no justice. Only the hunter... and the hunted.

The voice cut through me. I thought at first that it was my own, but there was a cruel resonance to it. As if it were echoing out of some vast, deep place. Through the ground, up through the soles of my feet. I turned, feeling again the wash of hot breath across my neck. My knife was out before I put two thoughts together.

The prey bares its teeth, as the hunter draws near.

The voice wasn't just deep, but slick, like lantern oil spreading on water. I could feel its amusement as I turned back and forth in the rain, on an empty street. I didn't recognise the street. That was no surprise. In the rain and the dark I'd got turned around. Or maybe the town had swallowed me up.

I spotted the dog a moment later. It watched me from an alleyway, all but hidden in a drape of shadow. Just a vague impression of an animal. Without thinking, I took a step towards it, and it retreated noiselessly. I paused. There was a smell on the air. Like flowers, just on the edge of rot. A whuff of sound – soft – made me turn back.

Another dog. This one stood beneath a moss-lantern, bathed in green light. It seemed... *wrong*. No. It *was* wrong. A dog that did not look like a dog ought to look.

Will you run for me again?

'Who are you?' I asked.

You know who I am.

The dog's skin moved in the light. It twisted and cracked as the beast took a step towards me, jaws sagging to reveal teeth like splinters of broken wood. It exhaled, and again I smelled the stink of almost-rotten flowers.

Will you run for me again?

I heard a splash of someone stepping in a puddle, and a soft curse. A wash of moss-light nearly blinded me, and through stinging eyes I saw a guard approaching.

'Something I can help you with?' he growled. He had the lantern in one hand, and his other on the hilt of his sword. He peered at me. 'I don't know you.'

'I don't know you either,' I said.

The guard frowned. 'You being smart?'

'Not at the moment.' I turned back. The dogs were gone. So was the voice. I realised my heart was pounding. I wondered if they had ever been there in the first place. I rubbed rain out of my face. The guard raised his lantern.

'Who are you? You aren't from around here.'

I interposed a hand between my eyes and the light. 'Just a traveller. Got turned around. Looking for the Stag's Head.'

'No food for vagrants, there,' the guard said. 'Your sort isn't welcome in Wald.'

'I have money.'

It was the wrong thing to say. The guard's eyes took on a sly glint. 'How much?'

I did a quick calculation. A wide net made quick work. 'Enough to reward someone for pointing me in the right direction,' I said, meaningfully.

The guard licked his lips. 'Down that street, take a left.' He held out his hand. I fished out a few coins and handed them over. The guard counted them slowly, his grin widening. It was likely more money than he earned in a month. The coins vanished. He looked at me. 'I know you now. You're the one the sheriff took to see his lordship.' He frowned. 'You look like shit. Go for a swim with the eels?'

'Something like that. I'm looking for someone. His name is Murn.'

He scratched his chin. 'He tried to kill his lordship.'

'So I hear. What can you tell me about it?'

'Why should I tell you anything?'

I rattled my coin pouch. He considered the matter, likely wondering whether he could just take it off me. Something told him that was a bad idea.

He looked around. 'Murn ambushed his lordship during a hunt. Tried to open him, split to spout. Didn't quite manage it, though, more's the pity.'

'You don't care for his lordship?'

His eyes went flat. 'I didn't say that.'

'My mistake. When?'

'Maybe I shouldn't be talking to you after all.'

'Maybe not.' I paused. 'His lordship asked me to look into the matter. Any help you could give, well, it'd be appreciated.'

He grunted. 'A few weeks ago. Murn's been hiding ever since.'

'Weeks,' I said. Around the time the coin had come. 'And you haven't found him?'

'Once or twice. Wald's bigger than it looks, and he's got friends.'

'And his lordship has enemies.'

The guard grinned. 'You might say that.'

I handed over another coin. 'Know any of them by name?'

The guard made the coin vanish. 'No.'

'Fair enough.' I held up another coin. 'You hear a name, maybe you let me know first, eh? There's plenty more where this came from.'

He took the last coin and weighed it speculatively. 'Why you want Murn? He do something?'

'Tried to kill me.'

He laughed. 'He's got the worst luck.'

'Better than some.'

I left the guard to his new-found wealth and made my way to better-lit streets. As I stepped from one to another, a burst of drunken laughter filled the space around me. Hunters cavorted in the street, stamping the mud, wearing antlered crowns on their heads. They charged each other, crashing together to fall in the mud as onlookers howled in merriment.

I avoided the rumpus and went to a nearby cistern. They were scattered throughout the town. One of the remnants of what Wald could have been. I scooped some water out of one of the basins that jutted from it. It was clean. The masons who'd devised them had created some form of purifying mechanism that scraped the water free of all but the basest sediment. I splashed my face and neck, and ran my dripping hands through my hair, trying to cleanse myself.

'You look like you fell in the swamp.'

I straightened, water dripping down my clothes. Deshler lounged nearby, beneath an overhang, a cheroot clutched between her teeth. The tip glowed cherry-red as she puffed it.

'What are you doing out here?' I asked.

She motioned to the drunks. 'Enjoying the festivities for a bit, before I head home. They'll be hunting a blinded leopard eel through this part of town in a few moments.'

'Sounds entertaining.'

'Always is. Smoke?' Deshler said, extending a cheroot. I took it, and joined her beneath the overhang. She looked me up and down. 'So... what happened?'

'I met his lordship.' I took the sparkstone she proffered and scraped my thumbnail across it, eliciting a flare of heat. I puffed on my cheroot until it lit. 'He's looking for my friend as well, turns out.'

Deshler took her sparkstone back and said nothing. I studied her.

'Funny running into you here,' I said, even though it wasn't. Word had already got around about my encounter with Fulder, and my ride with Sepesh. 'Do you want that second comet I owe you?'

'Not yet,' she said. 'Haven't had much chance to ask around.'

We stood in silence for a time, smoking our cheroots. A band of children in harvest masks raced past in pursuit of a stray dog. Not one of the ones I'd seen earlier. The dog was howling in fear and pain. The boy in the lead clutched a sickle, already wet with the animal's blood. Deshler spat as they vanished into the rain.

'Little bastards.'

'They teach them early, hereabouts,' I said.

She nodded and spat again, as if she were trying to get the taste of something out of her mouth. 'Harvest and hunt,' she said.

'Meant to ask earlier... what does that mean?'

Deshler straightened and gave me a funny look. 'Thought you didn't care about such things.' She puffed on her cheroot, putting a momentary wall of smoke between us.

'Maybe I'm curious about the local customs.'

Deshler laughed. 'I doubt that.'

'You'd be wrong.' I took a drag on the cheroot. 'Where's the Huntsman's Bower?'

She stopped laughing. 'Why do you want to know?'

'No reason.'

'Then I got no reason to say.' She pushed away from the wall. 'I'll keep an ear out, though. And you keep that coin handy.' I watched her go, hunched and swaying, as if she were still aboard her skiff.

I sat there a moment longer, until the cheroot was no longer enough to warm me. Then I headed back to the Stag's Head.

Gint was right where I'd left him, still playing with his cards. He looked up as I sat down, but made no comment on my appearance. 'Back so soon?' he said. He fanned his cards out in a broad sweep, and flipped them over, one at a time.

'Lord Wald invited me for a chat.' I didn't mention what I'd seen or heard on the walk back. It wasn't that I didn't want to – I simply couldn't.

Gint gave a low whistle. 'Aren't you the fancy one. He say anything interesting?'

'Nothing you need to worry about.'

Gint chuckled and nodded. 'No, I suppose not.' He looked around. 'What now?'

'Now? I need some sleep.'

'Sounds good. I'll take the hearth and you can take the table.'

'I was thinking I might rent a room. Given that I'll be staying here a while.' I put the pouch of coins his lordship had given me down on the table. Gint stopped playing with his cards and eyed it with interest.

'That sounds like a lot of money.'

'It's a retainer.'

'From Lord Wald?' Gint said doubtfully. 'Why?'

I shrugged and went to the bar. The silver-haired woman was wiping it down, trying hard not to look in our direction. Then, so were most of the patrons. Word travelled fast in places like this. She didn't look up when I knocked on the bar. 'I want a room,' I said.

'No rooms,' she replied, still not looking at me.

'I'll sleep in the stable.'

She laughed like I'd said something funny. 'No stables.'

'Attic?'

'You deaf?' one of the men at the bar growled. 'She said there's no room here.'

'I know what she said. I think she's mistaken.' I didn't look at him, but I could see him well enough out of the corner of my eye. He looked like he was spoiling for a fight. That was fine. After the night I'd had, so was I.

'I'll not have you cause trouble in here,' she said. Chairs scraped back at her words. I counted two of them. I cracked my neck, and stepped back just as the first one threw a punch. I caught his wrist and twisted about, driving my own blow into his kidney. He yelped, high and thin. I tripped him and sent him face first into the bar.

The second man tried to grapple me. I boxed his ears and he stumbled to his knees. Before he could get up, I had my knife to his throat. His eyes got wide, and he froze. The music died away as I became the centre of attention.

'I'd like a room,' I said again. 'Gint?'

'I'm not fussy, I'm happy to share,' Gint said. He was grinning widely.

'One room, then. Please.'

She licked her lips. Her eyes flicked up, away from me. I didn't turn around. I knew who I'd see.

'Give him a room,' Fulder said.

She nodded jerkily, and I took my knife from the man's throat. I sheathed it and turned. 'Very hospitable of you,' I said.

Fulder had an ugly look on his face. I gave him a broad smile. 'Careful you don't stoke those coals too hot,' Gint murmured.

'Let him burn,' I said.

Our room proved to be in what had once been an attic space, just beneath the eaves. In the light of the candle we'd been provided, I took in a bare triangle of wood. Rain slithered through the cracks in the tiles above, plopping into carefully arranged pots, jugs and tureens. Damp patches of thatch shifted audibly in the spots where the tiles had been replaced.

'Wet,' I said.

'No mice, though,' Gint countered.

'Plenty of bedbugs.' I kicked one of the straw pallets, and something scuttled out of sight. I'd slept on worse.

The room was mostly empty, save for the pallets, a rough table and a clay jug. There were bedpans as well, stacked under the table. The bedpans were rusty, and thin as paper in spots. I figured it'd be safer to piss out the single, circular window that occupied the far wall. A chimney breast provided some heat, though we had no fireplace of our own.

'I learned a fair few things while you were out making new friends,' Gint said. He sat back on his pallet and shuffled his cards. 'They were only too happy to talk to me, after you left. Funny that.'

I unrolled my bedroll over my pallet, hoping it would keep out the worst of the vermin. 'Maybe they felt sorry for you.'

He smiled. 'Maybe I'm just that charming. Or you're that charmless. Do you want to hear what I learned?'

'I don't know, do I?'

'You might.' He set his cards aside. 'They say that there're barges due in, in the next few days. Prison barges. From the Fastness.'

'So?' I rolled over and faced the wall.

Gint sighed. 'I thought it was interesting, at any rate.'

'You thought wrong.'

I pinched out the light, plunging the room into darkness.

CHAPTER FOURTEEN

PENDER

I was somewhere green. A harsh, sharp green, smelling of flowers and mud. The green of thorny briars and razor-leaves. The green of deep wells and mossy stones. The green of forgotten places.

I tried to move, but couldn't. My arms, my legs – nothing worked. A soft, sweet smell filled my nose, and my mouth tasted of blackberries. Something I couldn't see cooed gently in my ear as brambles caressed my cheek. I felt blood spill down my chin.

The constriction grew worse, the thorns biting deep, tearing through my clothes, my flesh, into the soft, red recesses of me. Brambles flexed against me like snakes, as the splinter-mouths twisted into clownish smiles – too wide and jagged by far. They whispered endearments as they bent themselves towards me, splinter-teeth worrying at me.

I felt my flesh rip like parchment. Something reached inside me, plucking at the pulsing, thumping sweetmeats within. I tried to writhe, to voice some final protest, but the only sound was the wet crinkle of my body as it was emptied of all that it contained.

I tried again, and my eyes opened, just as Gint made ready to shake me.

'I'm awake,' I said. My voice was barely a croak.

He looked down at the knife in my hand and swallowed. 'So I see. Do you always sleep with steel in your hand?'

'Do you not?' There was a sort of light, watery and grey though it was, pouring in through the round window. It crept across the floor, revealing the dismal extent of our lodgings. I rose and sheathed my knife.

'I've never been that afraid in my life, I'm happy to say.'

My clothes had mostly dried, and I pulled them back on after a cursory sniff. I didn't smell any worse than the rest of Wald, so I reckoned it was acceptable. 'It's not fear,' I said. 'It's experience. We're not in the city any more.'

'No, that is evident. Do you remember seeing that last night?' Gint pointed to the table. Something made of wood and corn-husk sat there.

'No,' I said softly. The shape reminded me of something. I reached for it, but Gint got to it first. He picked it up.

'Looks rather like a stag, don't you think?'

'I don't know what it looks like.'

He tossed it onto the floor and kicked it out of sight. 'No, neither do I. Tonight, I think we should shove the table against the door. Keep our hosts to their side of the fence, eh?'

I nodded. I hadn't heard anyone come in. I must have been more tired than I thought. Everything still ached from the night before, but I was hungry more than anything.

Gint looked me up and down. 'You look tired.'

'I am tired. And hungry. But I've got things to do.'

'No rest for the wicked, eh?' Gint said, grinning.

I laughed. 'You're one to talk.'

'I know of what I speak, Harran.' He rose to his feet. 'Still, you're right. Why waste the day lounging in luxury, when we could be seeing the sights?'

Downstairs, the common room was quiet. The fire burned low, and the troggoth was silent in its pit. The few patrons were studiously ignoring everything but their drinks. Most looked like death warmed over.

There was little as far as breakfast on offer at the bar. A few comets bought us day-old bread, a bit of cheese, and tea made from chicory root and crushed flowers – filling enough, if unsatisfying. Gint complained, even as he ate. I ignored him.

'What's the plan?' he asked, gnawing a rind of cheese.

'Shouldn't you be looking for your bride-to-be?'

He shuddered. 'Have you seen the women around here? I'd rather marry an eel.'

'Whatever makes you happy.' I rose to my feet. 'Just leave me out of it.'

He followed me to the door. 'Are you sure you won't let me help? I can be quite handy when I put my mind to it.'

I looked at him. I was tired of his wheedling. And as the old saying went, many hands made for swift work. I wanted to get out of Wald. That meant I had to find Murn. 'You want to help?'

'I'm offering, aren't I?'

'Fine.' I caught the front of his coat and dragged him close. 'If in the course of your day you happen to find out anything about a place called the Huntsman's Bower, I'd be obliged if you'd let me know.'

'And what's the Huntsman's Bower?'

'If I knew that, I wouldn't need your help, now would I?' I let him go.

'See you tonight,' he called after me.

The air was damp with drizzle, and tasted faintly of mould. I pulled my coat tighter about me and strode into the street. Music was playing somewhere, and several drunks, their masks askew, wandered the streets, singing a ballad of the Greentide Kingdoms. Vendors sold steaming bowls of broth to keep off the chill of the morning damp, or nebulous meats, chopped and rolled in flour and fried in lard.

The town wasn't quite bustling. But it was busy. I wasn't going anywhere in particular. I wanted to get a feel for Wald, before I started tearing the place apart. In the light of day, it sprawled around me like a thicket, denser in some places than others. Here and there I saw signs of recent fires – blackened beams, scorched stone – and in places the greenery that was so lush elsewhere was thin.

The further away from the tavern I drew, the more signs of what must have been the original village I saw. Stone foundations – the remains of the blockhouses that would have sheltered the loggers and engineers who always came first.

I turned a corner and a tangle of shops surrounded me – the sorts of places villages of any significant size had. An apothecary's shack nestled against a leatherworker's lean-to. I could hear the steady ring-beat of a blacksmith's hammer, echoing over the rooftops, and the whinnying of the shaggy ponies that the locals used to pull their carts.

But there was blood on the streets, and the smell of death was thick on the air. The bodies of slaughtered animals were being butchered over troughs, their still-wet bones stacked at intersections. I narrowly avoided being splashed with mud as a still-twitching wolf rat was dragged out from under a boardwalk by iron hooks and ropes, its killer clambering into the light with a triumphant shout.

I spied an old woman sitting on an overturned bucket, crafting an antler sigil out of bone and brambles. Her fingers moved deftly, and she smoked a pipe as she worked. Children chased one another with freshly flensed eel-jaws as they ran shrieking underfoot. I recognised the eelmonger's boy among them.

I made my way to the road agent's offices, but found them closed and shuttered. Another of the antler sigils hung from the door. I pulled it down.

It was only a little thing. But it had a weight greater than its size. Or maybe that was just my imagination. I heard the thud of great hooves as I looked at it. Smelled the rank odour of my pursuer of the previous night. What had Fulder said?

You've been marked.

Questions rattled in my head like wasps in an iron pot. I wasn't sure I wanted the answers. In fact, I was sure I didn't. What I wanted was to find Murn, and do what I'd come here to do. Then I wanted to leave the swamp and never come back.

I tossed the sigil into the street and turned away. There were more of them on the buildings all around. I got the feeling that someone was trying to tell me something. Or maybe not. Who knew how these people thought.

I decided to find Deshler. Even if she hadn't learned anything yet, there were things she could tell me. Murn trying to kill Lord Wald seemed like the sort of thing that would be common knowledge in a place like this. The Murn I remembered wouldn't have tried such a thing on his own. And the guard had implied that he wasn't the only one who'd wanted Lord Wald dead. It made me wonder why Deshler hadn't thought to mention the matter. Made me think that she wasn't as uninvolved in local politics as she'd claimed.

I followed the smell of water around the corner and out of the street. In the daylight, this part of the canal looked smaller. It was overlooked by weather-beaten statues of gods and heroes. A statue of Sigmar Heldenhammer that I hadn't noticed the day before presided over the assemblage, as was his right. The God-King knelt on his cracked plinth, as if weary from battle, leaning against the haft of his hammer. Moss crept over the stone, hiding the celestial sigils carved into it, and his face had been worn away, reduced to nothing by the rain and time. He wore a crown of antlers, and something that stank like blood had been smeared onto it – though whether in an act of desecration or veneration, I couldn't tell.

I stared at the statue, grateful that it had no face.

The jetty sagged on rotting pylons. Deshler's skiff was nowhere in sight.

A clink of metal made me glance back. Two men stood behind me, gripping cudgels. A third stepped into view opposite me, on the other side of the statue. Then two more, cutting me off from the rest of the docks. They were dressed in patchwork leather and stained clothes, looking as lean and nasty as jackals. Greywater Fastness was full of such men, always looking to make comets the easy way – by taking them out of someone else's pocket. It was no different here, I supposed.

'It's broad daylight,' I said. I knew who'd sent them without asking. I'd dropped a stone in a still pond the night before, and these were the first ripples. Five was more than I'd been expecting, though. Caspar Guno would have only sent one – me.

Three of them came in a rush, moving fast. A cudgel caught me on the shoulder, numbing my arm. I drew my knife with my good hand and slashed out, driving a second attacker back. As he retreated, I lunged forward, driving my shoulder into the chest of the third and bowling him over. The street was too narrow for a fight like this – too close to the water. They had all of the advantages. I needed to get away – somewhere more open.

I ducked my head and ran. The leg-breakers gave chase. Punters and vendors yelped and squalled as I pushed through the morning crowd, knife in hand, looking for a way out. Out of the corner of my eye, I saw one of my pursuers angling to cut me off.

I pointed at him and called out, 'Stop! Thief!'

The magic words in any market square. Hands were suddenly reaching for the leg-breaker from every direction. He cursed and fought, trying to escape the mob of concerned citizens. I wished him luck. I'd once seen a crowd like this pull down an unlucky cutpurse and stomp him to death in their frenzy.

I kicked an overeager fruit seller somewhere ripe and spilled the man's cart. Fruits and vegetables of all shapes and hues spilled across the rain-slick cobbles, along with the merchant's money-box. Comets and motes bounced gleaming into the gutters as the fruit seller wailed like a damned soul. People bent, snatching at the coins. I didn't stick around to watch the ensuing scrum.

I rounded a corner and stepped back against the wall. The street was a narrow, winding path curving beneath a roof of overhanging balconies and washing lines. I caught a whiff of something sickly-sweet, and thought I saw something move into the open at the other end of the street. Something taller than a man, with a crown of antlers. But it was gone the moment I tried to focus on it.

Footsteps drew near. Running now. I selected a handy chunk of wood from the ground and waited. The leg-breaker was close, cursing and panting in the same breath. He'd be the youngest of the quintet, or the newest member. Either way, the one with the most to prove – that was why he'd given chase without waiting for the others. That was always the way. The young and stupid ran in where the old and cunning feared to tread.

As his shadow stretched across the street, I tensed and sprang. I hit him hard, and he went down to one knee, shaking his head like a poleaxed ghyroch. I lifted what was left of the chunk of wood and brought it down again. It crumbled in my grip, but he fell with a soft, whining groan. I kicked him for good measure and turned, just as a second man charged towards me, cudgel held low.

I caught the first blow on my numbed shoulder and bit back

a yelp. This one was bigger than the first, heavier and grizzled. He ducked back as I swung at him. 'Don't be stupid,' he growled.

'Too late for that.' I tackled him, catching him around the midsection. My momentum carried us backwards, into the wall on the opposite side of the street. He grunted and tried to break my hold. I kept my head down and started punching.

I found the rhythm quickly, and his kidneys a few moments after that. He folded up with a disgruntled sigh, and sank down low enough for me to slam a knee into his nose. He fell over and I stomped on him a few times.

Always kick a man when he's down. That way, he's less likely to get up again. Another bit of wisdom bestowed unto me by Cassian.

Two down, three to go.

'He went that way – come on!'

They were close. I ducked down another side street. The little back alleys and passages all tangled back on one another like a rat's warren. A dozen streets were crammed into a space fit only for two or three. The canopy of overhanging roof-edges, balconies and makeshift walkways squeezed out the grey light of morning.

I coughed, smelling smoke. Old smoke, the stink clinging to the wood. The street was a dead artery. There were marks of fire everywhere, and ash-mould clogging the gutters and making strange shapes on the walls. Broken crates and barrels littered the ground. Abandoned stalls rose out of the rubbish like derelict ships, some still protected by ragged awnings, heavy with mildew.

I paused, listening. I heard rats skittering through the trash – and something else. Voices. No – echoes. Memories. Dreams. There was green everywhere. Growing out of the gutters, poking up beneath the ash and dripping from the roof-edges. The street was soft under my feet, and my boots squelched. I heard a growl echo from within a broken crate. I reached for my knife.

'There he is!'

I turned, narrowly avoiding the brutal thrust of a cudgel. A third leg-breaker had caught up with me.

'Nowhere to go,' he panted. He swung the cudgel in short, sharp arcs, brutal blows designed to cripple. This one knew how to fight – or was simply more cautious after bypassing his fellows.

'Looks that way,' I said.

The leg-breaker grinned. 'Think that pig-sticker is going to help?' He had a small, carved ruby in place of one of his front teeth, and eyes like a stoat. He tossed the cudgel from hand to hand, quick as thought. 'Give up. Come quietly.'

'Never been one for quiet.'

The man shrugged. 'Have it your way.' He snapped forwards. He was fast. But I was ready. I caught the blow on my forearm and whipped my knife across the leg-breaker's belly. The blade was sharp and it easily cut through the layers of cloth and leather to bite the skin beneath. The leg-breaker's eyes widened and a high, thin sound emerged from his puckered lips. I heard his companions arrive as he started to scream.

I don't like killing, normally. I got my fill of it when I wore the azure. And anyway, Guno doesn't pay me enough to kill people. But sometimes you have to make a point.

He fell against me, and the knife went in again, almost as an afterthought. Hot wetness spurted, engulfing my forearm. I felt the body twist and twitch, as everything let go at once and there was another grunting whine. I jerked the knife free, and things spilled out.

I leaned back as the dead man slid to the ground, leaving a swath of red down the front of my coat. For a moment, I was somewhere else.

I was a decade ago, and a realm away, with another dead man at my feet – only this one I knew. Had thought I'd known. But in that moment, with the rain beating down and the hammer heavy in my hands, I realised that I knew nothing at all. Screams echoed from cages of gold and iron, soon drowned out by the crackle of flames and the rumble of thunder.

The moment passed quickly. They always did.

The two who were left looked at me like I was their worst nightmare. Then they looked at one another and started to edge towards me. I stepped over their friend and went to meet them.

'This day isn't going the way you hoped, is it?' I said. 'You thought your morning consisted of a nice, quiet beating. Instead, I made a ruckus, and killed your friend here. I'm betting Wald isn't big enough that this sort of thing can escape notice.' I paused. 'I bet the guards are on their way, in fact. That's not going to end well for you.'

'You neither,' a voice said. The two men stopped, looks of relief on their faces. They stepped aside for the newcomer. 'Dabney, Sculo – drag Cusmir somewhere quiet, get him out of sight until Pepasho can bring a night-soil cart around.'

He was big, and ugly. His face had met fists one too many times, and now had a rough, unfinished look to it. I could tell he was the boss from the cut of his clothes. Better quality, but they didn't fit right. He was dressed like he thought a success- ful man ought to dress, but without any sense of taste or style.

'You beat up my boys pretty good.'

'They weren't much of a challenge,' I said.

He looked me up and down, and smirked. 'Think you're a tough one, do you?'

'Caspar Guno thinks I am.'

As I'd hoped, Guno's name carried weight, even out here. The big man blanched slightly and licked his lips. 'Guno? You... work for him?' He looked like he was starting to regret coming out here. He'd probably expected it to be more entertaining than this.

'On occasion.'

'Now?'

'No. I'm here on a personal matter.'

His relief was palpable. He looked around, trying to regain the advantage. 'So you beat up my men, kill one of them, and make noise by way of – what? An introduction?'

'If you like. I'm not a patient man and I wanted your attention.'

He grinned sourly. 'Well you've got it. Now give me one good reason not to have you dropped in the swamp.'

'Professional courtesy.'

'You killed one of my men.'

'I lightened your organisation of dead weight.'

He preened at that. He liked that someone associated with Guno thought that he had an organisation. In reality, I figured them for bandits who were too scared to hide in the swamp.

'Maybe. Truth to tell, I never liked Cusmir much. You want his job?'

'I've got my own. I'm looking for someone.'

'I know a few girls, if that's what you like.'

'Not a girl.'

'I got a few men as well.'

'Murn,' I said. 'Evrek Murn.'

His smile faltered. His eyes widened slightly. He wasn't very good at hiding his feelings. 'You want help? It'll cost you.'

I saw the walls go up, and decided I was done being cordial. 'What's your name?'

He frowned. 'I don't know if I want to tell you…'

'Maybe I should ask the sheriff.' I smiled. 'You probably know that she and I are good friends now.'

He flinched. It seemed that information was not new to him. He looked at me. 'You can call me Pender.' He paused. 'You really work for Guno?'

'Yes. Let me see your arms, Pender.'

'Why?'

'Humour me.' I'd had a thought, and I wanted to follow it through.

Frowning, he rolled up his sleeves and extended both arms. Plenty of scars, no tattoos. That made me feel better, though I couldn't say why.

'You know Murn?' I said.

'Maybe.'

'I want to speak to him. Where is he?'

'Don't know.' The way he said it told me he was lying.

I decided to ask more forcefully. He wasn't ready for it. Lazy, maybe. Or perhaps he thought the proximity of his men would protect him. The punch caught him in the abdomen, and he folded over my waiting arm, wheezing. He was soft in the middle – too much easy living. I caught his hair and jerked his head up.

'That's a shame. Caspar Guno would be grateful if you found out.'

'Y-you said this was personal,' he spluttered.

'Even so.' I yanked on his scalp. 'Someone in this misbegotten village must know where Murn is. You're going to find them for me. Or I'm going to be forced to get creative. You understand?'

'I-I understand.'

'Good.' I helped him stand. 'I'm at the Stag's Head.' I patted him with a bloody hand. 'I look forward to our next meeting.'

I left him there, bloody handprint on his cheek. As I departed, I thought I heard something laugh.

Or maybe it was the distant thunder of galloping hooves.

CHAPTER FIFTEEN

RED SEED

I didn't go back the way I'd come.

I found another cistern and washed my hands and coat as best I could. I wasn't the only person wandering around town with blood on him, but I felt better with it gone. No need to risk undue attention from the guards, even if I was on his lordship's payroll. When I was finished, I wandered back towards the far edge of town, where solid ground gave way to water and reeds, and the houses rested on stilts rather than stone foundations.

There wasn't much here. The town slid into the water, with new shacks built atop sunken roofs, or on the anchored shapes of barges and scuttled boats. Trees stretched over the fallen slopes, casting deep shadows onto the water.

It was quieter on this side of town. There weren't many people here. A few sat on porches, or on the docks and jetties, playing instruments, cooking or preparing meat. No one paid me any attention, or if they did, they kept it to themselves.

I figured I'd satisfactorily impressed the need for urgency on Pender. As far as he knew, I was trouble. The sooner he helped me, the sooner I was gone. Granted, he might try to kill me again, but I had him down as the type who wouldn't want to annoy someone like Caspar Guno. Either way, something would happen.

The key to finding someone who doesn't want to be found is to shake as many trees as possible and see what falls out. Murn was definitely hiding somewhere in town, and probably with help. Maybe Pender, maybe Deshler or someone else. That he was hiding from his lordship was obvious. Not from me, though, which made things easier.

I was still in the dark as to why he'd risked sending for me. I knew he wouldn't have done it without good reason. Maybe he expected me to help him escape whatever mess it was that he'd obviously got himself into. Or maybe...

A trap. Just not the one you thought.

I closed my eyes as the words sifted through my head. So soft, they might have been my own thoughts. If I'd been anyone other than who I was, I might have assumed just that. But Cassian had taught me how to hear when something was using my voice as camouflage. Daemons were tricky things.

You think me so small as that?

I didn't reply. I kept walking. I heard the ghost of an echo of great hooves, plodding in my wake. I didn't turn around. I knew there'd be nothing there.

I shaded my eyes against the glare on the water and peered across the swamp. The shrine sat at the top of the island. Azyrite shrines were often built on hills or crags – as close to the stars as possible. As close to Azyr and its God-King as possible.

Trees rose in thick, irregular rows, dominating the path and the island. I was reminded of an encroaching army, blocking off all retreat. As I observed them, I knew I was being observed in turn.

'They're watching you.'

Deshler. I glanced at the old woman. She was sitting on a nearby jetty, carefully stripping strands from a corn-husk. She chewed on a twig as she worked, her face set in an expression of placid concentration.

'Who is?'

'You know who.' Her tone was chiding. 'And not just them. You shouldn't have crossed old Fulder. He's got people following you.'

'Yeah.' I went over and leaned against a mooring post. 'I looked for you this morning. After our little talk last night, I got to thinking...'

'Always dangerous out here.'

'Maybe. Can you take me out to the Huntsman's Bower?'

She looked at me. 'Why would I do that?'

'I'm interested.'

'Why?'

'Does it matter?'

She snorted and went back to her work. 'You don't want to go there.'

'How about to the shrine? You'll take me over there?' I rattled my money pouch. She stopped what she was doing.

'I thought you were looking for this Murn, not playing realmwalker.'

'So you heard something, then?'

'I didn't say that.'

I paused. 'This is twice now you've popped up somewhere unexpected.'

'I live here.' She grinned. 'Why the worry? Think I'm following you?'

'Thought never crossed my mind. What are you making?'

'You know what I'm making.' She held up the familiar, antlered shape.

'What is it?'

'Something we've always made.'

'To celebrate?'

She smiled. 'In a manner of speaking.'

'Local traditions,' I said.

The old woman nodded. I looked back at the shrine. A part of me was sad to see it reduced so. Only a small part, but it was there. The church had its militant side – a good priest needed to be able to wield a hammer as well as they preached the word of heaven. But that wasn't its only purpose. It was simply the only one I'd cared about, back then.

I'd been young. New to the azure, and full of righteous fire. That had passed quickly enough, after my first few battles. The hammer had more weight than the word, out in the wilds. I'd brought judgement rather than salvation.

I remembered the roar of guns, and the screams. The smell of blood and powder, the taste of maggoty bread. I closed my eyes, banishing the memories back into the dark. Those days, that man – they were gone. I'd traded in my hammer and robes for simpler tools. Lighter burdens. It was better that way. That was what I told myself.

The one thing the realms didn't lack for was priests, after all.

The wind turned, and the trees shook. Water slapped against the jetty. Out in the swamp birds took flight.

Deshler squinted. 'They're singing again. Trying to sing the Old Stag to sleep.'

'Why?'

She shook her head. 'Don't know. Just stories.'

'I got time.'

She peered at me. 'Do you? You seemed awfully impatient last night.'

'That was last night.'

Her gaze sharpened. 'Something happened to you, didn't it?'

'You might say that. And now I'm in the mood for a story.' I drew my knife and began to clean the blood out from under my nails. She watched me, her expression uneasy. 'Tell me about the Old Stag. That a name for Kurnoth?'

Deshler made a sharp gesture. 'Hush! You want to draw his eye here?'

I shrugged. 'I'm sure he has better things to attend to than my lack of respect. I'm right though, aren't I?' Between what Lord Wald had implied, and what the sylvaneth had said, I was getting a picture of things. One I didn't like.

She nodded. 'That's the story.' She looked out over the water. 'It's said that when the Everqueen tamed the Old Stag, she flayed him. And out of the meat of him she pulled a single, red seed. And from that seed grew Kurnoth, the Huntsman.'

'And what happened to the rest of him?'

'She sank him in the mire, to sleep and dream red dreams forevermore.'

'Hunter's Bower,' I said.

She blinked. 'That's what they say. How'd you know?'

I scratched my chin. 'I pay attention. So there's a dead god planted in the swamp somewhere?' Or not so dead, maybe, given what I'd experienced of late.

Deshler nodded. 'That's why we make these. Helps propitiate him. Or so the old men say. Keeps Red Kern quiet, keeps him sated and slumbering.' She gestured to the town. 'That's the point of the celebration. Harvest and hunt. Harvest for the Everqueen, and the hunt for him.' She tossed me the sigil and stood. 'Only now, things are bad.'

'How so?'

'You've got eyes. You saw what I saw. You heard the stories.' She stood and shuffled to the edge of the jetty. She spat into the water. 'People go missing in the swamp all the time. More nowadays, though.' She looked at me. 'Best leave it be, whatever you're thinking.'

'Who said I'm thinking anything? I'm just making conversation.' I looked back at the shrine. 'How long has it been like that?'

'Since before my time.'

'So, a long time.'

Deshler laughed. 'You think you're funny.'

'No.'

'At least you know that much.' She stretched, old bones popping. She was hiding something. I could smell it on her. I decided to give her a prod.

'They say Murn tried to kill his lordship. Is that why you looked so nervous, when they ran up on us?'

'They didn't make you nervous?'

'Not as such. You didn't hear about it?'

'I'm not a gossip.'

'But you're popular.' I sighed. 'I think you know more than you admit. I think you know a lot about what goes on here. I think you know where Murn is.'

She fell silent. I flexed my hands, considering.

'And I think if I hurt you, you'd tell me what I want to know, quick enough.'

I let that sink in. I wanted her to have a good, long think on it. She swallowed. I smiled.

'I'm not going to, though. I'm going to do exactly what I said I was going to do. You hear anything, I'll pay you.'

'And if I don't?'

I pushed away from the mooring post. 'Think I'm going to go get a drink. See you around, Deshler. Keep those ears open.'

I felt her eyes on me as I ambled away. Deshler was one to keep an eye on. She was old enough to trust me at my word – and to know the only way to stop me was to put a knife in me.

I didn't think she would, though. Something told me things were progressing as they were meant to.

I didn't think it was a sham, all this secrecy. Murn was really hiding, and his allies – his friends – didn't know who to trust. I was certain that whatever his lordship had claimed, Sepesh was probably still hunting for Murn as well. I was just another beater in the bush. But unlike her, I knew Murn. Murn liked people. He was the sort who'd draw down on anyone who threatened his kith and kin.

The more threats I made, the more of a nuisance I made of myself, the more likely it was that I wouldn't have to find Murn. He'd find me. Then, I'd kill him and go home.

So certain. A hunter's pride.

I'd expected the voice, so I wasn't startled. I didn't reply. Didn't see the need. I didn't think it was a god. Gods don't talk to men like me.

It could be said that we speak to no one else.

I almost laughed at that, but I stopped myself. The presence – the pressure – receded. It was goading me. Making me curious. Making me angry. I knew it, and couldn't help but feel both. I wanted to know what it was. Why it was shadowing me.

Hunting me.

And then I wanted to put my knife right in whatever passed for its heart.

My head full of red thoughts, I made my way back to the Stag's Head. The harvest celebrations seemed more sedate today, and I didn't see as many people out on the streets as the day wore down to dark. Plenty of dead meat, though. Hanging from roof-edge hooks, or piled bleeding in carts. Flies gathered in black clouds, something in their buzzing reminding me of those terrible hoof-beats from the night before.

And the sigils too, of course. More of them every time I looked. Hanging from every door and in every window. Antlered faces, staring out at the red, red world the people of Wald had made. Blood slopped in the gutters, and dripped into barrels. Children sharpened knives on grindstones, so as to better carve up the street-curs and alley-strays they'd caught the previous night.

I saw masks, too. Masks with twists of bramble for manes, and carved scraps of wood for antlers. Men and women clapped and sang songs – not the ribald tunes I'd heard when we arrived, but something slower and statelier. An imploration, rather than a celebration. Sometimes the masks turned to watch me as I passed by, and I thought of Deshler's warning.

Let them follow me. Let them eavesdrop and spy. I'd deal with them, if I had to. And otherwise, what did it matter?

Even so, I felt a stirring in my gut as I reached the tavern. Not hunger, but something else. A feeling that was all too familiar. I'd had it once before, and long ago. And now I was having it again. A twinge of unease. Something was happening, out of sight and in silent places.

But this time I wasn't fool enough to go looking for it. That's what I told myself. Repeated it to myself, like a mantra. I was only here for Murn. Nothing else.

The common room was crowded again. Apparently the Stag's Head was popular. Or maybe it was the only real tavern in town.

Gint was sitting at our table when I arrived. He was raking in a pile of motes as angry fishermen rose, scowling and cursing under their breaths.

'Thank you for the game, gentle sirs – and all these lovely motes, as well,' he called out. He tossed two to a serving girl as she set a drink down at his elbow. 'Bring one for my friend as well,' he said. 'He looks like he could do with it.'

'Feeling generous?' I grabbed a chair and sat.

'I'm a rich man, by local standards. Pretty soon I expect his lordship to come and ask for a loan.' He swept the motes into a pouch and stuffed it into his shirt. 'Remind me to pay you back for the room.'

'You could get your own.'

'I asked. None to be had, I'm afraid. Besides, two sleep safer than one. Especially around here.' He leaned forward. 'I am not convinced by the local hospitality.'

I looked around. Gazes were hastily averted. 'No. Does seem to be precious little of it. Find anything out?'

'About your bower, you mean?' He shuffled his cards. 'Nothing much. It's a spot somewhere in the swamp. No one goes there, except when they do.'

'And when do they?'

'When a shipment comes in.'

I reached over and stopped his shuffling. 'Shipment of what?'

He grinned. 'People.'

I sat back as my drink arrived. 'People.'

'Prisoners. Prison barges.' He laid out a hand of cards, clucked his tongue and began to reshuffle them. 'Remember? I mentioned them. So did Deshler.'

'So you did.' I didn't ask him to elaborate. Outside the rain continued to fall. Someone stoked the firepit. I stared at it, listening to the crackle of burning wood. I closed my eyes. When I opened them, I felt stiff, and my mouth tasted sour. The fire was low and red. It was still raining outside, but the common room was almost empty now. I realised, with some surprise, that I'd fallen asleep.

Gint still sat across from me, his gaze speculative. 'Tired?'

'I don't know what you mean.' I sat up and stretched. Things popped and clicked in unsettling ways, and I couldn't help but grunt in pain. 'How long?'

'An hour or two. It's getting dark.' He reached for his cup. He cut his eyes towards the door. 'Well, there's a familiar face.'

I glanced back. The pickpocket I'd nearly drowned the day

before stood dithering in the entrance. He craned his neck, as if looking for someone. When he saw me, he approached, looking nervous.

'Come for another bath?' I said.

He swallowed. 'Pender... Pender said I was to tell you that someone wants to speak to you.' He retreated as I rose to my feet.

'That was quick'

I took a long pull from my drink and set it down.

'Lead the way.'

CHAPTER SIXTEEN

ROAD AGENT

The little pickpocket led me down a maze of side streets and back alleys. We found ourselves in sight of the palisades, as the grey of the day turned black. I could hear the guards shouting to one another as a queue of vessels sailed through the gates. Swamp-birds perched on the rooftops overhead, squawking raucously as they settled in for the night.

'This way,' my guide said. He stank of fear. His eyes darted around. I wondered whether he was scared of me, or something else. We stopped several times to let guards amble past. The glow of their lanterns washed across the walls, casting long shadows.

'More of them than I remember,' I said.

'They're stepping up patrols. Something has them nervous,' the pickpocket muttered.

'Any idea what?'

He frowned. 'Same as always. Treekin are agitated. They always get pernickety during harvest time. Snatch babies from their cribs, creep along the rooftops. Kill animals. Snatch people from the road.'

'No wonder you look nervous.'

'I'm not nervous. I'm scared shitless.' He glanced at me and licked his lips. 'You really work for Caspar Guno?'

'If I didn't, I'd be a fool to claim otherwise.'

He gave a sickly grin. 'That's the gods' own truth.' He ducked down a side street. 'This way. Is it true he once had a fellow split open, filled with hot coals and sewn back up?'

'Yes.' I knew because I'd helped toss the body afterwards. The victim had been a murderer – a cannibal. He'd eaten the wrong person, and Guno had lost a lot of money.

The pickpocket shuddered. 'Did he really have a... a Stormcast killed? One of the God-King's chosen warriors?'

I hesitated. That was the sort of question it was dangerous to answer. 'He did.'

'*How?*'

They always asked that. I gave the same answer I always did. 'We got lucky.'

The pickpocket's eyes bulged. 'You did it?'

'I was there.' I remembered the look on his face, the way his eyes blazed like caged lightning as we dragged him down with weighted nets. It had been the only way. Then, the spears and the hooks. Duardin-forged, gromril-tipped. Even then, it had taken too long.

I remembered the way Guno had clapped me on the back. The way I'd almost turned and spilled his fat guts on the street, right beside the scorch marks, where the lightning had struck. Mostly, though, I remembered the look on that Stormcast's face. The look in those awful, burning eyes. The look that said he'd remember me.

The pickpocket hesitated. 'Are they... are they as glorious as the stories say?'

'No. Yes.' I paused. 'They're not human.'

'That's obvious,' he said, with a nervous laugh.

'That's not what I meant. They're not human. They're... hollow, but full. Like jugs filled with naphtha. Break one, and the world burns.' I frowned, trying to articulate what I meant. It was hard, even now. 'You can smell it on them, in their sweat. Hear it in their voices. A storm, compacted into a ball and buried. But it is always fighting to free itself. They bleed lightning. They sweat rain. Their voices are like thunder. They are not... human.'

The pickpocket shook his head. 'They sound beautiful.' He sounded wistful.

'They aren't. The ones I knew were as ugly as sin, for all their features were perfect.' I gestured to my face. 'Too perfect, even with the scars. You can't look at them for long without seeing it. Even the women.'

'Women?' He looked horrified. 'Some of them are women?'

'They're not human,' I said again. 'Stop talking about it.'

He gulped and nodded, as another guard patrol sent us sidling into an alleyway. These were heading somewhere in a hurry. I watched them go, wondering who – or what – had drawn their attentions. We were still within sight of the palisades. I looked at my guide.

'If the guards have increased patrols, is it wise to be meeting here, under their noses?'

The pickpocket nodded jerkily. 'Pender has it covered. He always does. Takes good care of us, does Pender.'

'I bet. Wald doesn't strike me as big enough for a man like Pender.' I looked at my guide, noticed the hint of a tattoo poking out of one ratty sleeve. 'You were in Ironhole?'

He stopped, face pale. 'What?'

I grabbed his arm, and bent it up. 'Ironhole. The prison. You came here on a barge, then? Seems like a lot of you have.'

He snatched his arm back. 'What business is it of yours?'

'Just getting the lie of the land.' I tapped the pommel of my knife. 'Watch your tone, if you would. You might hurt my feelings, otherwise.'

'I came on a barge,' he said sulkily. 'So did Pender.'

'And how'd you manage to escape?'

He fell silent. I considered forcing the issue, but decided against it. It wasn't important. A moment later, I had a whole new concern. A guard was striding towards us, truncheon in one hand, lantern in the other. I stepped behind the pickpocket and reached for my knife. The pickpocket realised my intent and gestured frantically.

'No! It's fine. It's fine.'

'About time,' the guard said. He glanced at me, and his eyes narrowed. 'I know you.'

'I know you too.' We'd met the previous evening. He looked me up and down.

'You ever find the Stag's Head?'

'Right where you said it would be. You find what I'm looking for?'

'Why you think I'm here?' He gestured. 'Pender's waiting.'

I didn't move. 'You work for Pender?'

He grinned. 'His lordship can be a might stingy with wages.'

'I'm getting the feeling that he's not the most popular of potentates.' I looked him up and down. 'How many of you work for Pender, then?'

His smile faded. He slapped the back of his hand against my chest, lightly. 'Be quick. I can't pretend to patrol over here all afternoon. Buell's already on my back.'

'Buell,' I said. 'Small town.' I let the pickpocket lead me away.

Pender was waiting for us at the mouth of an alley leading to the quays. He stood with his back to the water, wearing heavy furs against the chill of the evening. He nodded to me and gestured.

'Be off with you, Scopa. Go find some pockets to rifle through.'
The pickpocket darted away, leaving us alone.

Pender scrubbed his jowls and looked at me. 'I did what you asked.'

'You found Murn.'

'I found someone who knows where he might be, at a certain time. If you so happen to be there, at that time...' He smiled, pleased with himself. I considered hitting him, just to keep him on his toes, but decided against it. As long as he was doing what I wanted, there was no need to bloody him.

'I get the picture.' I ran my hand over my head. My hair hadn't been dry in days. I would be glad when this was done. I planned on sitting in front of a fire and letting the chill bake out of my bones. 'You work quick.'

'Sooner I get you what you want, the sooner you leave.'

'Hard to argue with that logic. Who is it?'

'I look like I care about someone's name?' He frowned. 'She was trying to get out of town on a fishing barge. My boys caught her just before they left. She nearly put a knife in one of them.' He leaned over and spat into the water. 'She's scared. Never known an aelf to be scared.'

I almost laughed. After all, how many aelves could there be in a town like this?

'The road agent.'

He raised an eyebrow. 'You know her?'

'We've met. Where is she?'

'Just at the end of the quay, there. I told her I'd get her on a skiff, first thing in the morning. Only way she agreed to put her knife up.' He rubbed his face again. 'If this pays off... how much gratitude can I expect, do you think?'

'Depends on what happens after I find Murn.'

Pender frowned. 'That sounds vague.'

'It does, doesn't it?' I paused. 'You work quick, though. That's a point in your favour. Guno might have use for a fellow who accomplishes his tasks so quickly.'

Pender licked his lips. 'Yeah?'

I shrugged. 'There's always an opening or two.' I started down the quay. The evening was still. A murk rose from the dark water, hanging over everything. It muffled the sounds of the town and the swamp, making me feel as if my head were wrapped in cotton. There was a smell, as well. Thick and sour, like wood pulp left in the rain.

The other islands were indistinct masses, the trees but vague towers, piercing the gloom.

She was standing at the end of the quay, staring at the skiffs moored in the waters below. Her fingers played with the hilt of her knife, and I knew she was thinking about cutting a rope and stealing a boat and going... somewhere. She had a bottle in her hand – local rotgut, by the smell.

'Hello.'

She turned. 'You.' She didn't sound surprised. She swayed slightly.

'Me. I told you I'd speak to you again.'

'So you did.' She turned back to the water. 'What do you want?'

I pulled the coin – Murn's coin – out of my pocket and held it up, so she could see it. 'Word has it you know where Evrek Murn is.'

'Do I?' She lifted the bottle and took a long pull.

'Are you drunk?' I was getting impatient.

'Wouldn't you be?'

She had me there. I forced myself to relax. Even drunk, she was probably faster than me. I'd got a taste of it in her office. I wasn't looking for a second go-round.

'We weren't properly introduced last time. What's your name?'

She took a drink and stared at me.

I shrugged. 'Fine. My name's Harran. I'm looking for Evrek Murn. He sent me this coin. I want to know how it came to you.'

She was silent for a time. Then, 'I saw this place before it flooded, you know.'

I stuffed the coin back in my pocket. 'That's not what I asked.'

'It wasn't much prettier, but it was good enough. The air smelled like sawdust.' She frowned. 'Never liked that smell.' She took another drink. 'You humans... If you're not cutting up trees, you're cracking rocks and bending rivers out of shape.'

An old catechism rose unbidden to my lips. 'The realms are Sigmar's gift to man,' I said. 'His to oversee and whose bounty to best enjoy.'

She looked at me like I'd passed wind in the boudoir. 'Sigmar,' she said, and I recognised the tone. I'd spoken his name with the same venom myself, before it had all drained away. 'These lands are not his to give. These swamps, these forests, they do not belong to him or to you.'

'No. They don't. But we're here.' I looked around. 'Mostly.'

She smirked. 'For now.'

'Anyway, what do I care about forests? I'm only after one thing.'

She looked away. 'I remember when all this was dry... It was forest, then. An old forest, tangled and black. The sort of forest where those who aren't born there aren't welcome. Even aelves.'

'Forest or swamp, still doesn't matter. Tell me about Murn.'

'I liked him. He could talk, you know?' She shook her head. 'Talk about something other than eels or hunting. About cities, about other realms.' She took a drink. 'Shame he was married.'

'Married?'

She smiled in a dreamy way. 'Kersha,' she said, softly. 'That was her name.'

'Was?'

Her smile faded. 'Dead now. Sickness. Swamp-chill. Got into

her bones, turned her blood to water. Happens a lot out here.' She paused. 'She died and then their girl...'

'A child?' I said. I could hear the disbelief in my voice. Murn – with a child? I shook my head. 'He had a daughter?'

'Little baby girl,' she said. 'They used to throw babies in the water, here.' Her words were slightly slurred, now. 'Every harvest moon, in they'd go... one baby, two baby, three baby, four.' She took another swig and offered me the bottle.

I accepted it and took a swig. I nearly spat it out. It tasted like vinegar and chillies. 'Used to,' I said. 'Not any more?'

She shook her head. 'Not any more.' She leaned against the mooring post. 'I did it.'

'Did what?'

'Sent the coin.'

I paused, the bottle halfway to my lips. As I considered her words, I took a slow sip. I passed the bottle back to her. 'Why?'

'Murn asked me to.'

'Where is he?'

She took a long slug from the bottle and sent it sailing out over the water. 'I don't know,' she said. 'Have you checked his farm?'

'Farm?'

She snorted. 'Of course. He goes there to hide, sometimes. They've already searched it, so they don't pay it any attention.' She looked down at her hands. 'We used to worship her too, you know. The Everqueen.' She curled her fingers, as if gripping a sword. 'Only we turned from her, and she cast us out.' She glared at the trees rising from the shallows. 'She made the trees hate us. And then she turned from them too.' She looked at me. 'And some of them started to hate her, the way she hated us... all mixed with love.' She dropped her head, and was silent for long moments. I thought she was asleep until she said, 'They found new gods, then. Older gods, and bloodier by far.'

'Gods like Kurnoth.'

She gestured frantically. 'Hsst! Are you mad? Don't say that name, unless you want his hounds to catch your scent.'

'You're the second person to do that to me today,' I said in annoyance.

She looked around, visibly nervous. 'They're always listening. This place was his, long before it was hers…'

She stopped, head tilted as if listening to something. I knew aelves had better hearing than most, and my hand dropped to my knife. She swallowed convulsively, and stepped back from the water.

'I… I have to go.'

'Wait. What about this farm? Where is it?' I reached for her, but she twisted away, a feral expression on her face.

'I've already said too much!' She turned and began to hurry away. 'Tell Murn we're even. Tell him I don't want to hear from him again.'

As she vanished into the mists curling along the quay, I heard something splash, far out in the dark under the trees. When I turned in that direction, I saw only a hint of movement. A tree, I thought. Just a tree, swaying in the wind.

But what tree has antlers?

CHAPTER SEVENTEEN

THE FARM

My dreams were ugly, and full of red.

I dreamed of a woman so beautiful it hurt, and she was cutting me open. Slicing and slicing with knives of green as I struggled against chains of brambles and bark. She murmured to me as she flensed the meat from my bones, whispering words of endearment and longing as she stripped me to pieces.

This is a kindness, she said. *It is a kindness I do you. It is for love I harness you, and goad you. It is for love I make this pain.*

I heard her words and I wanted to believe, but I saw the ugliness beneath her pretty face. A longing no less needful than my own, a hunger no less consuming. And so I struggled and fought, as all around me her children tittered and pulled the cutting chains taught.

And she cut. And cut. And cut.

I was almost grateful when the grey light of day crept through the window and woke me. I rolled over, stiff and hurting. Gint was nowhere to be seen. But there was another antler sigil on the table. I tossed it out the window, dressed as quickly as I could manage and made my way downstairs.

The common room was all but deserted, and the firepit was nothing but ashes. Gint sat near the troggoth-pit, a bowl of oats and mash in front of him. 'They left us another gift in the night,' he said, as I sat.

'I know. I tossed it.'

He looked startled. 'Was that wise?' He pushed his bowl towards me. He hadn't eaten much, and I tucked in with gusto.

'I don't particularly care,' I said. 'How'd they get in?'

'I wish I knew. At least they didn't steal anything.' He looked over at the troggoth-pit. 'They took the poor beast out last night. Gods know where.'

'It was a troggoth.'

'I heard it whining when they hauled it out. Like a ghyrwolf pup, or a child.' He looked at me, his face drawn. 'Even a troggoth doesn't deserve that.'

I had no answer for that. Gint continued to surprise me. I pushed the empty bowl aside and sat back.

He set his cards on the table and tapped the deck. 'So what did you learn last night?' he asked.

'Nothing of interest.'

'I doubt that.' He leaned forward. 'Give me some credit, Harran. I'm not stupid. So what did you learn?'

I studied him for a moment. I wondered whether it was simple curiosity that had provoked his question, or something else. I decided to play along. 'Murn was married.'

'Explains why he stayed.'

'He had a child.'

'Had?'

'Dead, apparently.'

He looked at me. 'Not a flicker of sympathy, is there?'

'What?'

'Nothing in your eyes. Not even pity.'

'Murn tried to kill me once.'

Gint looked at his cards. 'Maybe he had a good reason.'

I thought about it a moment. 'He did. Doesn't mean I forgive him.' I took a card off the top of his deck and set it down face up. 'Why do you care, Gint? You don't know him.'

'I don't have to know him to feel bad for him.' He set a card down beside mine. 'You're here to kill him, aren't you?'

'Figured that out all by yourself?'

'Why?'

'He tried to kill me.' I paused. 'Among other reasons. That's my business, though.' I set another card down. 'What I can't figure is why any of this matters to you.'

'I told you – you saved my life. For better or worse, we're bound together.'

I looked down at the cards. 'I'm not good at card games. This a good hand?'

He shook his head. 'It's not finished yet.' He looked up, eyes narrowing.

I realised that everything had gone quiet. I turned and saw Sepesh standing in the doorway, her cloak running with rainwater. She spotted me and grinned. Two guards followed her inside, and took up positions to either side of the door. A soft murmur ran through the common room, but no one protested the implied threat.

Sepesh ambled towards me and took a seat. 'I understand you had some trouble.'

I gave her a wary look. 'Who says?'

'A little eel told me.' She leaned back. 'We found a body floating in the swamp. Somebody had done a bad job of weighing it down.' She gestured across her stomach. 'Someone else had cut him open.'

'Maybe it was self-defence.'

She nodded. 'I could see where that might be the case. He was a known troublemaker. A barge-escapee.' She sat up. 'We have a lot of those, hiding in the swamp. Living on the margins. Cost of doing business, I suppose.'

'I wouldn't know.'

'The same little eel told me that you were seen hanging around the palisades last night, talking to some unsavoury sorts. Care to explain that?'

'His lordship gave me a task. I am merely seeing it out.'

She snorted. 'Yeah. I bet. And I'm here, on his behalf, to ask for a report. So, report. What did you find?'

I considered not saying anything. But only for a moment. Sepesh was here as a reminder that Lord Wald wanted to know where Murn was as badly as I did.

'There's a farm,' I said. 'Murn owned it.'

She gave a dismissive wave. 'We already searched the farm. He's not there.'

'You might have missed something.'

She frowned. 'Like what?'

I shrugged. 'I've known Murn a long time. I might see something you didn't.' I doubted that, but it sounded good. And it was a bone to toss my new patron. Plus, if Murn did show up, it was all to the good.

She grunted and ran a hand through her hair. 'Maybe.' She looked at me. 'But I'm not letting you go out there alone.'

'Don't you trust me?'

She laughed. 'Not a bit.'

I nodded. 'Probably wise.'

'How'd you know about the farm?'

'A little eel told me.'

She smiled widely. 'Have it your way.' She pushed her chair back and rose. 'My coach is outside. The rain's picking up. Better to ride than walk.'

'You brought the coach?'

'I'm the sheriff. I don't walk.'

I looked at Gint. 'Try not to cheat anyone today.'

'No promises,' he said. I felt his eyes on me as we left.

'Your friend is a weaselly sort,' Sepesh said, as we stepped out into the rain.

'He's not my friend,' I said. 'More like a stray.' I pulled my hood up. 'Where's the farm?'

'Outskirts of the village, just south of the manor. Lots of dry land there, with good black soil, where the waters have receded over the years.'

Buell wasn't driving the coach this time. I recognised Pender's pet guard. He nodded to me amiably, without giving any sign of recognition. I reckoned I knew how Sepesh had found out about my meeting. I looked at her, and she gave me a knowing smile.

'Pender thinks he's clever, but he's only got as much rope as I give him.'

'You let him operate in town?'

She shrugged. 'There's always somebody. Better I know who he is.' She climbed aboard the coach, and I followed. 'Besides, Pender makes things entertaining. I get so bored out here.'

'Does he know?'

She laughed. 'Gods, no. If he did, he'd scarper quick. Pender's not the sort of man who fights a losing battle.'

'You ever think Murn might be hiding with him?'

She frowned. 'I'd considered it. But it didn't seem like the sort of thing Murn would do. Then, as you said, I don't know him as well as you.' She thumped on the roof, and the coach lurched into motion. 'How do you know him, anyway?'

'We're casual acquaintances.'

'Doesn't sound like it.' From the way she said it, I could tell she wasn't going to let it go. She drew a poniard from a sheath on her belt and began to clean her fingernails.

'How do you know him?' I countered.

She smirked. 'He's a troublemaker. Local rabble-rouser, though not as bad as that old bastard Fulder. You've met him, I think.'

'I've had that pleasure, yes.' I hadn't seen Fulder since the night I'd thumped his friends. I guessed he'd decided to stay out of my way after that. 'Who is he, by the way?'

'He's sort of the town father, you might say.'

'The hetman.'

She nodded. 'Fulder likes to think he's in charge, when his lordship is otherwise occupied with affairs of state. We let him, because he's diligent when it comes to keeping the peasants in line.'

'Except for Murn.'

'Except Murn. You didn't answer my question.'

'Yes. How rude of me.' I looked out the window. The coach rattled along a winding, marshy path through a corridor of close-set trees, passing farms and fishing shacks. The path was a berm of dirt, reinforced with pitch-soaked timbers and piled stones. I knew it must take constant effort to keep it from collapsing entirely. 'Who keeps these paths from crumbling?' I asked. 'I never see anyone working.'

'Harvest celebration. No one's working.'

'And when there's no celebration?'

'We use prisoners, mostly.'

'Slave labour, you mean.' I thought of what I'd heard about the barges. Was this what they were being used for, then? Prison labour wasn't unheard of. Greywater Fastness practically ran on it, though no one in their right mind admitted it.

'Perish the thought. Slavery is illegal under Azyrite law.'

'More than one type of slavery.' How many impoverished pilgrims and would-be colonists found themselves indentured to old masters in new realms? Too many to count. As many as there were stars in the sky.

'True,' she said, grinning. 'How many slaves did it take to build

Hammerhal? Ten million,' she continued, without waiting for me to reply. 'Ten million slaves, toiling day and night for almost a hundred years.'

I wanted to argue, but all I said was, 'You counted?'

'Someone did.'

'Good for them. What does that have to do with me?'

'Not a blessed thing. Someone's got to do the work.'

'Better them than you,' I said.

'Exactly.' She looked at me. 'Answer my question. How do you know Murn?'

'We served together.'

'What regiment?'

'Gold Gryphons.'

She raised an eyebrow. 'The regiment out of Vindicarum?'

'Hammerhal Aqsha,' I said. 'Tenth Cohort.'

'They get around.'

'A standard in every city, a comet in every purse,' I recited. 'What about you?'

'What makes you think I was a soldier?'

I looked her up and down. 'The way you've got your sword belted on. The boots you're wearing – Hammerhal issue, those.'

'Maybe I stole them.'

'Maybe. I doubt Lord Wald would make a thief his sheriff.'

'Maybe.' She paused. 'Faithful Blades, out of Hammerhal Ghyra. Surprised we never ran across one another.'

'I'm not. Hammerhal is a big place.' I looked out the window. The sky was only a thin sliver between the trees. But the rain fell steadily.

'True enough. I prefer it out here.'

I nodded. 'Quieter.'

'Too quiet. Especially of late.'

'I heard you were having trouble with the sylvaneth. Is that usual?'

'And where'd you hear that? Another little eel?'

'I like to know what's going on.' I watched the swamp. The further we drew from the main sprawl of the village the more rustic things became. The path was dotted with moss-lanterns, hanging from iron poles thrust into the sodden earth or into the shattered remnants of league-markers. A faint green radiance held back the murk, but only just.

Behind that radiance, something moved – stick-thin shapes that stretched and swayed from one copse to the next, in some fashion that I could only barely perceive. Sepesh followed my gaze.

'They never come any closer than that, if you're worried.'

She was wrong, but I didn't correct her. 'You saw them?'

'Hard not to, once you know what to look for.' She scratched her chin. 'Folk around here think that they caused the flood – that it was a punishment from the Lady of Leaves for their hubris.'

I could believe it. This far from the village, the swamp took on a pestilential aspect. The trees looked bloated, stretching long, crooked boughs over the rooftops of the few shacks. The water lapped at the edges of the path, washing over it in places. Out in the murk, I saw the shapes of sunken buildings and tumbled stones.

I wondered what it had looked like before the floods, before it had all gone sour. Would it have become a small city, in time, like Headwater Breach, or remained a way-station between metropolises? All that potential was lost now – drowned and buried. I looked at her.

'What do you think?'

'I think that if that's the case, she didn't do a very good job. They're still a prideful bunch, for a lot of eel-grubbing peasants.' She twirled her poniard with easy skill. The coach juddered as it ran over a fallen league-marker, and I heard the driver curse loudly and profanely.

'That includes Murn, I guess.'

'He's the worst of the bunch.'

'And why is that?'

'I thought you knew him.'

'He might have changed a bit, since we last spoke. Humour me.'

She eyed me. 'Used to be thick as thieves with Fulder and his bunch.' She smirked. 'Now he's got no friends at all.'

'Must have some.'

She nodded. 'Must have some. No clue who, though.' She peered at me. 'Sure you're not one of them? Maybe come to pull his fat out of the fire?'

'I want him dead more than you do.'

'For your sake, I hope so.' She leaned forward and craned her neck, peering out of the coach. 'Here we are.'

The coach slowed, and finally trundled to a stop with a splash. The horses were restive, causing the conveyance to creak as we climbed down.

The farmhouse was a squat, single-storey building, encircled by a low wall of piled stones. A larger structure that I took to be a barn or storehouse was visible off to the side, within the boundary of the wall. The farm sat atop the apex of a crumbling slope, and behind it the swamp spread out like an encroaching army.

'Only a few of the outlying farms survived the original flood,' Sepesh said. 'Those that were on higher ground than the others.' She gestured disinterestedly. 'Most of them are off that way. The swamp has grown up around them – they're like little islands, now. This is the only one you can reach on foot, and even that's dicey most days. The locals think it's a sign that the Lady of Leaves favoured the family – that includes our friend Murn now.'

'How so?'

'The old-fashioned way – he married into it,' Sepesh said. She looked the place over, her hand resting on her sword. 'Way I hear it, it surprised everyone. Especially Fulder.'

'Why is that?'

'Kersha was his niece. She was meant to marry someone the old man favoured. Instead she married some outsider, and popped out a brat...'

I was only half-listening. 'Bring a lantern,' I said, as I started towards the door. The farm looked... dead. Less like a home than a ruin.

But if Murn was here, I intended to find him.

CHAPTER EIGHTEEN

GREEN CORN

The courtyard was small – a soggy stretch of overgrown turf, with spindly trees rising up here and there. In the light of Sepesh's lantern I could see that the barn was collapsing in on itself, as if something massive had struck it at some point.

Bedraggled chickens glared at us from where they sheltered in the ruins. I had just started to wonder what they ate, when I saw a mouse streak from cover and scurry towards the house. Several of the fowl pounced, with eager clucks. The mouse never stood a chance.

'I hate chickens,' Sepesh said, as we watched the flock tear their prey apart and fall to squabbling over the pitiful remains.

'I'm surprised any of them are still alive.'

Out in the dark, something trilled. The chickens scattered with panicked indignation. Sepesh swung the lantern about, and there was a splash, close to hand. 'Leopard eel,' she said. 'Now we know what eats the chickens.'

'One mystery down,' I said. 'Come on' I pushed open the door of the farmhouse. The air inside smelled stale and damp. It was the sort of cold that said no fire had been kindled in the hearth in some time. So why the even spread of ashes? Why were they so thick?

I ran my hands along the stones of the hearth. Knotwork sigils had been carved into them. The sigils weren't those I'd seen in town, but they were familiar nonetheless. You couldn't live in Ghyran for long without coming to recognise symbols associated with the Everqueen. Sepesh watched me.

'Planning to start a fire?' she asked.

'No. When you said the locals thought the family was favoured – what did you mean?' I asked, as I stirred the ashes in the hearth. There were loose bricks there. An old trick, if you wanted to hide something. No way to check, however, with Sepesh standing behind me. I needed to get her to leave, somehow.

'Just that. Story was, they were jade-bloods, like his lordship. One of the old families, from before Azyrites set foot in the Greywater Reach.' She sniffed. 'Shabby place, though.'

'But dry,' I said. 'That suits me, at the moment.' I looked around.

The house was small. Not tidy, but clean. A kitchen, a larder, two bedrooms. More than most had, in villages like this. I was starting to see why Murn had stayed.

There were supplies in the larder, including a hock of salted pork that hadn't been touched by vermin, as yet. If Murn had left intentionally, he'd have taken food. That was the first thing you learned in the Freeguild – food was almost as important as your weapon.

I turned the pork on its hook, studying it. Someone had been at it with a knife. Possibly recently. I looked at the small shelves, and saw telltale gaps in the supplies – missing jars, open bags.

Someone was raiding these stores regularly. Murn might not be here, but he hadn't gone far.

The first bedroom was obviously Murn's. There was barely anything in it, beyond a sturdy bed and a heavy trunk. And books. Piles and piles of books. My gaze slid towards the pile nearest the bed. A hint of blue cloth poked out from the pile. I moved the books aside, revealing a blue bundle of cloth, striated with black char marks.

It had been a cloak, once. I recognised it easily enough, for it had been mine. How Murn had come by it, I couldn't say, but I knew it instantly. As I knew every rip and tear in it. Every mark.

Carefully, I unwrapped it. Inside were several items – a chain shirt and a breastplate, once gold, now turned black as if by a great heat; an astral compass that no longer functioned; a bit of marble that I knew had been chopped from a saint's tomb in Ghur; and a shawl made from coins – the traditional insignia of the Gold Gryphons.

I touched the coins, wondering why Murn had never spent them. Most of them were of Aqshian denomination. Some were from Ghur, others Ghyran. A coin from every battlefield we'd shed blood on, and a soldier's pension. One of the oldest traditions of the regiment, brought from the Hearthlands of Azyr.

For the regiment, tradition had been as much a weapon as a pike or handgun. It had been used to keep the troopers in line, and to browbeat clients. Tradition kept frightened soldiers in formation as much as discipline or the screams of officers. Tradition said the Gold Gryphons had never broken in open battle – oh, they'd made their fair share of fighting withdrawals and tactical retreats, but they'd never broken. Never fled like whipped curs. They'd died standing.

There was more besides – the burned remnants of a small book of catechisms, a fire-warped medallion. And the head of a warhammer, blasted by the same conflagration that had touched everything else.

My hammer.

I ran my fingers along the melted scenes carved into the sides of the hammer. Though they resembled nothing at all now, I remembered them well enough – Sigmar at war and at rest. Sigmar the Triumphant and Sigmar the Wrathful. I'd stared at them every day, trying to pull strength from them, into myself. Trying to make myself something more than just a man.

'What's that?' Sepesh asked, from behind me.

'Just some old junk.' I placed the hammer back amongst the other items. Slowly, I rewrapped them and put the bundle back beneath the pile. I turned my attention to the books.

They were on a variety of topics. I recognised a few of them. Without thinking, I reached out and picked one up. The book was old. The leather was cracked, the uneven pages crumbling.

'A book?' Sepesh asked.

'Not just any book. *The Sacred Bough*, by Ferek,' I said. 'I've only read the abridged version. This one…' I ran my fingers across the faded gilt on the spine. Ferek had been one of the first Azyrites to journey to Ghyran, after the Gates of Azyr opened. His treatises on the folkways and beliefs of the Jade Kingdoms had been so influential that the church had banned the book. I wondered where Murn had managed to acquire a copy – and why.

'You don't strike me as much of a reader,' Sepesh said.

'Not these days.' I eased through the pages, careful not to tear them. 'They say Ferek went mad, out in the wilderness.' A section on Kurnoth was marked. I read enough to see the words 'hunter's bower' before I snapped it closed. I set the book aside.

'Anything interesting?'

'Nothing you don't already know. How long has his lordship worshipped the god of the hunt?' I drew my knife and crouched beside the trunk. I made short work of the lock and popped it open. Inside was a folded uniform, a battered hauberk, an equally battered helm shaped like a gryphon's head, and a sheathed blade.

Sepesh leaned against the doorframe. 'You want to talk religion, now?'

'Might as well. Never met a worshipper of Kurnoth, this side of the Verdian Veldt.' I lifted the blade and unsheathed it. I ran my thumb along the edge. Dull. It hadn't seen a whetstone in years. I put it back.

'His people have always been here. Course, his lordship's father was a worshipper of the Everqueen.' She said the word like it was a curse. 'Most of the Walds were.'

'But not him.'

'Bit too much blood in the jade,' Sepesh said, and laughed at her own joke.

'And what about the people around here? Were they worshippers of the Lady of Leaves as well?'

'So they said.' She tapped the side of her nose. 'But the old ways came back quick enough when his lordship took over. He figured this had always been the Old Stag's territory, and it seemed a bit rude to worship another god.'

'Even if she was the one who tamed him,' I said. There were letters as well, wrapped in green ribbon. The writing on them was delicate – not Murn's.

Sepesh's eyes narrowed. 'You know the story.'

'I know lots of stories.' I considered the letters for a moment, and then closed the trunk. Whatever they contained was of no importance to me.

Sepesh kicked the trunk as I stood. 'Why would anyone leave a perfectly good weapon locked away like that?'

'Maybe he thought he didn't need it any more.' I scanned the shelves on the walls. Bric-a-brac covered them. Someone else's mementos, now covered in dust. I picked up a box, and opened it. Inside was a lock of hair, wrapped in a ribbon. Green as well. I didn't touch it. 'Let's check the other bedroom.'

The second bedroom belonged to a girl – young, I judged.

Barely more than a child. The crude decorations, the few homespun clothes, the corn-husk doll on the pallet, all of it spoke to
a girl, rather than a woman. Murn hadn't seemed the fatherly
type. Then again, people changed. I had, after all.

I felt the temperature in the room dip. Slowly, I turned.

The gheist stood in the corner, watching me. She was only a
child. She looked at me with black eyes and a hole-like mouth,
and clutched at her chest. There was something red there, and
I remembered my dream of the green place.

'Oh,' I said softly.

'Nothing in here,' Sepesh said, from behind me.

I blinked. The gheist was gone.

'You say something, Blackwood?'

'No.' I looked at her. 'When did they die?'

'A while ago.' She shrugged. 'Not my business.'

'No. I suppose not. This is a farm. What did they grow?'

'Now you're interested in agriculture?'

'I told you – I like to know things.'

Sepesh twitched her head. 'Out back'

I followed her through the house, to the back door. It opened
onto the swamp, but between the house and the trees was a
field of jade stalks.

'Green-corn,' I murmured. The stalks rose in irregular rows
from the shallow, emerald-stained waters, and stretched back into
the trees. They were higher than a man was tall, but splotched
and wilted looking.

The stalks rustled in the breeze, swaying above the waters,
revealing a stone archway and what might have been the top of a
wall. A ruin, sitting at the heart of the field. I felt a slight chill as
I studied the distant edifice, wondering what it had been before
time claimed it, just like the lumber mills and sunken houses.
Wald reminded me of a cheap death mask, stretched over the
bones of something greater.

Or like a hunter, wearing the skin of something they'd killed.

There were ancient paving stones beneath my feet, and league-markers that thrust upwards from the mire like narrow head-stones. Time had eaten this place, as it ate everything.

'It was bigger once,' I said.

'This whole town was bigger once,' Sepesh replied. 'Now it's a spoil-heap.' She looked at the corn.

'We should check the barn.'

'We've already checked it. We checked this whole place, remember?'

Around the front of the building, the chickens began to squawk. The driver of the coach yelled and we hurried around the side of the farmhouse.

'What are you yelping about, Fenk?' Sepesh shouted. She had her hand on her sword, and was looking at the trees rather than at her man. She seemed nervous, and that made me nervous.

Fenk pointed. 'I saw something go into the barn – something big.'

'A person?' I asked.

'I don't know. With the rain... it looked like a dog. I think it was a dog.' He trailed off, quailing slightly before Sepesh's glare.

'Keep a tight rein on those horses,' she snarled. She looked at the barn, and then at me. 'Your friend might have come back after all.'

'Maybe.' I tapped my knife. 'Let's say we find out.'

We entered the barn. Sepesh hung her lantern from a hook, casting a soft green light across the interior. The barn looked no bigger than the house from the outside, but the inside was cav-ernous in comparison. Cobwebs hung from the rafter beams and twitched in the wet breeze. The lofts above were all but black with shadow. The lantern-light didn't reach them.

A broken-down wagon sat near the far wall, its wooden pan-els plump with rot. A stack of rusted iron wheels occupied the

opposite corner. Chicken coops full of mouldy straw and grass
lined the closest wall. Crates of dusty bottles were stacked near
the doors. The dirt floor was scarred by the chicken tracks – and
something else. I crouched and traced what might have been a
boot-print. How old, I couldn't say.

'Someone has been here,' Sepesh said, standing over me.

'The question is, are they still here?' I stood. Above us, the
lofts creaked. I looked at Sepesh. 'Might just be the wind.'

'It's never the wind,' she said. She went to the closest ladder. 'Coming?'

'There's no light up there.'

She laughed and began to climb. I followed. Sepesh drew her
sword as she clambered onto the loft. 'Come out, come out,
wherever you are,' she half-sang. She was enjoying this. I was
starting to see why Murn might've run. I'd run too, if Sepesh
was after me.

The loft was dark, and smelled of wet hay. Sepesh was a blur,
creeping across the bales, stabbing her sword into every sizeable
clump. I stayed on the ladder. I could hear something skittering
in the dark. I assumed it was another mouse, hiding from the
chickens. But maybe not. My hand was on my knife.

When I spied the pale face, peering at me from a pile of
hay, I almost spoke. But a black, gnarled finger was pressed to
non-existent lips, and the words died in my throat. The face
curled up like strips of bark, and a long, wide crack of a smile
greeted my silence. The thing vanished a moment later. It hadn't
gone far.

I could hear them, now. They were creeping through the raft-
ers, and slithering along the walls, watching Sepesh stab the hay.
And they watched me as well, with eyes as black as pitch, for
all that they were hideously alive.

The smell of them – like a forest after a torrential downpour –
nearly overwhelmed me. They did not attack, but merely watched.

An attentive, silent audience. I hardly dared to move. Were they here for me again, to finish what they'd started in the mill?

One of them dropped silently to the loft and rose, marionette-like, behind Sepesh. As I watched, frozen, it mimicked her movements, much to the apparent amusement of its fellows. But so silently, so swiftly, that she didn't notice the shadow play going on a handbreadth away.

'Sepesh,' I said. I drew my knife slowly.

The word echoed more loudly than I expected. Even as it left my mouth, the treekin were gone. I looked around, but saw not even the slightest hint of their presence. They'd vanished utterly. I let out a slow breath.

'What?' Sepesh said, her frustration evident.

'I don't think there's anything up here.' I didn't think it wise to mention what I'd seen, not least because I wasn't sure the treekin wouldn't use it as an excuse to kill us both. 'Maybe it was just a chicken. Or an eel.'

Sepesh crouched at the edge of the loft and looked down. She frowned. 'Maybe.' She peered over her shoulder. 'I was certain someone was up here, though.'

'If they were, they're not here now,' I said as I descended the ladder. Sepesh followed a moment later. The barn felt different to how it had before. As if it were truly empty, now. I reckoned the treekin were gone. But I had no intention of testing that theory.

We left the barn. It was still raining, but with less intensity. In its place, the wind rushed down through the trees and stirred the corn. It reminded me of a voice I'd heard in my dreams, calling out from a great distance. I glanced back at the barn, and saw something pale watching us from the dark square of the doors. A gnarled taproot claw gestured to the farmhouse. The thing was gone a moment later.

'We should be getting back.' Sepesh started towards the coach. 'I'll take you back to the inn.'

'I can make my own way back But in the morning. I'm staying here tonight.'

She hesitated. Then she nodded slowly, her suspicion evident.
'I'll leave you to it, then But heed me... If Murn shows up, I
want to know about it. You understand?'

I gave a lazy salute. 'We're on the same side, sheriff.'

She swung herself up into the coach 'See that you remember
that, or it'll go badly for you.'

'Of that I have no doubt.'

The driver snapped the reins and the coach clattered out of
the yard. I watched it depart with a sense of relief. Murn had
wanted me here, that much was evident. I glanced back at the
barn, but the sylvaneth were gone. I wondered what part they
were playing in this. Maybe they were just observers.

I watched the chickens hunt mice.

'What have you got yourself into, Evrek? And why ask me to
get you out of it?'

There was no answer, save the soft whisper of rain

CHAPTER NINETEEN

MURN

I didn't often dream.

Or, rather, I had the same dream to the exclusion of all others. In it, I stood again in that ruined chapel, my nostrils full of smoke. I heard Osmal and Murn, Feyros and the others as they fought and the screams of those who were burning in their cages of iron and gold. Censers swung, filling the air with pungent incense, as the faithful, in their blue robes, turned towards us, their golden masks set in eternal scowls.

'Have you come to offer up your soul to him?' one asked. I recognised Arch Lector Cassian's voice. 'The war awaits. Sigmar calls.'

He always asked the same question. And as always, my answer was the same. I lifted my hammer and charged. Lightning flashed overhead, drawing up the shadows and illuminating the scene starkly. They came for me then and I fought. All of us fought.

But slowly, so slowly. Too slow to save those who were burning. Too slow to do anything but avenge them.

Blue-robed bodies dropped with every swing of my hammer. Golden masks crumpled and censers rolled forgotten across the cracked floor. Masks fell away, and I recognised the faces behind them. Men and women, officers and nobles, true Sigmarites all. So true that they'd decided to offer up as many souls to the God-King as possible. Worthy souls, fit to be remade in his image. That was what Cassian had claimed.

I swung the hammer until my arms were heavy and my heart raged in my chest. Rain fell in dark sheets through the broken roof. Screams echoed as greasy trails of smoke coagulated on the air. They called out the name of my god as they fought, and so did I. But they were false, and I was true. At least that was what I'd thought, in that moment. Later, I realised Sigmar had been listening. Just not to me.

Thunder rumbled. A god's roar.

Lightning split the sky.

And then I woke up. I always woke up at the same moment. Just before it all went wrong. I didn't know whether to be grateful to my subconscious, or annoyed.

Blearily, I looked around. For a moment I didn't know where I was. The air tasted of smoke, and I realised the fire I'd kindled in the hearth had died down to a red edge. I sat up carefully, my back and hips protesting. I'd fallen asleep at the table. The sun was a dull slash of grey-green on the horizon and the rain had slowed to a drizzle.

Several of the books I'd found in Murn's room sat on the table, open at various pages. Nothing in them was helpful. Some were volumes of herbology or traveller's guides to places I'd never heard of before, like Mhurghast. Others were various histories of the cantons of the Greywater Reach. Wald was barely mentioned in any of them. It had never been big. The swamps in this area had been home to a number of backwater clans – the sorts of people who'd survived by being unnoticed. Or because they'd had help.

Humans and treekin had an uneasy relationship at the best of times. Out here, it hadn't been the best of times for centuries. Greywater Fastness was a sore point – a tumour of iron and fire, grown in the green body of Ghyran. The treekin had done their best to excise it, more than once. They'd failed.

Elsewhere, however, they'd been more successful. Dozens of towns and camps had vanished overnight, almost a century ago, leaving the Fastness isolated and alone. Wald was one of the few surviving communities, and most historians put it down to the descendants of those original clans knowing how to appease the mercurial treekin. What form that propitiation took was vague – rumours and innuendo.

I was good at reading between the lines. Between what was in the books, and what I'd learned, I reasoned the treekin weren't protecting Wald so much as what the town was built on, or near.

Cassian had taught me many things. One of those lessons had been that you had to be careful, in places such as this – there was an order to things that couldn't be ignored or disrupted. The church had tried to do so early on – lectors and missionaries sent abroad in the realms, to bring the light of heaven to the faithful. They'd built shrines where none had been before – or worse, built over ones that already existed. Sigmar wasn't the only god, but some among the faithful thought he was the only one worth the name. And it wasn't only Sigmarites who thought that way. Nothing but trouble came of that sort of thinking, though. I knew that from hard experience.

I groaned and stretched. As if in reply, there was a clatter from the larder, and I realised what had woken me. I stood, quickly but quietly. The larder door was open, and stood between me and whoever was rifling through Murn's stocks. My hand fell to my knife. As I reached for it, however, the door was jerked closed, revealing a levelled pistol.

Murn looked older than I remembered. He was still tall, and built strong – a soldier's build. But age had worn him down. His pale hair was thinning, and his face was grizzled and seamed. He wore homespun clothes and heavy boots. Bracers of leather protected his forearms. His clothes were stained, and the scrum of beard on his face spoke of rough living. The pistol he held was single-shot, and of good quality, though an antique.

'Evrek,' I said, my hand frozen just shy of my knife.

'It's been a long time,' Murn said. The pistol didn't waver. 'Sit down, would you?'

I backed up and sat down. Murn circled the table and sat down opposite me.

'Well, now. I was wondering if you would wake up. You always were a sound sleeper.'

'I sleep the sleep of the just.'

Murn laughed. 'You never believed that, even when you were a priest.'

'True.'

'What are you calling yourself these days?'

'Blackwood. Harran Blackwood.'

'Blackwood?'

'I thought it sounded good.' I shrugged. 'How did you find me, Evrek? I haven't heard from you since you tried to kill me.'

'It took some doing.' He didn't elaborate.

I leaned back. 'Who else knows?'

'No one.' Murn frowned. 'I always figured that you wanted me to kill you, that day. That's why you didn't fight back.'

'I was drunk.'

Murn shook his head. 'I've seen you fight drunk. You could have stopped me. You didn't. You wanted me to kill you.'

'So why didn't you?' It came out like an accusation.

Murn looked away first, but he didn't lower the pistol. 'You came alone?'

'Who would I have come with?'

'Good point.'

'Why am I here, Evrek?' I said, watching him. I wondered whether I could get my knife into him before he pulled the trigger. 'So you can kill me?'

'No.' The gheist echoed Murn. She stood behind him, staring at me. I didn't like the way she looked at me. 'Why would you think that?' He sounded insulted.

'You seem to have done well for yourself.' I looked around. 'A wife, a daughter… a farm.' I smiled. 'Never figured you for the marrying kind. Or the farming kind.'

It was a cruel thing to say, and it showed in his face. The pistol twitched and I knew he wanted to shoot me. But he didn't.

'I'm neither, now.'

'My condolences.'

His expression didn't change. 'I wouldn't be here now if it hadn't been for you.'

'You didn't have to come with me that night, Evrek'

'Of course I did.' He bowed his head. 'And I'd do it again. It was the right thing to do.' He leaned back in his seat. All the anger seemed to have drained out of him and he looked exhausted. I wondered when he'd slept last.

'Why did you send the coin?' I asked. 'Why call me here, only to greet me with a loaded pistol? Why the runaround?' I paused. 'Did you really try to kill Lord Wald?'

'I did. And next time I'll finish the job,' he said. 'And as to the runaround… because I wasn't sure it was you. I didn't know whether you'd actually come.'

'Well, I did. Now set the pistol down and we'll talk'

Murn licked his lips. He looked tired. Hungry. A man on the run. The little gheist clung to Murn, and he shuddered slightly.

He didn't know she was there, but I knew he could feel her. He probably thought it was a draught, or nerves. I wondered how she'd died. From the look of her, I thought I knew the answer to that. If I was right, it also explained why Murn had tried to kill Lord Wald. Murn plucked at his bracer, and I saw a flash of ink.

'New tattoo?' I asked.

His eyes flicked down, and then up. 'Things got bad, before they got better.'

'How long were you in Ironhole?'

He paused. 'Long enough.'

'Is that how you ended up here? Did you come in on one of those barges people keep talking about?'

He shook his head. 'Not exactly. It doesn't matter. The barges – it's good you know about them. They're why I asked you here.' His expression became pleading. 'I need your help, Harran. It's all happening again.'

The gheist was crawling on the ceiling now, moving in skittering circles, like an insect caught by the light. She hissed at me, and stiffened abruptly. Outside, the corn rustled in the breeze. The chickens began to squawk.

Murn rose from his seat, eyes wide. 'You said you came alone,' he spat accusingly.

'I did.' I saw a shape flash past the window. I wondered if Sepesh had come back. If she had, she couldn't have picked a worse time.

Murn spoke quickly. 'They're here. You have to go. Don't let them catch you.' He turned as if to flee. I caught him by the arm.

'Who's here? What's going on, Evrek?' I dragged Murn around to face me. 'I can't help you if you don't tell me what's going on.' I had my knife half-drawn. I wouldn't get a better chance.

But I didn't. I couldn't. Something in his eyes stopped me. Maybe I had never really intended to do it. Maybe, faced with the point of no return, I found that I was still too much of the man I had been. Or maybe it was something else.

The moment came and went. Murn shoved me back. Surprised, I fell against the table, upending it.

'The fireplace, Harran,' he said, in a rush. 'Check the fireplace.' Then he darted for the back door.

I scrambled to my feet and gave chase. 'Evrek – wait! *Wait*, damn you!'

I heard the door thud behind me – someone was trying to get in. I ignored it and raced out to the field behind the house. The corn stalks hissed, swaying. I followed the motion. Something – someone – moved swiftly away from me, down into the corn.

I couldn't let Murn get away. Not now. Even if I had no idea what was going to happen when I caught up with him. I leapt down the muddy incline and plunged into the greenery. Water lapped at the bottoms of the stalks and slapped at my knees as I splashed through the rows. The stalks moved and shifted around me, as if guiding me in my pursuit. More than once, I slowed, thinking I'd seen something out of the corner of my eye. But it was only the stalks, twitching in the breeze.

Murn was making no attempt to hide his presence as he crashed through the rows, heading towards the heart of the field. I knew, somehow, that he was heading for the ruin there. I followed, shoving through the corn. Behind me I heard muffled shouts.

Instinct prompted me to slow as the ruin came fully into view. It sat on a hummock of raised earth, just above the waterline. No hint of what it had once been remained, for it was crumbled and overgrown now. Stone walls loomed amid a shroud of greenery and the archway of what had possibly once been a gate. A domed tower had collapsed in on itself, and its jade remains spilled across the paved ground beyond the archway.

Crows took flight from the walls as I emerged from the corn and hauled myself up onto the hummock. Their harsh cries

sounded almost like laughter. I moved towards the archway,
straining to hear. But the only sound was the hiss of the corn,
and the distant croaking of frogs. There was no sign of Murn.

Beyond the archway, the ruin was smaller than it had first
appeared. I wondered if it had been a chapel, once. A place of
worship, for whoever had built it. But whatever it had once been,
it was something else now.

Water dripped from fallen timbers, and ran in thin rivulets
across the cracked stones. There had been a fire here at some
point. Thick vines of swamp-ivy hung down the walls and a
shroud of greyish moss obscured the walltops. Bulbous mush-
rooms clumped in the corners or thrust up through the cracks
in the stone floor.

The remains of a cistern occupied the centre of the ruin, its
bronze lid turned emerald from verdigris. Corn-husk sigils in the
shape of an antlered head had been strung from the rim, all connected by a chain of woven vines. Ivy strangled the stone base,
and water stains streaked the parts of it that were still visible.
Golden grotesques wrought in the shape of a woman's face decorated the sides of the cistern. They peered at me through the
curtains of ivy, each face bearing a slightly different expression –
amusement, sadness... wrath.

'The Lady of Leaves,' a voice said from behind me.

I whirled. A wind kicked up, and the corn rippled like waves
of green water. I heard the ivy stir behind me, and tensed. Crows
hurtled upwards.

'She is here, even now, though this place is no longer hers.'
The voice echoed through the ruin. I recognised it now.

'Fulder.'

'Yes.'

I turned. He stood in the archway, wearing a half-mask made
from corn-husks, moss and vines, with two great antlers curling above his head. He was stripped to the waist, his weathered

frame marked with curling, bramble-like tattoos. He held a small
sickle in one hand, and flicked it out, chopping through a nearby
corn stalk.

As if that had been a signal, more of them appeared, standing in the corn, surrounding the ruin. They bore no weapons,
but they were all wearing similar masks. A dozen of them that
I could see. Perhaps more that I couldn't.

'You shouldn't be here,' Fulder said. 'This place isn't for such
as you.'

'No. I suppose not.' I raised my hands. 'What is this place?
A temple?'

'Once. Before the forces of Azyr came, with their talk of star-
light and iron. But when have the cold stars ever cared about
the doings of men?' The old man scraped the sickle across the
stones of the wall, as if to sharpen it. 'We live here, on this
land. We are born here, we bleed here and we die here, prey
for the Huntsman. The Old Stag is the only god that matters
to us, and we know that we matter to him. He needs us, and
we need him.'

'In the same way cattle need a farmer.'

Fulder shrugged. 'We eat of the land and the land eats of us,
and that's the way it's been since the first of us set foot here.
It's a fair enough bargain, the way we see it.'

'Better than the alternative, you mean.' I turned slightly. The
others were drawing closer now. Closing in on me. They sounded
as if they were singing softly under their breaths, though the
masks made it hard to tell.

I could hear something else, as well. The same sound I'd
heard in the barn. The corn swayed, as if unseen shapes moved
through it. I saw something creep past a gap in the wall on four
legs. The hounds of the Huntsman.

That was what they were, these twisted sylvaneth. The others might serve the Everqueen, but these had a bloodier master.

They were the hunting dogs of Kurnoth. As much as – or more so than – Fulder and his lot.

'They flooded us,' Fulder said. 'Drowned us and dragged us down. A hundred. Two hundred. Drops in the bucket, in those early days when the Lady of Leaves made war on Greywater Fastness.' He gestured with his sickle. 'My grandfather told me about it – he'd been just a child, then, but he'd seen the waters rise, and the swamp heave, and he heard the ground crack and twist, swallowing the lumber mills and the camps. The dark water getting higher and higher, people climbing onto their roofs, praying for help – begging, pleading...'

'But there was no help,' I said.

'There was help. But not from her. Someone heard us. Not who we thought. We had forgotten him, left him in the dark. But he heard us then, and answered.'

'Kurnoth,' I said. Outside, the sylvaneth set up a howl.

Fulder paused. 'You aren't fit to say that name.'

'Maybe not. But I said it anyway.'

'That is the least of your sins. Where's the traitor? Where's Murn?'

'Good question. Where is he?'

Fulder gave me a basilisk stare. 'I have no patience for games, city man. Tell me what I want to know, or I'll offer your heart up to the Huntsman myself.'

'You can try.'

Fulder grunted. 'Have it your way. Buell.'

I heard them before I saw them. Buell was clad like the others. But unlike them, he bore a truncheon, and swung it with brute efficiency. 'Now you'll pay,' he snarled. I caught the blow on my shoulder and fell back, against the wall.

Another blow struck me in the small of the back. I staggered, and a third blow turned me around. I swung wild, catching a man on the jaw and dropping him. Buell roared and swung at me again. I went for my knife.

Fists thudded into my side, and against my head, but I took them and struck out in return. The shrine was small and they fell over each other in the mud, shouting and cursing. I stomped on hands, and kicked heads. I whipped my knife out and Buell screamed. I saw him stagger back, clutching at his arm.

I took the opening. I turned and dived towards Fulder. He back-pedalled, his eyes widening in his mask. I tackled him – hard – and we went through the crumbling wall in a cloud of dust and stones. He gasped in pain as we rolled down into the corn. He lay, wheezing, as I staggered to my feet. The old man had absorbed the brunt of the impact, but I'd taken my share of bruises.

I kicked Fulder in the head as I stepped over him, breaking his antlers. I heard shouts, but I was fairly certain I could lose them in the corn. I doubted they'd follow me. After all, they knew where I lived.

The sylvaneth, on the other hand, had no reservations. As I ran, they gave chase – barely glimpsed, doglike shapes racing through the corn to either side of me. They made no sound, save the slap of stalks against shaggy limbs of bark and vine.

I headed for the farm. If I could get inside – barricade myself – I might stand a chance. Out in the open, I was as good as dead. My breath burned in my lungs as I ran.

A dog-shape burst from the stalks, lunging for me. The impact knocked me sprawling into the water. Jaws snapped for my throat. I stabbed the shape with my knife, hacking at the vines of its neck. It whipped away from me with a screech, and I didn't wait to see where it went. I struggled to my feet. The farm was in sight.

Teeth sank into my boot as I made to scramble up the incline. I clawed at the wet earth as it tried to drag me back into the corn. Cursing, I rolled onto my back and kicked it in the head. Wood cracked and it released me. I scrambled up the slope and flung myself towards the house.

I stopped just before the door, and turned. The dog-things crouched at the edge of the field, mossy tongues lolling. They whined and hissed as they paced back and forth. Something prevented them from coming any closer. I thought of the symbols I'd seen, cut into the hearth, and almost laughed. The shrine might have been dedicated to a new god, but not Murn's farm.

But while the sigils might have stopped the sylvaneth, I knew they'd have no effect on Fulder and his crew. I heard them closing in as I slammed the door and bolted it. It wouldn't hold for long. As I ran, I cast a glance at the hearth. But there was no time to stop.

One of them was waiting for me at the front door. As I opened it, he lunged for me with a corn-knife. I avoided the blow and responded in kind. I left him with his guts spilling onto the ground.

His screams – and the frustrated howls of the sylvaneth – followed me all the way back to the road.

CHAPTER TWENTY

THE SHAPE OF IT

'So they just... let you go?' Gint said.

I shrugged. 'They weren't after me. They wanted Murn.'

We'd retired to our room, after I'd made it back to town, soaked to the bone, aching and footsore. I'd wanted somewhere out of sight to think. Gint had come because he was nosy or bored, or both. Now he sat on his pallet, playing cards against himself, while I tried to figure out what I was going to do.

'How do you think they found you?'

'Fulder,' I said, scanning the street below. I'd sent off a message with Scopa, the pickpocket, earlier. Now I was waiting to hear back from Pender. If he could do what I asked, I'd have my next move. If not, I'd need to come up with another plan.

'Fulder. The old man?'

'That's the one. He's the local hetman. Or high priest, maybe.'

'Sometimes, it's the same thing,' Gint said.

I grunted. Maybe I could just leave. I could buy passage on a barge, get back to the main road. A few days of travel would take me to another canton. From there, I could arrange transport to Headwater Breach or even back to the city.

Even as I thought about it, I knew I wouldn't. I was in too deep now. Angry and curious in equal measure. I wanted to talk to Murn. I wanted to find out what was going on in this shitty town that stank of blood and death.

'Think he was acting on behalf of his lordship?'

'Maybe.' I thought about Buell. Would the big guard have been there without his lordship's approval – or Sepesh's for that matter? That didn't surprise me. I couldn't imagine a group like Fulder's existing without tacit approval from Lord Wald. 'Maybe he just decided to kill two birds with one stone.'

'So what did he say?' Gint asked. 'Murn, I mean.'

'Nothing much.' I stared out the window. There were lights in the streets. Something was going on. 'They interrupted us before he could tell me anything of substance.'

'Convenient.'

'Not really.' I turned to him. 'What's going on out there?'

'The barges are arriving soon. Or so I hear.' He was laying his cards down, one atop the next, all in a line. 'People line up on the quays to cheer as they come through this part of town.'

'Where do they go from here?'

Gint looked up. 'Apparently there's a quay out in the swamp, near where the old lumber mills were. They unload the barges and take the prisoners the rest of the way via skiff. Some are brought into town, others to the manor – and the rest...' He shrugged.

'What happens to the ones brought into town?'

'They work. Repairing bridges and paths, mostly.'

'And the manor?'

'I think we both know the answer to that.'

I thought about a man without a tongue, sewn into a bramble-horn skin. 'And the rest? What happens to them?'

'No idea.' He didn't look at me as he said it. He was either lying – or he had a theory.

'How did you find all this out?'

Gint scratched his chin. 'Amazing what people will tell you when they think they're winning.' He grinned. He shuffled his cards back into the deck and stood. 'Speaking of which, I have a game to get to. Will you be all right?'

'Why wouldn't I be?'

Gint smiled. 'No reason that I can think of. Other than your habit of getting jumped by people you've annoyed.'

'Get out of here before I shove those cards down your throat,' I said. He laughed and departed, leaving me alone with my thoughts. Not a place I enjoyed being.

I watched the rain pelt the window.

I was cold, more so than normal. After Aqshy, I had trouble with the cold. It never got this wet in the city. Too many roof-tops to catch the rain, too much heat billowing from the forges and bakeries.

The rain reminded me of being on campaign, of marching through the ruins of Greenglades. It had rained there as well. A hot rain, though. Sweltering. Rain so as to boil a man in his own skin. Not like this.

I thought about the last time I'd seen Murn. In the days after, before any of us realised the full implications of what we had done – not just spiritually, but legally. I had been confined to the local temple, as my superiors tried to learn the truth of the matter. The reverberations of the deed had echoed through the corridors of the church, not just in Hammerhal, but beyond – to Azyrheim itself. Or so I'd been told.

I'd killed an Arch Lector. I'd killed prominent people. It had happened before, but the accusations I'd made... the evidence...

Even the Order of Azyr couldn't hide it all. People started to whisper. And those whispers spread.

The others quit the regiment – or simply deserted – over the next few months. But Murn had come to see me. I'd been praying, I think. Seeking answers in the stars.

Sometimes I think Murn intended to free me that day. He'd always had a soft heart – and a soft head – when it came to that sort of thing. Killing me would have been a mercy, given what happened after. They'd questioned me for what felt like years, but had only been days. The light from the Lord-Veritant's lantern, eating away at my will like acid.

I remembered the scrape of his war-plate and the smell of him – like rainwater and melting snow. I remembered the look in his eyes. Stormcasts don't have human eyes, not really. Their eyes are windows to the eternal storm, and when I looked into them I knew that I had defied a god.

Worse, I had disappointed one.

My hands convulsed into fists. I pushed the memories back down, forcing them into a red box at the centre of my mind. The past was done. All that mattered was the here and now.

I didn't know what I was going to do if I saw Murn again. I didn't even know why I was still here. Leaving was the smart play. There was nothing for me here.

Oh, but there is. And you have its scent.

The voice seemed to echo through the room. I turned. There was another antler sigil on the table. I didn't know where they were coming from. They might all be the same one, as far as I could tell. I didn't pick it up.

You're on the trail now, and you can't stop. You have to see it through to the end, just like you did before.

I heard the thud of hooves from above, as if something were creeping across the roof. My mouth was dry, and my head echoed painfully with the drumbeat of those damned hooves.

Like it or not, you're a hunter, Harran. You catch a scent and you pursue your prey until you run them down.

It was in the room with me now. Something impossibly big, somehow squeezed into such a small space. It stank of rotting meat and animal musk. Teeth like square blades clicked as it spoke.

That's why I chose you, Harran. That's why I want you to find me.

It moved, the floorboards bending and whining beneath its weight. Its stink filled my nose and mouth as a ragged mass circled me, always just out of sight.

Do you remember your dream, Harran? The way she cut and cut and cut, until there seemed no end to the pain. And then a sleep of ages, in the soft, wet loam.

But I am awake now.

And I will have my due.

'Not me,' I said.

There was an animal snort, though whether it indicated amusement or frustration, I couldn't say and didn't care. I went for the door. It didn't stop me. Maybe it couldn't, in the same way it couldn't catch me on the bridge. I knew enough about gods to know that they wanted you to come to them. If they were hunters, they were the sort who sat waiting in trees, or weaving wide webs. Patient and eternal. It didn't make it any less bothersome to consider.

I could breathe easy in the corridor. The animal musk was there, but faint. It hung over the town, like the miasma of rot and swamp. I listened at the door, but heard nothing. I imagined it there, pressed to the other side, eyes narrowed, great teeth bared. A great black stag, all hunkered up and listening to me, listening to it.

I laughed, but shakily. I needed a drink. Something to wash my mouth out.

I made my way down to the common room. I wasn't surprised
to see that Pender was already waiting on me, at a table in the
corner. He looked nervous. I didn't blame him.

'You took your time,' he said, as I joined him.

'You work quick. Did you find them?'

'I did.' He reached into his furs and produced a battered notebook. A little leather field-journal, like officers carried. He pulled
it back out of my reach. 'It's full of sketches. Why do you want
it?'

'I don't know. Murn told me where it was.'

He frowned. 'You saw him, then?'

'I think you know damn well that I did. I think you set it up,
on his behalf. How long have you been helping him?'

'Quiet,' Pender growled. He looked around. 'We shouldn't have
met here. Too many ears listening, too many eyes looking.' I followed his gaze, but no one seemed to be paying us any undue
attention. The room wasn't crowded, and most of the patrons
were occupied with their drinks. I wondered how many of them –
if any – had been at the farm.

'It's as safe as your little meeting place near the palisades.
Sepesh knew all about that, by the way. Answer my question.'

He cursed. 'Murn's... a friend.'

'He has a lot of friends, it seems.'

'Including you.'

'I'm not feeling very friendly at the moment. Do you know
why he wants me to have that thing?' I gestured to the notebook.

Pender shook his head. 'No. And I don't care. I got problems
of my own.' He looked up as someone came in. 'And there's the
biggest one now.' I didn't have to ask who he meant. The way
the common room fell silent told me all I needed to know.

'Give us some privacy,' I murmured. He beat a hasty retreat.
I tried to concentrate on my drink as the newcomer approached
my table.

'Was that Pender I just saw?' Sepesh said, as she took his chair and spun it around, seating herself opposite me.

'Is that his name?'

'Funny. Your sense of humour is going to get you in trouble, if you're not careful. Speaking of which... what was all that this morning?'

'Nothing I couldn't handle,' I said.

'You left a dead man on the front porch of Murn's farm.'

'Did he die, then?' I shook my head. 'How sad.'

Sepesh smiled. 'Not really. Plenty more peasants where he came from.' She looked around the room as she said it, and I heard chairs scrape back as people tried to avoid her gaze. 'That's two murders you've committed since you arrived, by the way.'

'I'm glad someone is keeping track. What do you want?'

'To say thank you.'

'I didn't do anything.'

'Way I heard it, you flushed out our quarry.'

'And who told you that?' I leaned forward. 'How's Fulder, by the way? He took a nasty spill. I hope I didn't hurt him too badly.'

'You mean when you tackled him? Or when you kicked him in the head?'

'Either,' I said. 'What about Buell? I cut him good, I think.'

Sepesh's smile took on a sour tinge. 'You know, you could say thank you. If not for me riding herd on him, Buell would have already come after you. He holds a grudge something fierce.'

'We have that in common.'

She snorted. 'I've put men on the house. They'll watch it. If Murn comes back, they'll have him.' She frowned. 'I was wrong. We should have checked more closely.'

'Murn's audacious,' I said. 'Always has been.'

'What did he say to you, anyway?'

'Nothing about why he might've tried to kill Lord Wald, if that's what you're wondering.'

'I wasn't. Where did he go?'

'No idea. I was a bit distracted by the lunatics in corn-masks trying to kill me.' I paused. 'You should really keep a tighter leash on your hunting dogs, Sepesh. They're liable to hurt themselves if you let them run free like that.'

'I'll pass that along to his lordship, shall I?' She leaned over the back of the chair. 'Anyway, I've come with an offer. His lordship is looking for men. Strong sword-arms are lacking out here. Fishermen make lousy soldiers – as you've just pointed out.'

I didn't look up from my drink. 'And does he need soldiers, then?'

'Every lord does.'

'I don't carry a sword, and his lordship already hired me, remember?'

'You earned your money. Murn will be caught soon enough.'

'You sound confident.'

'Maybe I am.' Sepesh leaned close and eased my drink out of my hand. 'There's good money in it.' I looked at her and she took a swallow of my drink. 'Better than you can earn breaking legs in the Fastness. His lordship thinks you have potential.'

'I'm not looking for work at the moment.'

Sepesh set the drink down and smiled. It didn't reach her eyes. 'You should start. We don't care for vagrants around here.'

I knew a threat when I heard one, even if she was smiling as she said it. 'I'm not a vagrant. I have a room. I have money, thanks to his lordship. I'm practically a man of means. And I don't take kindly to threats.'

'No. I don't suppose you do. Then, neither does his lordship. Best you remember that, Harran.' She tipped my drink over with a flick of her finger, and we watched it splash to the floor. Then she stood and threw a coin on the table. 'For the drink.'

Pender came over to join me as soon as she'd swaggered out. 'Think she knows?'

'That's my problem. Now – give it to me.'

He proffered the notebook and I snatched it away. He looked around. 'There was something funny about that place.'

'There's something funny about this whole damn town. Did anyone see you?'

He shook his head. 'No. I made sure.'

'The sheriff mentioned that she put men all around it.'

He grinned. 'They decided to look the other way.' He rubbed his fingers together. 'Speaking of which... you owe me.'

I fished some coins out of my coat and set them down. Before he could grab them, I said, 'You're certain no one saw you?'

'If they did, I certainly didn't see them.'

'That is not a comforting statement, Pender.'

He sat back. 'You either trust me, or you don't. Besides, nobody cares now. As far as the guards are concerned, I was claiming the money Murn owed me.'

'And did you?'

He gave another grin. 'With interest.' He looked at the note-book. 'So how are sketches supposed to help anybody?'

'Depends on what they're of.' I opened the notebook. Murn had always been a better than decent artist. Rather than drawing a map, he'd sketched landmarks with a char-pencil. I recognised some of them – places around the canton, including Lord Wald's manor. Others were less familiar. I saw stockades, where figures sat in obvious misery; work-gangs toiling in the waters; proces-sions of riders, sketched from a safe distance.

The drawings weren't random. Murn wasn't the sort to waste time on idle fancies. If he'd bothered to sketch them, they were important.

'I recognise some of these places, but others...' I stopped.

One of the drawings was of a prison barge, resting alongside a crumbling quay. Obviously sketched from a point close by.

'The prison barges are arriving today, aren't they?' I asked.

'Three of them. One from the Fastness, even.'

I showed him the sketch. 'Do you know where this is?'

He shook his head. 'I don't go out in the swamp if I can help it.'

'Doesn't matter. I know who to ask.' I flipped over the page and froze. A black shape, silhouetted against the trees, stared up at me from the paper. Antlers stretched across the page's width, and the animal's bulk was obvious and unnatural.

I snapped the notebook closed and rose to my feet. I pushed the coin Sepesh had left towards Pender as I stood. 'Have a drink on me.'

He snatched it up. 'Don't mind if I do.'

I left, taking a moment to make sure I wasn't followed. Sepesh didn't strike me as being that subtle, but it only cost me a few moments to be sure. I thought about her offer as I strode through the rain.

Something had them worried. Not just Murn. They were worried about me, for reasons I couldn't fathom. I wondered if it had something to do with the Old Stag marking me, as Fulder had called it, whatever that meant. Between what I'd experienced since arriving, and my dreams, I knew that whatever supposedly slept in the Huntsman's Bower had its attentions fixed on me for reasons I couldn't understand.

Oh but you do, though, don't you, Harran? You understand better than you admit.

I stopped. I knew it was foolish, but I was tired and getting angry. 'Understand what?' I growled. 'What do you want?'

Silence. I looked around, to see if anyone had noticed. The street was empty, save for me and the rain. I could hear music, though. And a noise like beasts howling. But I knew the sound came from human mouths.

The third day of celebration is always a bit fraught. They know what is coming, and grow ecstatic. Like hounds on the scent.

'Who are you?'

You keep asking that question. You know who I am. You know what I want. Deny it all you like, but I will still be here, waiting, when you finally find your courage.

'My courage,' I spat. 'You're the one hiding in my head.'

I'm not hiding. I'm waiting. Sooner or later, we'll meet face-to-face, little priest. A man and his god. That'll be a fine time, and no doubt.

'I'm not a priest. And you're no god.'

But you could be. And so could I. All it takes is a bit of blood and bone. A pause, and an animal snuffle, like some great beast making itself comfortable in its surroundings. *I can wait, as I said.*

'Good. Keep waiting.'

There was no reply. I felt sick and went to a rain barrel, looking to splash water on my face. But there was no water to be had – just bones. I looked up, and let the rain cover me. Just for a moment. Just enough to feel clean.

I found Deshler near the quay, at her berth. She was loading up her skiff with supplies. I coughed and she looked up.

'Well. You look a sight.'

'Where's this?' I asked, holding up the sketch of the barge. Deshler frowned.

'Where'd you get that?'

'Answer the question.'

She squinted at the drawing. 'Out where the old lumber mills are, by the looks of it.'

'You can take me there.'

Deshler straightened. 'Maybe. Why should I?'

I pulled out a handful of coins from Lord Wald's retainer.

She frowned. 'Double it, and you've got a deal.'

'Fine. Half now, half when we get back.'

She grimaced, but nodded. I dropped the coins into her palm. 'You're lucky you caught me between trips,' she told me.

'Almost as if it's meant to be. When can we leave?'

Deshler looked around. 'Now, if you like.'

I paused. The crowds along the quay gave voice to a blood-thirsty ululation. To my ears, it sounded like the call of some monstrous stag.

'Yeah,' I said. 'Now's good.'

CHAPTER TWENTY-ONE

PRISON BARGES

The sky was a wash of greys and blacks when we set out. The sun reminded me of a candle hidden behind a shroud as it sank towards the treeline. Clouds rolled in, and the rain pelted in fits and starts.

'Bad day for a celebration,' I said, as we left the town behind.

'No such thing around here,' Deshler said. 'Word is you saw Murn.'

'Word gets around quick, here.'

'I keep my ears open.'

'Not well enough, apparently. You still haven't earned your coin.'

She looked at me. 'My bad luck, I guess.' She peered into the rising murk. I could hear the hunting trill of the eels as they prowled the shallows. 'Eels are out early. Bad omen.'

'Is it?' I said. I felt an itch between my shoulder blades. Our passage was not unobserved. But I saw no pale faces in knot-holes or vague doglike shapes in the undergrowth. Only the trees and the water, and the mist covering it all. That only made it worse. I shivered in my damp clothes.

'Cold?' Deshler asked.

'I feel like I'm never going to get warm again.'

'The sun doesn't shine down here,' Deshler said. 'The moon doesn't gleam beneath these black trees. The only light is under the water, and what we make.'

'Poetic.'

She sniffed. 'It was, actually. Not by me, though.'

'I've never been much for poetry,' I said. 'How long have you known Murn?'

She didn't answer.

'You met in Ironhole,' I continued. I tapped my arm. 'I saw the tattoo on Murn's arm. Just like yours. He must have run into trouble since I last saw him.'

Deshler looked away. 'Aye. I met him there.' She spat over the side. 'He kept me breathing, when he had no reason to worry about an old woman. Then, that was him.'

'Yes,' I said. 'Tell me about him.'

'Aren't you his friend?'

'I don't think we were ever friends. Just on the same side. Tell me about him.'

'Why?'

'Because I'm trying to decide whether or not to kill him.'

She peered at me. 'That's a lousy sense of humour you got.'

'So I've been told. But I'm not joking.' I folded back the edge of my coat and tapped the pommel of my knife. 'See, I came to kill him. He knows things he shouldn't know. But I'm starting to think that was just an excuse on my part.'

'Yeah?'

I nodded, and looked out over the water. 'Maybe. Or maybe

I mean what I say. Maybe the only reason I didn't stick this knife into him last time was because I missed the chance. You understand?'

'Yeah,' she said, lifting her pole like a club. She almost caught me with it, but I'd been half-expecting her to pull something similar since we'd met. I caught the blow on my palm and shoved her over the side. Then I sat back down and waited. She surfaced, spluttering in indignation. She reached for the skiff and I jabbed her with the pole.

'Not yet,' I said. Trilling filtered through the air. I whistled in reply. 'Listen to them.'

'Let me back on the skiff, damn you,' she said, splashing frantically.

'First, tell me how long you've been Murn's eyes and ears in town.'

'What?'

I jabbed her with the pole again. 'Did I stutter?'

'No! No, godsdamnit! For years,' she spat. The trills were louder now, and she looked around, eyes wide. 'Let me back up on the skiff, Blackwood, please...'

'In a moment. Why did Murn bring me here?'

'I don't know!'

'I'm no expert on eels, but they sound hungry to me. What about you?'

'Blackwood!' Panic was etched across her lined features. 'Please!'

'Just answer the question.' I could see a spotted, snake-like form slithering closer through the dark waters. I tightened my grip on the pole. I'd have to be quick. 'And I'd be quick about it, if I were you.'

'He needs help,' she shouted, grabbing for the skiff. 'Damn you, he needs help. He said you faced a god before and survived. He said... he said you were the only one who might be able to stop whatever is happening out there!'

'And why would I do that?'

She stared up at me in incomprehension. Before she could answer, the eel shot towards her. I thrust the pole down like a spear, punching it in the side of the head. It whipsawed away, shrieking. More closed in.

'Why the runaround, then?' I demanded. 'Just to piss me off?'

'We had to be sure it was you!' she gasped. 'He hasn't seen you in years.'

'Good enough.' I extended the pole towards her. She caught it gratefully and I dragged her aboard, just as a second eel made its run. It tried to follow her onto the skiff, and I belted it with the pole. The hardened wood bent and flexed in my grip as I sent the eel tumbling into the water, its skull cracked open.

Deshler was on her feet in moments, a knife in her hand. I swung the pole around and held a blow that would have crushed her throat. She froze.

'It was no coincidence you were out there the day I arrived, was it?'

'No,' she said, and swallowed. 'He wanted me to keep an eye out for you. Good thing I did, huh?'

'Yes.' The eels circled the skiff, trilling in frustration. One by one, they began to slide away, back into the dark. All but the dead one. 'And all those other times you popped up – were you following me?'

'Somebody had to,' she said. 'I drew the short straw.'

'How many of you are there?'

She frowned and sheathed her knife. 'Not many. Enough.'

'Enough for what?'

She looked away.

I sighed and held out the pole. 'Fine. Let's go. I'm sure Murn is getting impatient.'

She froze for a moment, and then looked at me.

'Don't look at me like that,' I said. 'You know as well as I do that he wants me to see these barges. He's probably waiting for us, wherever we're going. So let's go.'

Deshler continued to stare at me for a moment, and then nodded. 'You're an arse, Blackwood,' she said, as she set the pole into the water.

'That is the least among my sins.'

She took us deeper into the swamp, towards the old lumber mills. Not the same way I'd come before, but by a more roundabout path, through thick copses and past the skeletal remnants of sunken barges, left to rot in the still waters. We didn't speak. The silence was too oppressive. The afternoon wore into evening, as the sky went the colour of smoke.

Our destination proved to be the remnants of a crumbled watchtower, its stone foundations sunk so deep that not even the swamp could shift them. Trees clustered about its jagged base, and grew among the fallen stones higher up like barnacles. We left the skiff moored to the entry-post, and Deshler led me through the hollows of the structure's bones. There was little natural light, but the walk was easy, compared to some. Roots grew so thick in the water that I was reminded of the mangrove swamps near Anvilgard.

A moss-lantern, covered by a hood of burlap, hung from a broken support beam. In the light, I saw that someone had made a hunter's hide from the innards of the tower. I saw supplies and bedding, as well as the disassembled pieces of a handgun. The weapon had been drenched, and its mechanisms were badly rusted.

'I've never been good at fixing these things,' Murn said, from somewhere out of sight.

I turned, scanning the shadows. 'Never very good at using them, either. That's why they gave you a pike, as I recall.'

He laughed softly and stepped into the light. He looked worse than when I'd last seen him. A bandage was knotted about one bicep and he was limping. Dried blood matted his hair. He had his pistol in one hand and a sword belted at his waist. It was the same blade I'd seen in his house. 'You're here,' he said, as if not believing his own eyes.

'I am.'

'I wasn't sure that you'd be willing.'

I stepped past him. What had once been a tower now resembled a scattering of broken stone, brambles and greenery. Murn had carefully cleared a space within the ruin so that someone could spy on the structures across the water, where the trees thinned, without being seen themselves.

'The old quay,' I said. 'Funny thing to be out here.' The old quay was a flat platform of stone, dotted with the broken remnants of pillars or statues. Braziers had been set up along the edge of the platform, illuminating the area with a flickering jade light.

Murn joined me. 'They used to load lumber onto barges there. Now it has a different purpose.' He pointed. 'Lights. Deshler, hood the lantern.'

She pulled the burlap tight, cutting the radiance. We were plunged into a deepening gloom. I looked around, barely able to make the others out.

'A pretty little hideaway, Evrek. What do you use it for?'

'Reconnaissance. Now, lower your voice. Sound carries strangely out here.'

I did as he bade. The lights were getting closer. I heard the steady thump of poles striking the water, and voices calling out depths. Barges found the swamp more difficult to navigate than skiffs. The wide-hulled vessels moved slowly, scraping against trees and the tops of sunken ruins. Each was strung with lanterns that bathed the surrounding waters in a harsh light. As they approached the quay, someone sounded a hunting horn.

The sound sent a chill through me. It echoed over the swamp, and was answered in kind from the quay. Guards shuffled into sight, carrying crossbows. More guards stood atop the barges. These were armed with handguns.

'Well armed,' I murmured.

Murn nodded. 'The sylvaneth have been attacking the barges.'

'Why?'

Murn didn't reply. 'They're starting to unload,' he said. The barges had anchored themselves near the quay. Gangplanks extended from each. Each of the vessels held maybe a few dozen men and women. Some held less, others held more. None of them looked in particularly healthy condition.

Sepesh stood atop the lead barge, overseeing the unloading. Murn muttered something I didn't catch. I wondered how close Sepesh had come to capturing him, before I arrived. The prisoners from the first barge were ushered onto the quay. They were forced into a ragged line by the guards.

'And there's Lord Wald himself,' Murn said. I followed his gaze. Lord Wald strode across the quay with a coterie of followers trailing at his heels. They were clothed this time. Lord Wald walked down the line of prisoners, checking them over as if they were livestock.

'What's he doing?' I asked.

'Taking his pick.' Murn's grip tightened on the hilt of his sword. 'Wish I had a crossbow. One good shot is all I need...'

'You're a terrible shot,' I said.

'I got better.'

'Even if you killed him, there's still Fulder,' Deshler said. 'It wouldn't change anything.'

Murn frowned. 'I know. That's why I only tried the one time.'

'That and he surrounded himself with all those lunatics,' Deshler said. Murn glanced at her, and she gave a gap-toothed grin. 'Well, he did,' she added.

Murn shook his head. 'His lordship takes his pick first. Then the rest are divvied up. The strongest are used for labour. The rest...'

'What about them?'

'I don't know,' Murn said softly. 'Most of them vanish. Just... gone. As if they never were.' He ran a shaky hand through his hair. 'I think they take them somewhere, deep in the swamp. But I haven't been able to find out where.' He looked at me. After a moment, he said, 'I'm sorry.'

'Why?'

'I tried to kill you.'

'Are you sorry because you tried, or because you failed?'

He was silent for a time. Then, 'Both, maybe. I was scared.'

'Scared I might talk?'

'Scared you might kill us.' He looked at me. 'You went mad. Utterly and completely mad, after that night. You prayed for three days straight, no food, no water, no sleep. And when I found you in that shrine, you had an awful light in your eyes. I was almost... glad, when they took you away.'

'Why?'

He coughed. 'I wanted to see you punished. For what you'd done. What you made us do.' He laughed. 'Only you didn't make us. We went willingly, and we did what we did because it was the right thing to do.'

There was an ache in my head, like the reverberation of a hammer striking an anvil. I ran a hand through my hair, trying to rub away the pain. 'You think that?'

'Don't you?'

'I try not to think about it at all.' I met his gaze, and something in mine made him flinch. 'I'm not who I was, Evrek. And neither are you. I don't think I was ever who I pretended to be. Not really.'

'Maybe not. But you could be.'

I laughed. An ugly sound. Hoarse and savage. 'Why did you come here, Evrek?'

'I don't know,' Murn said. He let his hand fall. 'I thought it might be safe.' He turned away. 'But nowhere is safe, is it?'

'Not for men like us.'

'Like we used to be.' He looked at me. 'It's happening again. A different place, a different god, but it's the same story. Only now I'm the one asking for your help. That's why I sent the coin.'

'I can't.'

'Why?'

'Because I'm not who I was. I can't fight a god... not again.' The words tasted like ashes in my mouth. The little gheist was back, sitting nearby, her hands covering the wound in her chest. I wondered what had happened to Murn's daughter, but I didn't ask. It didn't seem the time. 'I don't have it in me to do it again.'

Murn grimaced. 'Then why did you come? Why track me at all?'

And I had no answer for him. Not one that I could articulate. Instead, I said, 'What were you planning to do here? Were you just going to watch?'

He frowned. 'No. I was going to try and track the ones they take to the Huntsman's Bower. To see what they do there – and hopefully stop it.'

'By yourself?'

'I hoped you'd help, at least.'

I shook my head and turned back to the barges below... just in time to see the first of the sylvaneth slip out of the murk and head towards the vessels.

At first I took the creature for a floating log. But then it rose up, shedding water. More followed it. Ten, a dozen, twice that. An army. They sprouted from the dark water like the trees they resembled. A sound rose up with them – a crawling susurrus, like leaves rustling across wet stones. It spread outwards ahead of them, and I saw the guards on the quay stiffen in alarm. Horns blew, alerting everyone to the danger.

Lord Wald was quickly surrounded by his coterie and nearby guards. He was ushered towards a waiting skiff, his face a mask of rage, even as the first of the sylvaneth reached the barges. Atop the barge, Sepesh snatched her blade from its sheath. She chopped through a clawlike branch before turning back to her men and shouting orders.

Handguns barked from the tops of the barges, and sylvaneth shrieked in pain. Clay canisters that I knew contained black powder and lamp oil were hurled into the trees. I'd used similar explosives once or twice while with the regiment. Fire bloomed, burning back the shadows. Treekin screamed in agony, swaying and burning.

My hand tightened on my knife as I watched sylvaneth clamber aboard a barge, ripping the cell doors off. Screams erupted from within as the treekin flooded into the hold. I looked at Murn. 'Was this what you wanted me to see?'

'No,' he said. He was pale. 'No. The sylvaneth are angry. I thought I could talk to them – keep them out of it. But they don't listen. Maybe they never did.'

'Why are they angry?'

'Lord Wald has flouted their authority. He's not just feeding the Old Stag... He's trying to wake him...'

'I think he already has,' I said.

Murn stared at me. 'What?'

'I think he's already awake, whether Lord Wald knows it or not.' I laughed and sat back. 'I think this little crusade of yours was doomed before it began. The gods won the toss before we even knew we were in the game.'

Murn's gaze drifted away from me, into the trees. He flinched at the crack of gunfire, and the screams from the barges. 'But... but they said...'

'Who said?' I grabbed him. 'Who said? Who told you to do this?'

He struggled against my grip. 'The sylvaneth – the servants of the Everqueen! They needed help. Wald used to worship her, but not any more. Lord Wald, Fulder – they'd led the village astray. And now, every harvest, the Old Stag grows stronger and the Everqueen's binding grows weaker...'

I thrust him back and let him go. I shook my head. 'And so what? How is he any worse than she is?'

'It's not about worse or better,' Murn said. 'It's about right and wrong.' He closed his eyes as the guns continued to crash. 'We have to do the right thing, whatever the consequences.'

'That's a damn fool thing to say.'

'You're the one who said it.'

I froze. Just for a moment. Murn looked away. He climbed to his feet and drew his sword. 'I have to do something. I might be able to save some of them, at least.'

'It's suicide,' Deshler hissed, grabbing his arm.

He shook her off. 'I have to do this.'

I hit him on the back of the head. He fell forward with a groan. 'Get his sword,' I said as I dropped onto him and twisted his arm up behind his back.

Deshler wrestled the sword from his hand and tossed it into the mud. 'What are you doing?' she said.

'Keeping him alive.' Murn struggled, but I was stronger. I always had been. Down below, the sylvaneth were falling back. The barges had become abattoirs. Chained prisoners were no match for enraged treekin. The guards fared somewhat better. They were used to fighting sylvaneth. 'If he goes down there, he'll get himself killed.'

'I thought that's what you wanted,' Deshler said.

'I changed my mind. We need to get out of here.' I lifted him up. 'Help me get him back to the skiff.'

'Wait… wait,' Murn mumbled. He slumped against me, still dazed from my blow. 'You have to help me. I can't do it alone. We have to go to the Huntsman's Bower. We have to stop it. The sacrifice…'

Out in the dark, something growled. I stopped, and looked up. Doglike shapes prowled across the top of the fallen tower, splinter-jaws wide, tongues of bark lolling. Their eyes gleamed as they glared down at us.

'Friends of yours?' Deshler asked, her voice hoarse with fear.

I ignored her and retrieved Murn's sword. I looked down the length of the blade. He'd sharpened it, at least. 'On your feet, Evrek.' With Deshler's help, I hauled him towards the skiff. The dog-things prowled after us, moving with an ugly, sideways motion that wasn't natural in the slightest. They crawled across the walls and broken beams, circling us.

'What do they want?' she asked, casting fearful glances at our pursuers.

'To kill him. Or me. Or both of us.'

'Why? I thought…' She trailed off as one of the dog-things dropped down before us. It shrilled a warning growl. I slashed at it, driving it back. It scrambled away, snarling.

'Think later. Move now.' I hefted Murn and half-dragged him towards the skiff. When we reached it Deshler helped me bundle him into it. 'Get him out of here,' I said. The dog-things were creeping closer. I turned to face them, Murn's sword in my hand. 'I'll buy you some time.'

Murn caught my hand. 'Deshler… Deshler will know where I am,' he said. 'Don't take too long to think it over. If what you say is true, we're running out of time. If you decide to meet me… ask Deshler to bring you.' He looked at me. 'We have to stop it. Too many have died already…'

With that, Deshler set the skiff into motion, carrying them away, into the swamp. I didn't watch them go.

The dog-things crouched, studying me. I didn't think they'd come for Murn at all. A moment later, one of them leapt for me, its teeth catching my wrist and jerking me off my feet. I hit the water, and lost hold of the sword. The hound-thing backed away, still gripping my wrist, trying to drag me into the dark where the others awaited. I grabbed my knife and slashed at it, trying to break its hold.

It released me as I carved a gouge across its skull. Before it could attack again, something tall and dreadful rose up over us. Like a tree that had forgotten what it was, and dreamed of being a man. A face of cracks and splinters shifted.

No.

The voice was like the wind in the branches, rustling and rasping. The hound-things hunched, hissing. They retreated before the newcomer.

He is not ripe. Not ripe. Not ready for the reaping. Not yet. Not yet. Go.

The dog-things snarled and gibbered, obviously unhappy with this. One edged towards me, but the newcomer extended a hand, blocking its path.

No. Your master is not yet ruler here. Go.

They retreated, vanishing one by one into the gloom. That awful face turned towards me, and seemed to smile. I wondered if the look was supposed to be comforting.

A moment later, I was alone.

CHAPTER TWENTY-TWO

GINT

I was in the green place again, but things were different now. The cathedral of trees had swelled and bent outwards. The walls were full of hissing, screaming leopard eels, and doglike sylvaneth crept along in robes made from human skin, flayed and bloody.

I was running, but getting nowhere. Something stalked in my wake, every footfall like the boom of a drum, or a roll of thunder. I didn't look back, but I knew what I'd see regardless – something like a stag, but horribly, hideously *not*. As it hunted me through the green church it spoke in honied tones, though I refused to listen to its words. I knew that if I did, it would have me.

No matter how fast I ran, I couldn't get away. The shadow of the hunter stretched across my path and its – *his* – voice followed me wherever I went. The wooden hounds were always nipping at my heels, driving me further and faster onto the torturous track laid out before me.

And then, suddenly, there was nowhere to go. Only trees full of writhing, snapping eel-shapes and water swirling about my legs, crawling to my waist and chest. Brambles pressed close, like the hands of lovers whose names I'd forgotten.

The shadow fell, washing over me, and I gagged, my nose and mouth full of the sickly-sweet stink of rotting meat and sap. Despite myself, I turned – and screamed.

A moment later, I sat up, chest heaving, unable to draw breath. I felt as if I had been held under the water for a moment longer than I could bear. Sweat popped on my pores, and slicked my hair to my scalp.

'You're awake, then?' Gint asked, from somewhere in the dark.

'Close enough.'

'Sounded like you were having a nightmare.' He lit the candle.

'Just a dream,' I said. I blinked. 'Where'd you get that pistol?'

'From my bedroll.' He cocked it. 'Something is on the roof. Listen.'

I did. I heard the scratch of something sharp on the thatch. Digging its way down. I reached for my knife, but it wasn't there.

Gint lifted it from his lap. 'Looking for this?'

'Give it back.'

'Not yet.' He aimed the pistol – not at the roof, but at me. 'Where were you tonight?'

'Why do you care?' It had taken me hours to walk back, and my legs and back were a tangle of aches and pains. My clothes were stiff with grime, and crackled as I shifted position. I still wasn't sure how I'd managed to find my way back. Good luck, maybe.

'I don't, particularly,' said Gint. 'But it's one more piece of the puzzle. What happened out there – with the barges? That's where you were, isn't it?'

'Who can say?' The scratching was getting louder, or closer, or both. Whatever it was, it was impatient. I could hear a raspy, rustling wheeze, like the panting of a dog. 'Maybe I went for a stroll in the swamp.'

'Keep joking.' Gint tilted his head, listening. 'I think it's here for you. You annoyed them tonight. That takes skill.'

'You sound like you'd know.'

Gint smiled, but it wasn't his usual grin. This was a cold thing. 'I know a lot of things. I know about Murn. I know that Blackwood isn't your real name.' He leaned close. 'And I know what you did in Aqshy.'

Suddenly, I wasn't so worried about the thing scratching to get in. I licked my lips. 'You don't know anything about me, Gint. We're barely acquaintances.'

'Oh, we're more than that by now, I think.' He twitched the pistol as a bit of thatch fell from above onto the barrel. 'We're *accomplices.*'

'Take that gun out of my face, Gint, or I'll feed it to you.'

His eyes narrowed, and that cold smile slipped. 'You'd do it too, wouldn't you?' His finger caressed the trigger. 'Maybe I ought to just shoot you now and save myself the trouble later.'

Thatch was falling like snow now. I could feel the rain, and hear the harsh scrape of wooden claws. I didn't look up. Gint did, just for a moment. His mistake.

I was on him before he could fire. Gint was stronger than he looked, but not by much. I hit him hard on the side of the jaw and he went over. I twisted the pistol out of his hand just as the thatch gave way and something crashed down onto the floor. The impact knocked the candle over, and all I could make out were knotted, root-like limbs and splinter-like teeth. Eyes like hag-lights burned in knothole sockets as it took a skitter-step towards me, moving too lightly for something so large.

I fired as it sprang. I was no Greycap gunner, but even I couldn't miss at that range. I heard wood crack, and the thing fell, screaming and twisting. Something that might have been a tail whipsawed out, parting the air just over my head as it tried to get its paws under it. It snapped its jaws at me as I scrambled back.

The room was too small for it to manoeuvre. That bought me enough time to find an opening and bring the butt of the pistol down on its head. It wasn't a hammer, but it was heavy enough to do the trick. The crack my shot had made widened, oozing sap. I hit it again and again as it tried to drag me to the floor. Every blow further enlarged the sticky wound.

It screamed – whether in pain or frustration, I couldn't say – and knocked me sprawling. It was gone a moment later, back out the way it had come. I looked down. Sap stained my arm to my elbow.

'That was… impressive,' Gint said. I turned. He was on his feet, my knife in his hand. He extended the pommel to me. 'I'll trade you.'

If he'd been smiling, I might have tried to bash his skull in too. Instead, I snatched the knife from his hand and pressed it to his throat. He frowned. 'What do you know?' I demanded. 'What's going on in this damn place?'

'That's what I'm here to find out.'

'You're from the Fastness,' I said.

'No. I work for an interested party.'

The way he said it made me wary. I stepped back, but didn't lower my knife. 'You're not just a card sharp, are you?'

'No. Which is why you can trust me when I say we need to leave. Soon.' He extended his hand. 'May I have my pistol back, now?'

I handed the weapon back to him. 'And go where?'

'That's up to you.' He began to reload the pistol. 'I suggest out of this village, to start with.' He paused. 'That's odd.'

'What?'

'With all the racket that thing was making, you'd think someone would have come up here to check on us.'

'Maybe they're hoping it killed us,' I said.

'Or maybe they're getting ready to finish the job.'

I sheathed my knife. 'No sense waiting around to find out. Come on.' I indicated the hole in the thatch. 'I'll give you a boost, you pull me out.'

'Are you certain I won't just leave you?'

'As certain as I am that there're no more of those things waiting for us up there.' I smiled at him. 'How about you?'

He gave me a weak smile. 'Fair enough. Up we go.'

He scrambled through the hole, and helped me up. The rain sheeted down, instantly drenching us. 'What now?' he said.

'Across the rooftops. Head for the quay.'

'Why?'

'I've come to a decision.' I started across the roof, moving slowly across the wet thatch. 'You can come if you want, or make your own way out of town. Up to you.'

'Fate has thrown us together. I see no reason to dissolve the partnership.' He hurried after me, nearly sliding down the incline of the roof in his haste. I caught him and dragged him towards me. He wasn't as good at this as I might have otherwise expected.

'Are you sure you're a witch hunter?' I asked, with some disbelief.

'I don't hunt witches. Never claimed to. I am, however, an agent of the Order of Azyr.' He pushed past me, and half-crawled along the line of the roof. I followed, taking care not to fall myself. The thatch gave way to slates, which made the going somewhat easier.

'So why follow me?'

'You were good cover. And you seemed competent. More so than I expected. It was only once I knew who you were looking for that I realised who you were.' He looked like he wanted to ask a question, but he had the good grace not to. 'I almost shot you there and then.'

'Why didn't you?'

'I thought you might prove useful. Looks like I was right. My job was a lot easier with you blundering around, threatening people and kicking over anthills.'

'And the business with the hag-lights?'

Gint shrugged. 'I was trying to talk to the sylvaneth. Sometimes it's worth a go.'

'Not this time,' I said.

He frowned. 'No. Not this time.' He looked at me. 'Why did you save me, by the way? Seems a touch out of character for you, if you don't mind me saying.'

'We all make mistakes,' I said. There was a crash from behind us, and I knew someone had decided to investigate. I dragged him into the lee of a chimney, and he sank down. 'Quiet,' I murmured. I peered around the edge of the chimney.

I heard shouts, muffled by distance and rain. Saw heads poke through the thatch. Guards. Including a familiar face.

'Buell,' I muttered.

'Oh, he's a bad one,' Gint said. 'Not well loved, Buell.'

'He's one of Fulder's.'

'A cultist as well as a guard. For shame.' Gint lifted his pistol. 'I hate that sort of double-dipping. It shows a lack of professionalism.'

I pushed the barrel down. 'You've only got one shot. Don't waste it on him.'

'We can't just let them harry us across the rooftops.'

'No.' I pressed my hands to the chimney. It was heavy, but loose. Old. Ready to tip, with the right encouragement. I looked at Gint. 'Let them see you,' I said.

'What?'

'I want them to come closer. Let them see you.'

Gint stared at me for a moment. He shook his head. 'I hope you know what you're doing.' He slid down the incline of the roof.

'Why start now?' I muttered. I leaned into the chimney, working it back and forth. The stones ground against one another and the mortar powdered against my sleeve. One good push would be all that was needed – that and the right timing.

Gint yelped, as if he'd lost his balance. Buell and the guards turned, alert as hounds. They started across the roof, shouting. Gint clambered away from them, moving just slow enough to keep them in pursuit. Buell was in the lead, cursing the entire way. The guards weren't any better with the roof than Gint had been.

When I'd judged that they were close enough, I slammed my shoulder against the chimney. The stones shifted and broke apart. Dust and smoke boiled upwards, nearly blinding me. Guards cried out as they were knocked from the roof by the minor avalanche.

I staggered down the slope of the roof. A shape rose up, coughing and cursing. Buell. His eyes widened as he saw me.

'You!' His truncheon sliced out through the smoke. I ducked aside, nearly losing my footing. Buell loomed over me as I regained my balance. 'Got you now, you bastard.' He raised the club. 'Time to pay your debts.'

I threw myself aside as the blow fell. Buell cursed and swung around, trying to catch me. He swung wild. I turned and caught the blow on my palms. It hurt, but I held on. 'Let go,' he snarled. He drove a big fist into my side and I grunted. He hit me again, not thinking to simply let go of his weapon.

We reeled back and forth across the slippery roof for a moment, before I managed to wrench the truncheon from the big man's grip. Buell staggered, surprised.

I reversed the truncheon and drove it into his midsection, doubling him over. As he sank down, wheezing, I cracked him across the back of the head, dropping him flat onto the tiles. He grabbed at my legs, and I stomped on his hands.

I reached down and caught a handful of the guard's hair. I

wrenched Buell's head up, and he choked out an obscenity. I hit him again. It felt good, so I did it a third time. The guard's nose burst in a spurt of red, and he sagged with a wet groan. I let him.

I looked down at the truncheon, weighing it. It was a solid piece – good for breaking bones and not much else. I used it to send him rolling off the roof, to join his men. The fall probably wouldn't kill him, but I didn't have time to make sure.

I waved the truncheon through the smoke, trying to disperse it. 'Gint?'

'Here,' he coughed. 'Rain and smoke, never a good mix.'

'You get used to it.' I caught his arm. 'Let's go.'

'That won't stop them,' Gint said, as I propelled him ahead of me.

'No, but it'll make them think twice about following us over the rooftops. Come on.'

'Where are we going?'

'I told you – the quays. Why is an agent of the Order of Azyr interested in Wald?'

'The prison barges,' he said, puffing.

'What about them?'

'Not all of them are from the Fastness. Lord Wald made a deal with some of the other cantons. They give him their undesirables, he keeps the sylvaneth from their walls.'

'How?'

He gave me a flat look. 'How do you think?' Panting, he looked towards the swamp. 'They've got a taste for it, now, you see. Maybe they always did.'

'And someone is – what? – upset that a bunch of prisoners went missing?'

'Not just prisoners. Tithe-collectors. Pilgrims. Merchants. Anyone and everyone that gets near Wald, without his lordship's permission. Years of disappearances.'

'If that were true, the Greycaps and the Ironweld would have blown this village off the map,' I said, but I could hear the doubt in my own voice.

Gint shook his head. 'Lord Wald has friends in the Grand Conclave. He's convinced them that he can make nice with the sylvaneth, and get them to loosen their grip on the swamps. At least just enough to make Wald a sort of way-station for trade.'

He was about to continue when I clamped a hand over his mouth. I'd seen something, slinking through the rain, across a distant rooftop. I met his questioning gaze and tapped my lips. He nodded and lifted his pistol.

Thankfully, the hounds passed us by a few moments later. 'Sylvaneth?' he asked.

'Of a sort.'

He frowned. 'I think the treekin are confused. I think the ones here are like... garrison troops. Or prison warders. They're bored and they've been listening to the wrong people. Some of them, at least.' Gint shook his head. 'There's a schism, of some sort. Between one grove and another. Or maybe that's just me trying to make sense of something that's ultimately senseless.'

'How long?'

'How long what?'

'How long have you known?'

'Not long. Otherwise I might have come in with an army, truce be damned. But like I said, Lord Wald has friends.'

'They always have friends,' I said. I wiped rain from my face. 'We need to find Deshler. Then we need to find Murn.'

'And then?'

'And then we're going to end this. One way or another.'

CHAPTER TWENTY-THREE

SHRINE

We stayed to the backstreets, following the quay. The rain made it easy to keep out of sight. It was heavier than it had been, falling in silvery sheets that brought mist with it.

Lord Wald's guards were out in force. I saw the soft, green glow of moss-lanterns bobbing along the streets opposite us, and heard rough voices, and fists pounding on doors, followed by shouts and the sound of skulls cracking. I tightened my grip on the truncheon.

'Rounding up conspirators,' Gint said. 'Anyone associated with Murn.'

'How many could there be?'

'From what I gathered, Murn has his supporters.' Gint peered at me. 'Not many, but I have no doubt this has been in the works for a while. We should hurry. I'd hate to get caught up in a sweep.'

When we reached the quay, I saw fishermen and barge-crews

hurriedly loading supplies onto their vessels, as if fearing they'd be the next to face Lord Wald's wrath. Masked acolytes lingered in the shadows, watching in silence.

'Everyone who can leave is doing so,' Gint said.

'Rats leaving a sinking ship.'

'More like they're being cast out.' Gint frowned. 'I've seen this before. Lord Wald's sealing the canton. Driving out anyone whose loyalty might be suspect. Something is happening. Something we're not seeing.'

'What do you mean?'

Gint caught my arm and forced me to stop. 'Think. He's had all this time to find Murn. Why is it so urgent now? And Murn – why call for help *now*?' He tapped the side of his head. 'Think.'

'The harvest,' I said dully. 'Something to do with the harvest.'

'The barges,' he said. 'Did anyone survive?'

'The prisoners, you mean? No. Not that I saw. Maybe a few.'

Gint nodded. 'There it is. He needs bodies. Why?'

'A sacrifice,' I said softly. Gint nodded again.

'I think so. Maybe the timing is important, or maybe it's just ceremonial, but there's an urgency. Things have come to a head. Now we need to figure what to do about it.'

I pushed past him. 'First, we need to find Deshler.'

'The woman with the skiff? Why?'

'Because she can take me to Murn. And Murn is at the heart of all of this.'

We hurried along the quay, accompanied by the sounds of breaking glass, splintering wood and screams. Gint was right. I could feel something brewing, not just in the air, but inside me as well. A bane was on me, and there was a reek in my nose. In the glow of the moss-lanterns, my shadow seemed to stretch and flower into something unrecognisable. Something with a crown of antlers.

That reek is my breath on your neck. I am at your heels, Harran, and this hunt draws to a close. You have been most cunning, for prey. But you won't be able to avoid me forever.

'Shut up,' I muttered.

Gint looked at me. 'What?'

'Nothing. There's her berth.' I led him across the street, towards the end of the quay. Deshler was there, as I had expected. She was loading her skiff down with supplies. She looked up as we approached, one hand on her knife.

'Blackwood,' she said. 'Thought you'd be gone by now. Or dead.'

'No such luck. Where's Murn?'

'Safe.'

'I want to see him. Murn said you'd know where to bring me.'

Deshler twitched. 'Maybe. That mean you've decided whose side you're on?'

'Close enough.' I leaned towards her. 'Can you take me to him?'

After a moment's hesitation, she nodded. 'If you're certain.'

'I am.'

'What about me?' Gint said, peering into the rain. We were being watched. Masked faces loitered too close for comfort. I wondered whether one of them was Fulder.

'You find Pender.'

Gint looked at me. I had no doubt he could do as I'd asked. 'What? Why?'

'Because he's in on it, isn't he?' I said, not taking my eyes from Deshler. 'He's one of yours. Or Murn's. That's why he was helping you hide Murn.' Her eyes widened, and I knew I'd hit the mark. 'He didn't come out of Ironhole, but he came here on a barge nonetheless, I'd bet. One of the few to escape.'

'Murn helped him. Same as he helped me,' she said.

Gint whistled. 'I'm starting to wish this Murn were here instead of you, Blackwood.'

'Prison changes a man. Evidently, sometimes for the better.' I turned to him. 'Find Pender. Bring him.'

'Where? And how?'

'You're a witch hunter. Scare him. And he'll know where to go...' I looked at Deshler, and she nodded.

'He does,' she said, as she climbed down onto the skiff. 'We meet there sometimes.'

'I'm not a witch hunter,' Gint said, irritated, but he didn't argue further. 'What are you planning, Harran?'

'I don't know yet. But when I figure it out, I'll let you know. Until then, get Pender. I have a feeling we're going to need all the help we can get.' I heard the sound of glass breaking nearby. Shouts. Running feet. Something was on fire. 'And do it quickly.'

Deshler loosened the mooring line. 'If we're going to go, now's the time.'

I leapt onto the skiff. Gint was already gone by the time I looked back. As Deshler poled us away from the quay, I spied figures hammering on nearby doors. Some were guards. Others were not. They wore masks of corn and bramble.

'Going to be a busy night,' I said.

'Lord Wald is angry,' Deshler said. 'He thinks – well, who knows what he thinks.' She leaned into her pole. 'He's after Murn, and anyone associated with him. Surprised he didn't pick you two up.'

'I think he left it to others to handle.'

'Guess they weren't up to it.'

'Not so far. How many of you were there?'

'Not many, I told you. Maybe a handful. Most of them like me – just trying to get along. We hid Murn, got him supplies, but nothing more than that.'

'Apparently it was enough. Gint was right – this has been coming for a while, from the looks of it. That attack last night was the last straw.' I laughed. 'If I'd known what I was walking into, I might not have come.'

'Might have been better if you hadn't,' Deshler said. 'So far, all you've done is make things worse. At least Murn is trying to help.'

'That doesn't sound like the Murn I remember.'

'Maybe your memory isn't all you think it is,' she said harshly. 'Or maybe he changed. All I know is he's a good man. Better than this shithole deserves.'

Instead of replying, I settled back into the skiff. We didn't speak as we left the town behind. When the shrine came into sight, I almost sighed. Of course Murn would choose to hide there. The one place no one would think to look for him.

'Doesn't seem like much of a hiding spot.'

'The sylvaneth claimed it a long time ago,' Deshler said. 'If Murn is safe anywhere, it's there.' I followed her gaze, half-expecting someone or something to be watching us from the trees. But there was nothing. Not even a sound, save the raucous clamour of birds. The island was silent – but not dead. Not that. Not here. It was the silence of patience – or something waiting.

'Last night – something he said... He made a bargain with them, didn't he?'

She shook her head. 'I don't know. They've been keeping him safe, I think. Or maybe it's the other way around.' She paused. 'His wife... she was of the old blood. She knew how to talk to them. When she died, they sang for days and days, out in the swamp.' She swallowed. 'They haven't sung much, since.'

'What about when his daughter died?'

She didn't look at me. 'He tell you about it?'

'No. How did she die?'

'Do you care?'

'No. Tell me anyway.'

Deshler shook her head. 'They used to drown babies – children – in the bower.'

'So I heard.'

She looked at me. 'Sometimes they still do.'

'Is that why he tried to kill Lord Wald?'

She nodded. 'Murn tried to stop them. They nearly killed him. Maybe they thought they had. By the time he recovered... it was too late.'

'Why her?'

'Fulder,' Deshler said. She spat over the side. 'He was always a petty bastard.'

I sat back. I had more questions, but I didn't see the point in asking them. The girl was dead and nothing was going to change that. The reasons why didn't matter.

When we reached the shrine, I helped her drag the skiff ashore. 'What's your plan?' she asked.

I shook my head. 'What makes you think I have a plan?'

I started up the muddy slope towards the shrine. The ruin was a solid weight on the island's back. The marble walls were black with grime, and so overgrown that the edifice was barely recognisable as a building. The broken path led straight to the doors. The shattered remains of statues lined the last few yards.

The doors were the only thing free of growth. The wood was warped by damp and rotting at the edges, the hinges and latches rusted through, but they were still in one piece. Curling knotwork sigils had been daubed onto them in blood, layer after layer, year after year, until the pale wood had been dyed a dark brown.

I paused. Some of them were familiar. I'd seen them before, in the pages of Murn's books. Marks of oaths and bindings, of promises kept and debts owed – like the ones on Murn's hearth. The Jade Kingdoms were full of such markings – it seemed every waystone and cistern had them. I could feel the power in them from where I stood. The whole structure seemed to reverberate with a clenched anticipation – and an ugly, savage hunger.

I hesitated, and then sheathed my knife and set my hands against the doors.

'Wait,' Deshler began. 'Something's wrong...'

I forced the doors open. They swung inwards with an echoing groan. The smell of rampant life, raw and vibrant, enveloped me. Shafts of light pierced the darkness beyond, like the candles of the faithful. My hands tingled, as if I'd grasped something too hot, or too cold.

The shrine was overgrown and harrowed. The stones of the floor had burst asunder, and the trunks of great fen-trees rose upwards like contorted pillars. Thick, serpentine roots spread through the floors and walls. The altar had been subsumed into the trunk of the largest of the trees, the pale, azure-veined stone all but hidden within the folds of bark. Branches stretched from wall to wall, or pierced the roof, and rain fell freely into the nave. Wide puddles filled the gaps between broken stones, and deep pools had formed in the aisle. Frogs croaked somewhere out of sight, and things splashed in the dark.

I turned, taking in the primal dilapidation. I reached out to touch one of the trees, but stopped myself at the last moment. Thick, black sap boiled from the fibrous pores of the tree. In the weak light, it looked like blood. I felt something – a silent reverberation. Like a heartbeat. Or the thunder of galloping hooves.

Deshler said something, but I didn't hear her. The reverberation pulsed all around me, inaudible but omnipresent. It pressed against me from all sides, growing stronger and stronger. Something wet squelched beneath my feet. I looked down.

We were too late.

What was left of Murn floated here and there on the water, bobbing like flotsam and jetsam. Something had torn him apart, and used his blood to mark the walls and sigils. Desecration – or perhaps an act of reconsecration.

The little gheist stood over her father, head tilted. I wondered if she'd seen the whole thing. If she'd watched as they'd torn him apart and scattered him like offal. I met her gaze, and saw a flicker of… something. Sadness, maybe. Or fear. Then she was gone, like dust caught on a strong wind.

In the darkness, something growled. Dog-shapes prowled into view, blood staining their wooden jaws. I backed away. 'Back to the skiff,' I said, without taking my eyes off them.

'Is he…?' she began.

'Back to the godsdamned skiff,' I snarled. Splinter-teeth snapped in anticipation. I picked up the pace, and they followed me, slinking down and down, moving like oil on glass. They loped in my wake, splinter-jaws wide, tongues of bark lolling.

At the last moment, I turned and flung myself at the doors. I heard a frustrated snarl, and felt something tug at my coat. Then I was rolling across the broken stones, out of the shrine. I rose and spun, heart thudding, desperation lending me speed and strength. I grasped the doors and yanked them shut as my pursuers leapt. When the doors slammed into place, their shrill cries were silenced.

I stepped back, shaky with relief. I turned on Deshler.

Someone drove a fist into my side, doubling me over. Coughing, I barely saw the sickle as it gashed me across the head. I fell to my hands and knees, the world turning red. I looked up. 'Too late,' Fulder said.

Through a veil of blood, I saw three more of them crowding around Deshler. One held a knife to her throat. Fulder squatted beside me, knife in one hand, sickle in the other. Both weapons were bloody, and I knew then who was responsible for the butchery inside the shrine. 'Last time, you nearly broke my face. This time will be different.'

I eased the truncheon out of my coat. 'I wouldn't count on it.' I snapped the club up, and Fulder jerked back, surprised. He fell on his arse and I kicked him hard as I rose. I brought the truncheon down on his arm, knocking the knife from his grip. I snatched it up as two of the others stalked towards me.

The first came at me with his sickle. I caught the blow on the truncheon and sank the knife into the gap between his neck and his shoulder. He spasmed and staggered as I wrenched it loose and turned to the other. The second cultist crashed into me, knocking me prone. I caught his wrist as he tried to sink a blade into me, and he caught mine as I tried to do the same. We wrestled in the mud, him on top of me.

'Don't kill him,' Fulder panted. 'The Old Stag wants him alive – and his lordship as well. We need a living sacrifice!'

The cultist paused, and that gave me the opening I needed. I lurched up, and slammed my head into his. His mask gave him precious little protection and he slumped back I tore my hand free of his grip and rammed the knife into his throat.

'No!' Fulder started forward as I staggered upright. I took a two-handed grip on the truncheon and slammed it into his mid-section, hard enough to break it. Fulder sagged, wheezing, and I shoved him to the ground. I turned on the remaining cultist.

'Stay back, or I'll kill this old bitch,' he said. I could hear the panic in his voice. He pressed the knife tight to her throat, drawing a thin seam of blood.

'Fine,' I said. 'Saves me having to pay her.'

Deshler glared at me. 'Bastard,' she spat. Her captor hesitated, and she stamped on his foot, twisting away as his grip loosened. He groped for her, and she slid her own knife into him He gave a strangled yelp and fell, nearly dragging her from her feet. I steadied her, and she shoved my hand away.

'Don't touch me.' She turned, and her eyes widened. 'Blackwood!'

Alert to her warning, I twisted aside. Fulder's sickle hissed down between us. I turned and drove a fist into his jaw, snapping his head back He fell down, senseless.

Branches cracked behind us. I spun, and saw a fourth cultist step out of the trees. He raised a handgun Time slowed. There was a roar.

The cultist fell.

Gint stepped out from the trees and lowered his smoking pistol. 'Looks like I caught up with you just in time,' he said.

'Just,' I said. 'Pender?' I asked, but I already knew the answer.

'Arrested. Or dead. Sepesh and her men are making the rounds, it seems. Strange time to become diligent, if you ask me.' He paused. 'Murn?'

I shook my head.

Gint cursed softly. 'What now?'

I turned towards the swamp. I thought I saw a towering, ant-lered shape watching from among the trees. But it was gone a moment later, and I wondered if I had truly seen it at all.

'Only one place left to go,' I said. 'The place I've been avoiding since I got here.'

In my head, something growled in pleasure.

'Huntsman's Bower.'

CHAPTER TWENTY-FOUR

HUNTSMAN'S BOWER

Deshler protested, but I was insistent. Gint said nothing. He left his stolen skiff where he'd moored it, and helped me get Fulder's dead weight into Deshler's vessel. When we were at last in motion, I'd woken Fulder with a few stiff blows.

It hadn't taken as much convincing as I'd expected to get Fulder to show us the way to the Huntsman's Bower. Indeed, he seemed almost eager to do so.

'I don't trust him,' Gint murmured, as we edged beneath the trees.

'Neither do I. Which is why whatever happens, he's not coming out.'

Gint smiled. 'I knew I liked you, Harran. If we get out of this – well, I might have a job for a man like you.'

'Even knowing what you know?'

His smile faltered. 'Men in my line can't afford to be picky about the tools Sigmar places before us.'

'You think this is his doing?'

'I think… it depends on what happens next,' he said.

I laughed. I was starting to like him, despite myself. Out in the swamp, the croaking of the frogs ceased. Something was moving through the trees, circling us. Padding lightly on inhuman paws. I could see only the barest hint of it, the slinking undulation of a low form.

'I think we're expected,' Gint said.

Deshler laughed, the sound brittle with fear. 'Somebody is, at any rate.'

The movement stopped. I could feel it watching us. Waiting, perhaps, to see what we did next. I looked down at Fulder. 'Is this it?'

He nodded. 'It is.'

'Good. Get up. You're taking me on a tour.' I looked at Gint and Deshler. 'Both of you wait here.'

Deshler shook her head. 'This isn't wise.' She looked around. 'He's dead, Blackwood. There's nothing left to do but ride it out.'

'I hate to say it, but she might be right,' Gint said. 'Whatever is going on here, it's beyond our resources. We should go back to the Fastness – I can make a report…'

'And then what?' I said, studying the trees. I looked at him. 'Would anyone care?'

Gint looked away.

I nodded. 'I figure I'm owed something, at least.' I stepped onto the hummock, pushing Fulder ahead of me. Hag-lights danced all about us, casting a dim radiance over everything.

The wind fell still. But the leaves continued to rustle. I didn't see her at first, not until she moved. Then she was rising out of the water, her wrinkled features twisting into what was either a grimace or a smile. I supposed she wasn't as attached to the lumber mill as I'd thought. Fulder sank to his knees and began to pray. The sylvaneth ignored him.

'Go no further.'

'Murn's dead,' I said, flatly.

...*dead*...

...*dead*...

She tittered. 'That is the way of meat, is it not?'

'Way of all life,' I said. 'Even green growing things.'

She stopped laughing. They all did. 'We did not kill him.'

'No. But you could have stopped it.'

'Yes.'

...*yes*...

...*yes*...

'Why didn't you?' I demanded. I was angry. Angry at myself, at them. At everything. If I'd listened to Murn... gone with him... done something differently, he'd be alive. Or maybe we'd both be dead. 'You started him on this path. Set him off. And for what?'

No answer. But I could feel their amusement. Their disdain. Gint was right. Whatever they had once been, they'd become corrupt. Venal, if not in any way I understood. I tried a different tack.

'How did they wake the Old Stag up?'

'Blood.' She lingered over the word.

...*blood*...

...*blood*...

I expected the echoes this time, and didn't flinch. The sylvaneth were playing with me. Taunting me. Maybe they were looking for an excuse. I intended to give them one.

'You told me before that you could help me. What did you mean?'

She eyed me. 'Why, only that we would be merciful and kill you before he had the chance. What did you think we meant?' She shook her boughs in merriment. 'This is an old game, meat. One your kind has no business playing in. The Old Stag stirs in his bower, and we seek to stymie him – to lull him back to sleep.'

'By killing people. All those folk on the barges. Others.'

She shook her leaves. It might have been a shrug. 'If he scents prey, he stirs. So we take it from him. We spill the blood in the water, and feed his eels. *But not him.*'

I nodded. 'Only Lord Wald decided enough was enough. He bought guns and powder. Fire to burn you out.' I was talking more to myself now, feeling it out. Putting the pieces together, as Gint had said. 'Murn figured out what he was up to. He was trying to stop it.'

'Yes,' the sylvaneth hissed. 'He was good meat.'

'And you let him die.'

She smiled, and I felt sick. Sap dripped down the line of her smile and plopped into the water. 'Yes. The others chopped him up and sent his soul screaming into the bower of the black stag. The old beast crunched him up-up-up.'

I paused, fighting back the sudden flare of rage. 'That night on the bridge... you drew me to you. Away from him. Did you save me just to kill me yourself?'

'To see you,' she said. 'To taste your blood. You are... special. He bugles your name from his den, and marks you from afar. It is your scent he has, your meat and bone he desires. You are his quarry. We wished to know... why.'

'And?'

The bark of her face ripped as her smile widened. Her eyes gleamed so bright that I could not meet them. 'Did it hurt?' she cooed.

'What?'

'When the God-King cast you down?' She extended herself towards me, and I took a step back without thinking. 'Did it burn, when he smote you with the fury of the storm?' A claw stretched out and dug into my chest. 'It still burns there – an ember, a spark. A bit of wrath, crackling like blue flame in the hollows of you. If we gut you, will it spill out and consume us? Or will it make us verdant and strong?'

I shook my head. 'There's no fire in me, witch. No spark. I'm as empty as night.'

'You should know better than most that the night is never empty.'

As if to emphasise her point, something roared. A stag's roar. The gathered sylvaneth fell silent. She turned, and stared into the darkness, as if in silent communion with whatever lurked there. A moment later, they were gone.

I kicked Fulder. 'On your feet.' As he stood, he looked around in what I took to be relief. I shoved him forward. 'Get going.'

He lurched into motion as best he could with his hands tied. 'You would have got here eventually,' he said. 'We would have brought you gladly, if you'd but asked.'

'Very hospitable of you. Did grand-niece ask to come?'

He looked at me in confusion. 'What?'

'Your niece, Kersha,' I said. 'She married Murn. They had a daughter. What was her name, by the way?'

'Calla,' he said softly.

'Calla. Pretty name. When did you decide to feed her to the Old Stag?'

He didn't answer. I kept talking.

'Did he ask you to?' I leaned close. 'Or did you do it of your own free will?'

'What does it matter?'

'It doesn't,' I said. 'I just wanted to know what sort of bastard you were.'

The trees thinned and the waters fell. We were entering a grove, hidden by the vast swathe of the swamp. Trees, flattened centuries before, acted as water breaks, and I had the impression that something had fallen here long ago, striking with great force. I looked up, but the stars were nowhere in sight.

'What makes this place so sacred?' I asked, more to make noise than because I wanted an answer.

'Blood,' Fulder said. 'A hundred generations or more. We seeded the soil with our blood and the Old Stag waxed strong.'

I remembered what the aelf had said about babies being tossed into the water, and felt my gut twist and strain. 'Of course.'

Something in the way I said it must have pricked his pride. 'That's why I offered her up. My blood, my kin. No greater sacrifice than that. A blood sacrifice requires a sacred foundation. Otherwise it's nothing but murder.'

'You have something against murder?' I said, giving him a shove.

Fulder looked at me like I was something he'd stepped in. 'One is a show of faith. The other is selfish.'

I shoved him again. Harder this time. He stumbled and nearly fell. 'You say that like faith isn't selfish,' I said. I wanted to hit him again. I wanted to hit him until his old bones turned brittle and broke, but I restrained myself.

'You don't know anything,' he said.

'I know that worship is just another word for appeasement. You shove blood into a god's maw, hoping to fill his belly before he turns those greedy eyes on you.' I smiled and something in my expression made him recoil. 'How many died here, other than Calla, to make this place sacred? A hundred? Two hundred?'

'Generations, as I said,' he spat.

'Good. Then you'll have plenty of company. Keep moving.'

The grove spread out around us, and with a sickening sensation I realised why it all looked so familiar. Here was the green place of my dreams, but horribly real and reeking of blood and piss. Animal smells. The smell of the hunter and the hunted. There was a foetid stink to the dark sap that sweated from the trees.

The ground dipped again in the centre of the grove, and the water was almost waist-deep here. The trees rose overhead like the arches of a cathedral. There were shapes I took for statues at first, but these were soon revealed to be the fossilised stumps of even larger trees, hewn down at some point in the dim past.

Strange knotwork sigils and leering faces were carved into the looming stumps, illuminated by the balls of hag-light that floated across the surface of the water. The trees that clustered about the edges of the grove were gnarled and cankerous, their roots sunk deep and their branches twisted into patterns that hurt my eyes.

There were bones as well. Hanging from the trees, tied together with vines and husks. Skulls secreted in knotholes or peering out from within the curvature of the roots. Most of them old and brown, but some yellow or even white. Too many to count.

'There's more under our feet,' Fulder said, with an air of pride. 'Our devotion healed his wounds and in return, he fed the land.'

'And then you forgot,' I said.

...forgot...

...forgot...

My words echoed back to me, twisted up into sharp yelps and hisses. The trees creaked, and I thought I saw pale faces watching from the uppermost branches. Fulder spat.

'Not all of us.'

'But enough.' I leaned close. 'Did you celebrate, when Sigmar came to Ghyran? Did you hold a feast of corn and fish in his name?' I glanced up. Pitiless stars now glared down through the trees, cold and sharp.

'What have they ever cared for men?' Fulder murmured.

'No more than the trees,' I said softly. We looked at one another, and for a moment we were not captor and captive, but simply two men caught between irresistible forces. The gods smashed at the world, beating it into a shape pleasing to themselves. They did the same to men, often breaking them beyond repair in the process.

The moment passed swiftly. Fulder was who he was, and I was who I am, and the gulf between us was as vast as the distance between the sky and the trees. He must have read something in my eyes or my face, for he sighed. 'I told you before, the Old Stag has marked you. You're his, whether you admit it or not. Killing me won't free you.'

'What about burning this place to the ground? That might do the trick.'

And something in the great, hungry darkness stirred, and laughed at my presumption. Fulder stiffened and sighed. He went on, as if I hadn't spoken. 'We knew how to placate the spirits of the trees and the wild. And they remembered too. They remembered what was planted here, in the time before the Lady of Leaves slumbered… and what might grow, with the proper tending.'

As he spoke, a tremor ran through the glade. It reverberated up my legs and spine. An impossible note, echoing up from far depths. As if something were stirring, deep in the earth. There were gheists in the trees. Little souls, consigned to the black waters down the long course of years, crying out soundlessly for parents who would never come. Children. Babies. I remembered what the aelf had told me, as I spun him around and shoved him back against one of the fossilised stumps. 'The sacrifice – when does it take place?'

The gheists were close now. Not all of them were young. I saw bent ancients, their withered necks hung with strangling vines, and the bodies of those who might have been warriors, princes and kings. There were men and women; humans, aelves and other things, wholly unrecognisable, their shapes worn to rags and tatters by time and the manner of their passing. Their blood and life taken to feed whatever slumbered here. And all of them watching me with hollow gazes, their eyes nothing more than black pits in waxen masks.

Fulder was silent. I pressed the tip of the knife against the hollow of his throat. I wanted to kill him, but resisted the urge. 'Talk, or I'll leave you here with the rest of the dead.'

'You won't kill me.'

'No? Willing to bet on it?' The knife-tip drew a bead of blood from his leathery flesh. Fulder swallowed reflexively. But there was no fear in his eyes. Not even a hint of nervousness.

'You won't kill me because he won't let you.'

The dead pressed close, silent. Moving like stuttering shadow images, cast by candlelight. I blinked, trying not to see, but they insisted. Soon, I could see nothing else but them, all around me. Mouths moved, but no sound emerged, save the chitter of insects. I thought maybe they were trying to warn me.

I realised I was cold. It bit into me like a blade, twisting and tearing. Abruptly, the gheists scattered, vanishing as quickly as they'd come. Like small animals fleeing the approach of a predator.

I heard a sound, like the hoarse breathing of an animal. It filled the glade, and the branches twisted in the resulting breeze. I smelled something rank – like rotting meat and sap. Whispers crowded my hearing, and I spied broken, gaunt shapes creeping among the stumps. Not attacking. Just watching.

Waiting.

Fulder smiled. 'He's coming. You defile his bower with your presence, and now he comes to claim you himself. You should run while you can. Run away, little man. Run. Run!' He grabbed hold of my arm, and we tussled for a second, lurching back and forth in the water. I thought he was going for my knife at first, but he was just trying to get away.

Then there was a sound, like many seedpods bursting open. A tide of sap-like effluvia rushed out of the dark, bearing dozens of small, mummified forms across the water. I looked down at them, at their faces contorted by death into leathery masks.

All had been sucked dry, reduced to compact husks, their chest cavities split and emptied. Harvested. Their blood and life taken to feed whatever slumbered beneath the waters here.

Fulder cackled. 'You see? This is what awaits those he marks. Soon you too will sleep beneath the mud.'

Something tangled my leg and I fell heavily among the dead, the water slopping around my chest and chin. I kept hold of my knife, though. Fulder splashed past me, calling out to the dark, hands raised in supplication. I managed to get upright just as he reached the far edge of the glade.

'Fulder,' I snarled. I didn't know what I was going to do. His name died on my lips when the thing he was calling lurched into the open.

From a distance, it resembled a stag. A big, black beast, taller than a man, its crown of antlers rising up and vanishing into the shadowed boughs above. But in the soft radiance, I could see that its hide was shaggy with moss and there were knotholes in its flanks. Leopard eels gambolled in the frothing waters at its hooves, hissing and singing as if in rapturous celebration.

Its face was the worst of it. Like someone had tried to carve a man's features out of a rotten log and stopped halfway. Its mouth was nothing more than a splintered crack stretching the width of its overlarge skull. Its eyes wept rivulets of dark sap, and more glistened on the cracks in its limbs and body. As it splashed into the light, I saw that there were faces of green moss sprouting from its shoulders and chest. The faces seemed to flex and writhe in the radiance of the hag-lights – as if they were crying out in pain.

When it spoke, its voice was a single black note. I felt my ears pop and I slumped back against a tree, cradling my head. The note echoed outwards, setting the boughs to nodding and the waters to swirling. I felt it in my bones, and my stomach twisted in protest.

Fulder cried out, as if in ecstasy. Head bowed, he fell to his knees in the water, which lapped at his shoulders and neck.

The stag-thing bent down over the kneeling man and its jaws unfurled, and then there was a crunching sound and what was left of Fulder sank beneath the water, out of sight with the rest of the dead. Hag-light eyes rolled in their sockets and came to rest on me, standing among the dead oaks.

I turned and ran.

I heard a shrill cry and then the splash of heavy hooves as it pursued. Again came the winding cry, like that of a rutting stag or a hunter's horn or a wolf's howl, or maybe all three. The glade shook with the thunder of its passing and I cast about, looking for a place to hide. I felt the wash of its rancid breath roll over me, and I gagged.

Even as I ran, I wondered why it had killed Fulder. Maybe his talk of trespass within the thing's bower being forbidden had been truer than he suspected. Or maybe it was simply hungry.

I ran on, until my heart felt like a weight in my chest and my lungs strained. The water made it hard, made every step an effort. I stumbled, and something caught me. I dragged my knife from its sheath and slashed out.

'Damn it, Harran! I'm just trying to help.'

Gint. I staggered back, hands raised. I'd run all the way back, somehow. Maybe it had let me go. Maybe the game was still going.

'We have to get out of here,' I said, panting. Deshler looked at me, her eyes wide.

'What is it? What did you see?'

My reply was interrupted by an ugly, wooden sound. A crossbow bolt sank into her back. Her mouth opened, but no sound came out. She toppled into the water, causing the skiff to rock. She was gone as quickly as that.

Gint turned and fired his pistol. Out in the mist, someone screamed. More crossbows twanged in reply. Bolts thudded into the skiff and the trunks of nearby trees. I caught hold of him and rolled us off the skiff, into the water. I flipped the skiff over as I surfaced, using it to cover us both.

'What are you doing?' he spluttered.

'Trying to keep us breathing for a few more minutes. Come on.'

Bolts punched through the skiff as we swam away from our attackers. 'Where are we going?' Gint demanded.

'Away,' I said. 'Beyond that I have no idea.' I flinched back as a bolt cracked through the wood, scraping my cheek. 'Keep moving.'

'What did you see back there – in the glade?'

'That's not what you need to be worrying about.'

'Answer the question!'

'I don't know what it was... a sylvaneth, maybe. Or something older.' I swallowed back a rush of bile at the memory of it. 'It killed Fulder.'

'I guessed, given that he didn't come back with you.'

The skiff shuddered on our shoulders as bolts peppered it. Gint flinched with every one.

'This won't stop them for long... Do you have a plan?'

'You're the witch hunter, not me. Plans are your thing.'

'I told you, I'm not a bloody witch hunter. I– Ah! Damn it!'

I turned. A bolt had nearly pierced his hand and he swayed to the side, causing the skiff to spin with him. The mud beneath my feet gave way and I slipped under the black water.

When I surfaced, the skiff was floating away, out of reach. Gint was cursing, floundering towards solid ground. With nowhere else to go, I followed him. He hauled himself up onto the grass, and turned to help me up.

'I'm starting to think we need to get out of here,' he panted. 'Back to the city. I'll find help. I'll bring the wrath and storm of Sigmar himself down on this place.' He stood.

There was a wet sound, and a length of steel emerged from his chest. His eyes widened. He toppled forward into the dark waters.

'Should have left, Harran,' Sepesh said. She smiled, and there was something that might have been regret in it. 'Too late now, though.'

CHAPTER TWENTY-FIVE

CELEBRATION

The cage was cramped. A cube of thick wooden bars, held together by strips of shrunken leather. There was barely enough room for me to crouch and keep my head above the water. My cage was one of several sunk into the shallows, among the reeds and grasses below the rear of the manor. The other cages were empty. I was alone, save for the hum of insects and the faint music of the celebrants in the gardens above.

I tensed my muscles, trying to head off the cramps I felt building in my arms and legs. My back already hurt, and my head was pounding. It was a constant effort to stay upright. The motion of the water caused the cage to rock slightly.

I heard a creak, and glanced up at the gibbets hanging from the branches above. A dozen of them, some occupied, some not. I recognised the pickpocket, Scopa, languishing in one. He didn't respond when I called out to him. There were other faces

I recognised as well, from the Stag's Head. I suspected Pender had finally come to the end of his rope.

I squinted through the mist and damp. The shallows ended at a broken wall of stone – the base of the island's original keep. There might have been a jetty there, once. Now it was nothing more than a spillage of cut stone, mouldy and half-sunk in the waters. A makeshift bridge, crafted from slats of wood, extended across it from a gaping hole in the wall.

Past the hole, I could see a set of slabbed steps, rising upwards into the dark of the keep's lower levels. They'd dragged me down those steps, and I had a bruise for each.

Behind me, the swamp waited.

It was watching me. I could feel it. Faces in the swaying grasses, leers in the branches. Laughing at me. Enjoying my predicament.

'Is this fun for you, then?' I said, turning to face the closest trees. 'Is it a game? If so, I'd be obliged if you told me the rules…'

'Run fast, rabbit,' Sepesh said, from behind me.

I turned back to the jetty. She stood on the steps, a slight smile on her face.

'Those are the only rules around here. Run fast, earn a few hours more of life. But no more than that.'

'Not exactly fair.'

'Take it up with the dead. We play by the rules they made, centuries ago.' She spat into the water. 'Hunt and harvest.' She peered about her. 'They used to drown babies, here. One at harvest time. An offering to the treekin. Part of the old pact, or so his lordship says.'

'And now you have a new one.'

'That's life – can't get something for nothing. Always got to give a bit, to get a bit.' She pulled an apple out of her jerkin and shined it on her sleeve. 'If more people understood that, things would be a lot better.'

'Or maybe there'd just be more dead children.'

She drew her knife and deftly began to peel the apple. 'Maybe. Then again, peasants breed like rabbits. Always more where they came from.'

'Spoken like true gentry everywhere.'

Sepesh smiled and sank to her haunches. She extended a slice of apple, impaled on the tip of her knife. My stomach gurgled, and I snatched it eagerly. It tasted sour, but I devoured it without hesitation.

'Wald's a jade-blood,' she said. 'That old-time religion runs through him. The Lady of Leaves and the Stag-King. The Huntsman.'

'Yes, we've met,' I said. I leaned against the bars of the cage.

Sepesh gestured with her knife. 'Lord Wald isn't a bad master, but he *is* the master. You understand?'

'I do.'

'Either you serve him – or you leave.' She paused and peered off into the swamp. 'That goes for them out there, too. Soon, we'll burn their glades and scatter their seeds into the swamp. Plant new groves, to replace the old.'

'They won't like that.'

'They won't have much choice. We have a god on our side. His time is coming, and every living thing will have to pick a side. You're either predator – or prey.' She peered at me. 'Which are you?'

'I'll let you know when I figure it out.'

She laughed and stood. 'Best be quick about it.' She whistled. Two guards ambled down the steps. 'Get him out of there. His lordship wants to speak to him, before we head out to the bower.'

'The bower?' I said.

She looked down at me. 'Huntsman's Bower. The sylvaneth deprived us of our yearly offering. His lordship reckons you'll do for a replacement.'

The guards dragged me from my cage none too gently. They weren't taking any chances, and I got a punch to the kidneys to keep me busy. Sepesh followed at a distance, her hand on her sword. 'It's a shame, really,' she continued. 'I was starting to like you.'

'I was starting to like me too,' I said. That earned me a blow to the head, and for the next few moments all I saw was stars. They cuffed and kicked me, keeping me moving. I counted every blow, intending to pay them back with interest.

Lord Wald's guests watched with predatory eagerness as I was hauled through the garden. Despite their general lack of clothing, they had the look of gentry – well fed, clean, healthy. They had a soft leanness to them, like pampered hounds. Many were covered in strange, atavistic tattoos – not the knotwork patterns signifying growth and renewal that worshippers of the Lady of Leaves often bore, but more savage markings, signs of the hunt. Of blood and fear.

There were statues of Kurnoth scattered about the gardens, carved from living wood much like the one in Lord Wald's library. But these were daubed with blood and offal, and each was wrought to represent a different aspect of the god.

Kurnoth the Huntsman, man and beast conjoined in one form; Kurnoth the Killer, clad in ironoak armour and bearing a hunter's spear; Kurnoth the Seducer, clad in ivy and bearing a crown of stag horns. And others, less identifiable. Including one that resembled a great stag, its antlers a jagged crown. I stared at it as I was hauled past, and thought for a moment that it returned my glare. In my head, something laughed.

At the feet of the statues, the celebrants showed their devotion in the ways that suited them. Men and women copulated atop the bloody hides of freshly slaughtered bramblehorns, or devoured the creatures' raw flesh. Others sharpened primitive, ceremonial weapons of stone or bronze. Some danced about ritual firepits, shaking bone-rattles, turning and hopping as if in parody of a wounded animal. A few stopped what they were doing and made as if to snatch me from my captors, but Sepesh saw them off with curses and blows. Her men dragged me in her wake, holding tight to my arms and hair.

If I tried to pull away from my captors, I got a swift blow in the ribs. They dragged me into the main courtyard, overlooking the lower gardens. It was open to the elements – a flat, grassy space, marked by a few crooked trees growing from the stonework Lord Wald awaited us there.

He sat at a table, running a whetstone along the length of a single-edged sword. I recognised it as Murn's – the one I'd lost in the swamp Unlike his followers, he was dressed as before, in furs and robes. A trembling servant held a rain-break over his head, keeping him from getting wet. Wald looked up as I was shoved to the ground before the table.

'Did you know that back before the flood my ancestors had planted orchards behind the keep? A whole swathe of them, stretching back to the then-edges of the swamp Apples, mostly. There's a sort of little sour apple that grows in the Ghoul Mere. Very tasty, especially when baked. Nice with a bit of good cheese, like that crumbly sort they make in Headwater Breach You know the kind I mean?'

'Not big on cheese,' I said, as I dragged myself into a sitting position

'No matter. Get him to his feet.'

Two men roughly hauled me upright and shoved me forward. Lord Wald went back to sharpening the sword.

'I'm told Evrek Murn is dead at last.'

I said nothing. Lord Wald continued as if I had. 'You might ask why this is significant. Murn was one of the last worshippers of the Everqueen left in this canton Now, at last, it belongs to Kurnoth once more.' His adherents set up a raucous cheer that set my ears to aching. Lord Wald calmed them with a gesture.

He looked at me. 'He has always been worshipped here, of

course. Even before Sigmar disturbed Alarielle's slumber, the Old Stag roamed these swamps, and his worshippers rejoiced in his bloody reign. They offered up the choicest parts of their own kills to him, and when prey was scarce, they gave up their own flesh and blood to assuage him. And now those beautiful, bloody days are here again.'

He stood, leaving the sword on the table. He was showing off for his followers. 'The Everqueen wanes,' he said. 'Her season is done. It is time for Kurnoth to rise. Not the pale shard of him that Alarielle holds leashed, but the true Kurnoth – the Old Stag himself, who slumbers beneath these shadowed waters. We water his seed with blood taken in the hunt, or offered up in sacrifice, so that he might awaken and lead us in a hunt such as the Jade Kingdoms have never seen.'

At his words, his followers cheered again – wilder, this time. More like animal howls than the cries of men. He turned, playing to the crowd. 'We feed him, so that he grows strong. We glut him, fill him to bursting, and he returns the favour...'

'What do you get out of it?' I said.

Lord Wald stopped and turned to me, frowning at the interruption. 'All the eels you can eat?'

'Isn't it obvious?' Lord Wald said. He spread his arms. 'This canton barely existed before. Now it flourishes. Roughly, crudely, but it grows. It lives. In time, it will grow mighty. And any who seek to interfere, to meddle, will become prey. Murn made himself prey and paid the price. Kurnoth demanded it, and we were bound to obey.' Lord Wald leaned close. 'You helped us with that, of course. For which I am grateful. That is why I was willing to allow you a chance, as a courtesy.'

'Meaning?'

'A hunt,' Lord Wald said, smiling. 'One last hunt, before the harvest ends. But this time the prey will not be some malnourished sneak-thief or debtor, but prey worthy of us.'

'Is that supposed to be a compliment?'

'I can think of none greater.'

I glanced at Sepesh. She fingered the pommel of her sword. She was enjoying herself. I wondered if she was hoping I'd make a play for the sword. I hated to disappoint her. 'I can think of a few,' I said.

Lord Wald grinned. 'I'm sure you can. But prey is meant for the hunt. And you are prey. The god has decreed such.'

'Funny, he never said anything to me.' Even as I spoke, I leapt for the sword. I caught the hilt and flung myself over the top of the table, putting distance between myself and the startled guards. I upended the table and sent it crashing down.

Lord Wald applauded politely. 'Very good. I do hope I sharpened it enough for you.' He waved the guards back. 'The hunt begins now. Escape if you can. We shall harry you to exhaustion and then cut your throat and offer up your heart to the Old Stag.'

'Or maybe I'll just kill you.'

Whatever they'd been expecting, what I did next wasn't it. I went for his lordship, and I saw his eyes widen in startlement. He fell back, and Sepesh intercepted me, her blade against mine.

She laughed. 'I like you, Harran. I really do. I knew you were something special the moment I saw you.'

I glanced around, trying to find an exit route that wasn't blocked by a guard. Plenty of ways out, but I didn't want to go. Something held me in place. Held me here. I was a beast at bay, surrounded by hunters. Ready to die, so long as I could take a few of them with me.

Only… not really. I didn't want to die. I knew what was waiting for me if I did.

'Do I make good prey, then?' I said, tightening my grip on the sword's hilt.

'I don't know. Let's find out,' Sepesh said. We broke apart and she came in quick and low. Old instincts kicked in, and I blocked her first blow. She was surprised, and I leaned into her, driving an elbow into her chest. She fell back, coughing.

Wald waved the guards back. Some looked like they were enjoying the show. Others seemed to be wagering on the outcome. Wald himself seemed coolly amused. I wanted nothing more than to bury Murn's sword in his skull, but Sepesh was still between us.

She came at me again. This time it wasn't so easy to surprise her. I was no swordsman, and it showed. Her blows came almost too quickly to predict, and soon I was bleeding from a number of nicks and scratches – each of them a blow that might have killed me, had she wished. Our blades connected with an awkward shriek, and she kicked me in the knee. I fell and narrowly avoided a thrust that might have crippled me.

Lord Wald applauded. 'Excellent, excellent,' he called out. His coterie had gathered now, filling the space, hemming us in. Someone began to pound a drum.

I scrambled to my feet and backed away. Sepesh paced after me, grinning wildly. 'You should have run, Harran. You might have lived a little longer.'

'I've run enough,' I panted. My chest was heaving. I was sucking air. I was out of practice, exhausted – running on adrenaline. But I was angry.

Sepesh shrugged. 'Your choice.' She leapt and I was hard-pressed to divert her blow. She snatched her poniard from her belt and nearly opened my thigh with it. I was forced to grab her wrist. I was stronger, but she was ready for it. She stomped on my instep and swung at me, forcing me to interpose my sword.

I fell back before her. She was used to fighting men with greater reach, more strength – she was like a wolf wearing down an elk. Snapping and tearing, weakening me, pushing me back and back. Worst of all, she was barely panting. If I was going to survive, I needed to surprise her. I glanced to the side. Lord Wald was within reach, watching avidly.

I leapt. Sepesh cursed, but she was too far away. Lord Wald cursed too, as I caught him and swung him around, putting him between myself and Sepesh. I laid the edge of my sword against his throat and backed towards the edges of the courtyard. The garden spread out below me, maybe twenty feet down. Not an easy drop, but I'd survived worse.

'Release me,' Lord Wald said as he struggled in my grip. I ignored him. If I could make it to the trees, then maybe the town... from there the road. It sounded simple in my head. The music still rose from below. The celebrants down there hadn't noticed what was going on. Before I could make the jump, Lord Wald slammed an elbow into my midsection and tore himself from my grip.

'Sepesh – kill him!'

I turned and leapt, falling down into the gardens below. I struck one of the statues and buried my sword in its bestial head, briefly anchoring myself. The statue tottered on its plinth, rolling this way and that, before finally toppling into a firepit. Burning embers scattered across the wet grass, eliciting a shroud of smoke.

I rolled across the uneven ground, every bone in my body singing in alarm. But I was on my feet a moment later, muscle memory moving me. The garden was smaller than the courtyard, but crowded with statuary, benches and ornamental archways. I sought cover as celebrants scattered in surprise.

Through the pall of smoke, I saw Sepesh race down the steps to the garden, followed by several guards. Too many to fight. I squinted through the thinning smoke and spotted a set of slabbed steps, going down into the dark of the keep's lower levels. My escape route. If I could reach it. I looked around.

The garden was in uproar thanks to the smoke and the fallen statue. The appearance of the guards only added to the confusion, as Lord Wald's guests either sought safety, or went for their weapons. I heard Sepesh shouting, trying to calm the situation.

I put my shoulder against another statue and heaved. It tilted and slammed down, shattering a bench and scattering guards.

I darted through them, deeper into the smoke, heading for the steps. A root caught my foot, knocking me to one knee against a pillar. As I stumbled to my feet, I heard a high-pitched laugh. The treekin were watching. I could feel it.

Sepesh came at me fast, and I pushed myself away from the pillar. Her blade drew sparks as I lost myself in the smoke. I slid around a statue, heart thudding. Loose stones crunched beneath her feet. She was getting closer. I tried to gauge the distance to the steps.

I circled towards where I thought she was. I froze as I spotted the bulky outline of a guard edging towards me through the smoke. I turned to deal with him, and Sepesh leapt from her hiding place with a wild yell.

I barely parried the blow, and lost my sword in the process. I fell back, as she recovered and came for me again. I twisted aside as she lunged, and her sword plunged into the bark of a tree, embedding itself. She stepped back, surprised. I caught her a blow on the side of the head while she was distracted, dropping her to her knees.

She rose, knife in hand, but by then I had my arm around her throat. I caught the back of her head. Her knife slashed out, becoming tangled in my coat. I felt it gash my stomach, not deep, but enough to hurt.

I snapped her neck.

The guards reached me as I let her fall. Truncheons thudded into my back and arms, staggering me. I fell back against a statue, trying to twist away from the blows, but to no avail. They hit me again and again, until I went down.

'Get him up.'

The guards jerked me to my feet, none too gently. Everything hurt, but it was better than being dead. Lord Wald looked down at Sepesh, an expression that might have been regret on his face. 'She was worth a dozen of you,' he said softly. He had Murn's sword in his hand.

I didn't say anything. Lord Wald turned his gaze on me. His eyes blazed beast-hot for a moment. 'I think we will forego the hunt this time,' he said. He raised the sword in both hands, and I closed my eyes.

Out in the swamp, something cried out. A wolf-stag shriek. The sound hung on the air, and as I opened my eyes I saw that the revellers had fallen to their knees. Only Lord Wald still stood, his sword hanging forgotten in his hand.

'Kurnoth stirs,' he said. He smiled and looked down at me. 'Before this night is done, you might wish you had let Sepesh take your head, Blackwood.' He turned to his guards. 'Bind him. It is time to offer up the Huntsman his due.'

There was a sound like falling trees. Or cracking ice. We all turned, captive and captor alike. The ground shuddered as something stepped into the open, shouldering aside the remaining statues and sending them toppling. Men and women scrambled back from the apparition as its great hooves cracked the stones and gouged the earth.

'He is here,' Lord Wald said. He sank slowly to one knee. 'The god has come.'

The Old Stag loomed over us, slaver dripping in loose ropes from the almost human jaws. Its gaze bored into me.

Hello, Harran. It seems our hunt has come to an end.

CHAPTER TWENTY-SIX

HARVEST'S END

I wanted to look away, but I couldn't. It held my gaze with ease, forcing me to meet its hellspark eyes.

Here we are, back again. As I said.

The sound of its voice was like a knife scraping bone. I knew that I was the only one so blessed as to hear it. Lord Wald and his followers were still singing and chanting. Too busy making noise to listen to the object of their prayers.

Why would I speak with them? Of what possible interest is the whimpering of whipped dogs to their master?

'But you'll talk to me?'

Lord Wald started, and looked at me. But he made no attempt to silence me. From the look on his face, I think he suspected.

You are special.

I felt revulsion at the word. A twisting in my guts, as if someone

had shoved a knife in and stirred it about. 'I don't feel special,'
I said.

And yet you are. An ineffable mystery.

The man-face on the stag-neck twisted up in a lopsided grin.
It was amused. That only made the nausea worse. It stank of
standing water and blood. Of generations of death. Spite-grubs
crawled through the cracks in its flesh, and I heard the trilling
of leopard eels echoing up from the waters below the gardens.

'Let me know when you figure it out,' I said, forcing the words
out. There was no courage in my defiance – only the snarls of
an animal in the trap.

*I owned you the moment you entered these swamps, Harran.
Your course was set the instant Murn asked for help.*

Teeth like shards of burnt wood scraped together, inches from
my ear. I couldn't help but flinch.

Let's have a look at you, then.

It met my gaze and in that moment, I felt as if I were drowning.
It peeled back my skull and looked inside, as if I were nothing
more than a dead beast for the harvesting. Would it drink my
blood, the way it had Murn's?

*Fresh blood is best. Heart's blood, squeezed steaming from the
prey. Or baby's blood, sweet and clean. Girl's blood, pure and
honied.*

I thought of the little gheist in Murn's house – of Calla – and
felt sick.

She was sweet, that one. A true delicacy. Like you, Harran.

The great tongue, like a lash of corrugated leather, licked across
my face. Tasting me. Tasting the fear that gibbered and snarled
down deep in my heart.

*The blood is the life. They know that, my caretakers. My hounds.
They've always known. A bit of blood makes the green things
grow. A bit of blood to feed me in my respite. Is that so much to
ask, in return for my blessings?*

'You're not a god,' I said, or thought I said. I couldn't tell whether I spoke aloud, or only in my head. It didn't seem to matter. The stag-thing laughed, a hateful, guttural sound.

No. But I once was. And I might be again.

It pressed itself close, nostrils cracking and flaring. It sucked in my scent, gulping it up as if it had never smelled anything so sweet.

After all, even a wretched seed might grow into a darksome tree.

Teeth like knives scraped down my cheek, opening the skin. Blood welled and spilled. I bit back a scream.

In time. With the right nourishment.

The lips squirmed and it made a sound like a geyser as it spat my blood into the water.

Which you are not.

I blinked. That sounded like a reprieve, or as close as I was going to get. 'What?' I croaked. It looked down at me, a peculiar expression on its unfinished features. A sound like a sigh emerged from its ragged lips and it shook its great antlers.

You are not yet ripe. How unfortunate.

I started to laugh as the stag-thing stepped back. Lord Wald's face was a picture of shock. 'What...?' he began.

'You can't give it what you don't have,' I said. I forced myself to my feet, body aching. The stag-thing – the shard of Kurnoth – snorted and rattled its antlers as if in agreement. I tried not to meet that hellish gaze again, tried not to see the savage amusement that burned there. I wondered if it was truly as annoyed by this as it seemed. Maybe it had grown tired of Lord Wald's games, or maybe it was simply fickle, in the way of the sylvaneth.

Lord Wald bared his teeth. 'Stay where you are.'

I took a step towards him. He stared at me, a look of incomprehension on his face. He hadn't figured it out yet. He didn't understand. But I did. I wished I didn't, but I did.

My soul already belonged to another.

The great black stag reared up and loosed a shrill, bugling roar. The manor shook to its foundations, and howls sounded in the distant trees. Pale-faced things emerged from the shadows of the garden, laughing cruelly as they bounded towards us. One of the treekin pounced on a member of Wald's coterie, bearing the screaming man to the ground.

'No – our bargain,' Lord Wald began, looking around wildly.

'No more bargain,' I said. I drove my shoulder into the nearest guard and knocked him sprawling. As he thrashed, I crushed his throat with my knee and went for his knife. I had just managed to slit my bindings, freeing my hands, when Lord Wald lunged for me, sword raised. I rolled aside and sent the knife hurtling towards him, forcing him to bat it aside. While he was distracted, I went for the guard's sword.

I snatched the blade up, and Lord Wald extended his own. 'This is wrong,' he said, shaking his head. 'This isn't how it goes.' He looked at me. 'Fine. Fine. I'll spill your guts at his feet, for him to feast on at his leisure.' He started towards me, eyes glinting with malice.

I laughed. 'If a god couldn't kill me, what makes you think you've got a chance?'

Lord Wald hesitated – and I stamped forward, blade singing out in a wide arc. He parried the blow instinctively, but staggered back, off balance.

'Two gods, in fact,' I said. I paced after him, grinning like I was mad. In that moment, I think I was. 'Two gods had the chance to end me – and they both decided that they had better things to do, the bastards.'

Our blades met with stately grace. I was bigger than him; I hadn't realised it before, and I don't think he had, either. I was bigger, and at that moment, I was sure as hell meaner. He went on the defensive, and his eyes flicked this way and that, looking for a way out.

They always do. The prey, I mean. It's a thing of beauty, that look. That desperation makes the meat tough, but I do love it so.

Lord Wald's eyes widened, and I knew he'd heard the whistle-rasp voice. The black stag circled us with slow, plodding steps. 'I served you,' he said. Desperate now. Pleading, almost. 'I am your huntsman!'

What do you take me for, little lord? Some pampered king, in need of servants to do his hunting for him? You were my hound, nothing more. And every dog has its day. Yours has passed. You should be pleased – is this not a magnificent ending? The hunter, slain by the hunted. The circle is complete.

'No,' Lord Wald growled. 'No!' He lunged, wildly and without finesse. I slapped his sword aside and sent him sprawling with a cuff to the back of his head.

'Up,' I said.

He writhed in the mud and came up swinging. Howling. I tripped him and the Old Stag gave a guttural, echoing laugh.

That's the way, that's the way. Let him fight. They always fight.

'Shut up,' I said, not looking at it. 'This isn't for your benefit.'

How little you know, Harran. How small you are, in comparison to me. I could trample your soul into flinders so infinitesimal that not even the Undying King could sieve them from the mud.

I ignored it. I kept my eyes fixed on Lord Wald, as he struggled upright. He was frothing at the mouth, his eyes starting from their sockets. His body shook, as if with ague, and he twitched towards me, trying to hammer me flat with each blow. I retreated, drawing him towards the edge of the garden. He was babbling as he fought, and I wondered if I'd acted the same the day my god abandoned me.

No wonder poor Murn tried to put you down. He probably thought it a mercy.

'Shut up,' I snarled. Lord Wald charged me, screeching. Our

blades locked and we stumbled back and forth along the garden's edge. Lord Wald's face contorted into something bestial – and utterly mad. He champed his teeth, savaging the air. He leaned into me, trapping our blades between us.

I turned, hurling him back. I tossed my sword aside as he rose, and hit him – hard – in the sternum. Something cracked, and he staggered, suddenly white-faced. His sword slipped from his fingers and I caught him by the throat.

It is traditional to spill blood.

'This isn't for you,' I grunted, as his lordship's hands clawed at my forearms.

Ah. A personal matter, then. Very well. I'll allow it.

I tightened my grip about Lord Wald's neck. His thrashing had become more frantic. I watched as his expression became lucid – and then terrified. That was good. I wanted him to understand what was happening. To know what was coming.

This wasn't a fight. It wasn't even an execution.

But it was damn satisfying.

Eventually, he stopped struggling. Lord Wald stared upwards, blank and empty. I let him go and stepped back, as the Old Stag dipped its antlers.

For a time, I favoured him above all others.

The god-thing retrieved the limp body and lifted it almost gently.

But times change. The seasons turn.

With a flick of its head, it flung the body into the deepest part of the waters below, where the leopard eels waited. They trilled in pleasure, and Lord Wald soon vanished into red foam.

The Old Stag turned its attentions to me.

Well then.

'Well,' I said.

What do you plan on doing for an encore, Harran Blackwood?

I spied a bench and went and sat. 'I'm tired,' I said. I looked around. I was the only living man in the garden. All of Lord Wald's companions, the guards, were dead or gone. What was left of them was hung about from the nearby trees and pillars, glistening strands of meat and muscle dangling over the gardens like solstice decorations. 'They served you,' I said.

They still do, though the manner of that service has changed.

I laughed. There was a shrill edge to it. I choked it back. 'Yes. So it has. Murn tried to stop you. Tried to stop the sacrifices. That's why he called me. We did it before, him and me. He thought we might get lucky a second time.'

The only certainty when it comes to luck is that it inevitably runs out.

'That go for me too?' I looked up at the god-thing, and felt the ashes of my fear stir. But only a bit. It had all been burned out of me, for the moment. The creature seemed to understand, because it gave me an awful smile as it bent over me.

Oh no. No, no easy end for you, Harran Blackwood. No red moment of mercy, in this life or the next. You are destined for a more awesome and hideous end than even such as I can conceive.

I bared my teeth. 'I think if you set your mind to it, you could make an end of me here. Why not give it a try?'

It laughed, and I wanted to weep.

No. Even damnation pales next to what I see ahead of you. Be glad and rejoice, for not every man earns such a mighty doom.

The black stag swung its antlers away and turned. It gave a great, horrible cry and the sylvaneth faded away, as swift as whispers. This place was no longer theirs, but the Huntsman's. Maybe it always had been, whatever the Everqueen had hoped. The god-thing glanced back at me. Its eyes shone like stars gone feral, and I felt the cold heat of them in the hollow places of my soul. It was smiling, as if privy to some private jest.

When that day comes, you will wish I had devoured you.

And then, it was gone.

I sat for a time, in the rain. I still had Murn's coin, and I looked at it for a while, turning it over. At some point, I dropped it in the water. I didn't bother to search for it.

When the sun rose, I left, trying to ignore the gheists that followed me.

The swamp was full of them. They were everywhere, perched in the trees and staring up at me from beneath the water. Weak things drawn to the scent of my blood. They knew I was hurt, and so they gathered like carrion birds.

The girl was among them. She watched me, her lips wriggling like nightcrawlers. And Gint was there as well, a tattered shadow of who he had been. His mouth moved. I knew what he was asking, though I couldn't hear him. *A game...? A game...?*

I looked away.

Wald was quiet. No one tried to stop me as I bartered passage on a barge heading upriver. No one seemed to realise what had happened. Maybe nothing had. One lord was as good as another, and the Old Stag was a familiar master, at least.

Either way, I didn't give a damn whether Wald flourished or perished. I'd done what I'd come to do. Murn was dead, and my past with him.

The man I had been was dead. Only Harran Blackwood remained.

Or so I told myself as I kept my eyes on the trees, watching for any sign of the sylvaneth as I left. They kept out of sight, but something that might have been a stag trailed the skiff to Wald's border, and watched me as the trees hid all sign of the town from sight.

The god-thing did not speak to me again. Maybe it had said all it needed to say.

When that day comes, you will wish I had devoured you.

The words prowled through me, and I knew that though the

harvest was over, and the hunt was ended, there was always another harvest.

And another hunt.

ABOUT THE AUTHOR

Josh Reynolds' extensive Black Library back
catalogue includes the Horus Heresy Primarchs
novel *Fulgrim: The Palatine Phoenix*, and
three Horus Heresy audio dramas featuring the
Blackshields. His Warhammer 40,000 work includes
the Space Marine Conquests novel *Apocalypse*,
Lukas the Trickster and the Fabius Bile novels. He
has written many stories set in the Age of Sigmar,
including the novels *Shadespire: The Mirrored City*,
Soul Wars, *Eight Lamentations: Spear of Shadows*,
the Hallowed Knights novels *Plague Garden* and
Black Pyramid, and *Nagash: The Undying King*. His
Warhammer Horror story, *The Beast in the Trenches*,
is featured in the portmanteau novel *The Wicked
and the Damned*, and he has recently penned the
Necromunda novel *Kal Jerico: Sinner's Bounty*. He
lives and works in Sheffield.

YOUR
NEXT READ

WARHAMMER™ HORROR

CASTLE OF BLOOD
by C L Werner

Seven families arrive at the ancient castle of Mhurghast, each with their own dark secret and hidden agenda, each marked for revenge. Doomed to discover the depths of horror and despair, it is not a night of revelry that awaits them, but a night of unprecedented terror.

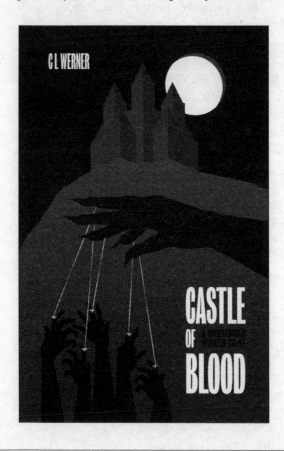

YOUR
NEXT READ

THE HOUSE OF NIGHT AND CHAIN
by David Annandale

At the edge of the city of Valgaast, Malveil awaits. It is a house of darkness, its halls filled with history and pain. It knows all secrets, and no weakness can escape its insidious gaze.
Now it stirs eagerly at the approach of prey.

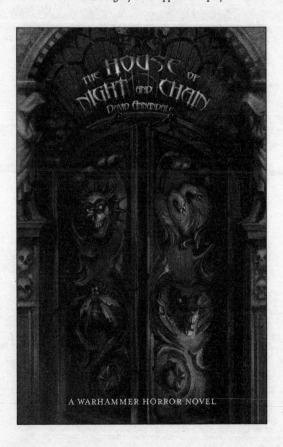

A WARHAMMER HORROR NOVEL